I0544245

Murder in Darnley Glen

ALSO BY DANIEL SELLERS

DCI LOLA HARRIS

Daniel Sellers

MURDER IN DARNLEY GLEN

JOFFE BOOKS

Joffe Books, London
www.joffebooks.com

First published in Great Britain in 2025

© Daniel Sellers

This book is a work of fiction. Names, characters,
businesses, organisations, places and events are either
the product of the author's imagination or are used
fictitiously. Any resemblance to actual persons, living
or dead, events or locales is entirely coincidental.
The spelling used is British English except where fidelity
to the author's rendering of accent or dialect supersedes this.
The right of Daniel Sellers to be identified as author of this
work has been asserted in accordance with the Copyright,
Designs and Patents Act 1988.

No part of this book may be used or reproduced
in any manner for the purpose of training artificial
intelligence technologies or systems. In accordance
with Article 4(3) of the Digital Single Market
Directive 2019/790, Joffe Books expressly reserves this
work from the text and data mining exception.

Cover art by Nebojša Zorić

ISBN: 978-1-80573-375-1

For Kirsty Lawie

AUTHOR'S NOTE

Some places in this novel are real, as are some institutions. The characters and the events are fictional. Clyde University is entirely my creation.

Please follow me on X (@djsellersauthor) and on Instagram (@danielsellersauthor). You can also sign up for my newsletter on my website: www.danielsellers.co.uk

#WhatWouldLolaHarrisDo?

CHAPTER ONE

Saturday 25 October
8.45 p.m.

Lola had gone with her friend Sorcha to a new French restaurant in Glasgow's West End. It wasn't a special occasion, but they liked to go out from time to time, to gossip and drink wine. Their evenings were always fun, with inconsequential chat — usually about Sorcha's enormous townhouse and the trouble she was having with workmen.

But tonight, from the moment she got here, Lola had sensed Sorcha was strained. She denied anything was wrong but, when they were on coffees, finally came out with it.

'You'll kill me, Lola, but I need some advice. The professional kind, but unofficial.'

'Go on,' Lola said drily.

Sorcha bit her lip and looked embarrassed. 'You know my old auntie out in Giffnock, Jeanie?'

Lola smiled. 'The one who's forever trying to adopt other people's cats?'

'Yes. Well, she's worried about her neighbour. A young woman called Marta. She's Estonian but married to a Scottish bloke who's quite a bit older than her. Anyway, they've got a

1

young baby and Marta's got it into her head that someone's watching her. Watching the house too. Lola, she thinks someone's after the baby.'

'Why does she think that?' Lola asked.

'I don't know. She claims someone was watching her when she took a shortcut home through woods near the house, and that someone's been driving past the house from time to time.'

'Sounds . . . tenuous.'

'Auntie Jeanie says Marta's terrified. Whether it's true or not . . .'

'Has she reported it?'

'No. She wants to, but get this.' Her friend sat back, as if for dramatic effect. 'Her husband won't let her.'

'Because he doesn't believe her, or . . . ?'

'I don't know. Maybe he thinks he can protect them himself — like, an ego thing? You know what some men are like. And *no*,' she said, peering hard at Lola, 'she's not mad or depressed either — not according to Jeanie, anyway. And Jeanie should know; she had post-natal depression that lasted over a year after my cousin was born.'

'How old is Marta's baby?'

'Two months. Jeanie has her over for coffee sometimes. She feels sorry for her. She hardly knows a soul in Scotland. The weird thing is, Marta's husband has just installed a lot of new security: fencing, a new gate, cameras everywhere. He's even hired a man to be there during the day — you know, like a private security guard — and he's told Marta on no account to go out. He's even forbidden her from going round to Jeanie's. Which seems to indicate he's worried too. And yet . . .'

'And yet he won't let her report it to the police? Seems rather . . . controlling.'

'Can you do anything — look into it unofficially, I mean?'

'Hardly. We can't investigate things that haven't been reported. You must realise that.'

'I suppose I do. But that poor girl . . .'

Lola fell silent, picking over what Sorcha had told her.

'What are you thinking?' Sorcha asked.

'I'm thinking that I'm much more concerned about the fact Marta's husband is keeping her locked up in her house than I am about possible stalkers.'

'There is that!' Sorcha made a face.

'Tell Jeanie that Marta must report her concerns. Alternatively, she could talk to someone. I'm thinking of organisations like Women's Aid. Someone who could advise her. Help her feel strong enough to push back.'

Sorcha nodded, eyes down.

'I get it,' she said and swilled coffee round her cup.

Lola sighed, relenting. 'Look, tell me their names and their address. I'll pass the info to one of my colleagues in our public protection unit. Have them run a few checks.'

'She's Marta Dixon. He's called Lawrence though he goes by Lawrie.' Sorcha saw Lola's expression. 'What — do you know him?'

'Lawrie Dixon? It seems familiar. What does he do?'

'Cyber security something-or-other. He had a company and sold it for millions. Now he's started a new one.'

'I may have come across him at work . . .'

'They live in Baslow Gardens in Giffnock. In a hideous modern house specially designed for them. Auntie Jeanie's in a bog-standard 1930s semi next door. She says it's like living next to NASA. She's number seventeen.' She gave a sheepish smile. 'Thanks, Lola. I do appreciate this and I hate to ask. I'll get the bill.'

'You don't have to do that.' She sighed. 'I'll talk to my colleagues, like I say. Try not to worry.'

Next day Lola sent an email to Sergeant Jackie Bennett, a colleague in the public protection unit whom she liked and trusted. She had every intention of checking in with Jackie after a day or so — except that evening Sandy dropped his bombshell and everything changed. Sorcha, her aunt and her aunt's neighbour were put firmly out of Lola's head.

3

CHAPTER TWO

Wednesday 29 October
7.21 a.m.

Lola came out of the shower to find her work mobile ringing. She saw who it was and picked it up.

'Morning, boss, we've got a murder,' DI Anna Vaughan told her. 'Young female victim found by a dog walker in woodland at Darnley this morning.'

'Where in Darnley?'

'The very bottom end of Darnley Glen country park, by the entrance off Waukglen Road.'

'Are you there now?'

'I got here twenty minutes ago. I've called Identification Bureau and they're on their way. Jonno's with me and Kirstie will be here in a few minutes.' These were two of the detective constables. 'I've got cordons in place and we've closed off access to the woods.'

'Okay. Thanks, Anna. Any ID on the woman?'

'Nothing yet, boss. White, late twenties or early thirties. Above-average height, I'd say. Slavic or Nordic look about her, maybe.'

Lola caught her own eye in the mirrored wardrobe door.

'Boss, you there?'

'Aye, I'm here. Any . . . any reports of missing persons matching that description?'

'Nothing according to Control, but I've made sure there's a note on the system to catch anything that comes in.'

'Okay, Anna. I'll set off straight away. See you there.'

She got dressed quickly, telling herself not to overthink — not ahead of the facts.

* * *

7.46 a.m.

Waukglen Road wound up from the main road towards an estate of big modern houses. Just before the estate, on the right, was an entrance to Darnley Glen. There were cars everywhere, some marked, some unmarked, and a cordon in place to stop anyone entering the woods. A number of residents had emerged from their houses and were watching the activity.

Lola got out of her car and made her way to the cordon. It was chilly and overcast but dry. A light breeze stirred the tops of the trees, dislodging the occasional yellowed leaf.

'Morning, boss,' an officer at the cordon said gloomily.

'Morning,' she replied, no more cheerful.

'Mind your way down the slope,' he told her. 'Wee bit slippy. Go left at the bottom and it's about a hundred yards or so.'

She found the place: a hive of quiet activity under a canopy of trees overhanging a reedy pond. Identification Bureau — or IB — officers were engaged in setting up a tent. Two white-suited figures stood to one side. One of them pulled down its hood and removed its mask — DI Anna Vaughan nodded at Lola and came over.

'What do we know?' Lola asked.

'A dog walker found her just after six fifteen,' Anna said. 'His dog was barking at something at the edge of the pond. He came over, saw the body and nearly fainted.'

'Was she in the water?'

'No. Among reeds at the side. Quite dry. Want a look?'

Lola nodded, steeling herself. Anna called to an IB colleague and the officer fetched Lola a suit, overshoes, gloves and mask. Lola dressed quickly, then let Anna lead the way. The officers who'd been setting up the tent paused and moved away to give them room. Lola stopped a metre away from the corpse.

The dead woman lay on her side, knees up to her chest, arms straight out before her face so that one shoulder obscured the lower part of her face. She was clothed in dark leggings, a warm-looking black jacket and black trainers. A black elasticated bandana lay loosely round her throat. There was blood everywhere about her face and clotted in her dark hair. On her pale hands too. A wound in her temple showed bone.

'No ID on her,' Anna said. 'Not that we've found, anyway.'

Lola studied what features she could make out, noting the woman's high, broad cheekbones and the slightly upturned eyes. She saw what Anna had meant about her having a Nordic appearance.

'IB have given us a rough estimate for the time of death,' Anna said. 'Between four and six hours ago, so between approximately two and four in the morning. And they don't think she was killed here. Just dumped.'

'She'd have to have been carried,' Lola said, considering the narrow and uneven path through the woods. 'Still no missing persons who match the description?'

'No.'

'Look at the way she's dressed,' Lola said, surveying again the sleek black outfit, the tough trainers, the elasticated bandana. 'She's dressed like someone doing one of those "iron man" contests.'

'Boss,' a voice interrupted her. It was DC Jonno Gillies, his phone in hand and looking excited. 'I've just spoken to Control. They took a report just after two this morning from a taxi driver about a distressed woman he'd seen running by

Rouken Glen Park. The driver pulled over and tried to talk to her but she told him to leave her alone and kept running. Dressed in black, he said, hair tied back.' He licked his lips and looked nervous. 'Bloke couldn't be sure, but he told Control . . . he thought she was carrying a baby.'

'A baby?' Lola asked, her heart rate picking up.

'That's what he said.'

Lola and Anna exchanged shocked glances.

'Have you got the witness's details?' Lola asked.

Jonno nodded. 'Stays in a flat in Thornliebank, so not far from here.'

'I'll go see him,' Lola said. She turned to Anna. 'I'll take Kirstie, if that suits you.'

'Of course,' Anna said. 'Jonno, fetch Kirstie, would you?'

While Lola waited she went into her phone and looked at a map. Rouken Glen Park was only a mile or so from here. Giffnock was maybe another mile beyond that. What was that address Sorcha had told her . . . ?

'Boss, are you okay?' Anna asked, frowning.

'Yes,' she said, still distracted. 'Yes, I'm fine. Get onto Corporate Comms while I'm away, would you? Ask them to draft a short appeal for information. Email the draft to me. I'd like to get something out on social media as soon as possible. Oh, and get one of the DCs onto the local authority. See if they've got any CCTV footage from Rouken Glen Road about two this morning.'

CHAPTER THREE

9.27 a.m.

Rab McCreedy wasn't long out of his bed, he told them apologetically. He was sixty-something, grey and unshaven — and seemed disproportionately embarrassed about it.

'This about that young lassie, then?' he asked, scratching his chin as he led them into his kitchenette.

'It is.'

'You're taking it serious, then?'

'Shall we sit down?' Lola suggested.

'Aye, of course. Sorry.' He busied uselessly about, pulling out chairs they could have got for themselves. 'It's such a mess here. The wife left me twenty years ago and stuff just piles up.'

Lola avoided catching Kirstie's eye. The place was indeed cluttered, with piles of newspapers, boxes and food cartons on the floor — and empty beer bottles protruding from a crate by the kitchen door.

'Can I get you a tea, or a coffee, perhaps?'

'We're fine,' Lola said quickly. 'We need to talk to you about what happened last night.'

'Aye. Aye, of course.'

He sat then hunched forward in his seat and eyed them cautiously. 'I'm no in any trouble, am I? I only tried to help the lassie. She . . . she hasn't made a complaint or anything?'

Lola pondered the question. 'Why would you think that, Mr McCreedy?'

'Sorry, I know it sounds paranoid. It's just, cab drivers do get malicious complaints from time to time — usually from the worst-behaved passengers.'

'We just want you to talk us through what happened, what you saw, what you said to each other, that sort of thing. DC Campbell will take some notes. We'll likely ask you to make a formal statement at some point, but for now we just want to talk. Does that sound okay?'

He nodded but looked uncomfortable.

'Mr McCreedy—'

'Rab, please.'

'Rab, you made a report to 101 in the early hours of this morning. Can you tell us what that was about?'

'Aye, it was about this young lassie. I seen her tearing along in a panic, and I thought to myself, that's no right. So I pulled a U-turn—'

'Sorry, where was this?'

'On Rouken Glen Road. The A727. Its name changes every roundabout or so. This was the stretch by the park.'

'Which way was she running?'

'West. I was heading east to a call in Clarkston and she was coming towards me. I saw she was in a panic and — well, like I said when I called it in — I got the impression she was carrying a bairn. I said to myself, "Rab, you cannae ignore that," so I swung round as soon as there was a gap and I drove back the way. I jumped out and yelled across the road, "Is everything all right?" She stopped — just froze — and gaped at me. Poor thing looked petrified. I shouted, "Are you in some kind of trouble? I'm a cabbie," I said. "I can take you somewhere if you like." She just stood there, staring at me, all

9

wide-eyed and her hair coming loose, holding this — well, this *bundle* to her chest like this.' He demonstrated.

Lola's skin prickled.

'Did you actually see a baby?'

'No. I started to cross the road, only she sort of backed away. I know when someone's scared, so I stayed in the central reservation, but I knew she was thinking about it — about accepting my offer, I mean. I tried again. I said, "I know a lady cabbie. My pal Lynn. I could call her if you like. Fare's on me." "We'll be fine," she says.'

'"We"? She definitely said "we"?'

'Aye. Meaning her and the bairn, so I reckon.'

'Did she sound local to you?'

The question seemed to surprise him and he frowned. 'No. No, she didn't. She sounded, well . . . foreign, I'd say. She had — well, you know, an accent.'

'Right.' Lola swallowed.

He nodded. 'I thought she was one of they Polish lassies . . . Or Czechoslovakian or somewhere like that. I don't know. She kept looking back the way along the road. I asked, "Is someone after you?" and she just looked at me like — well, like an animal that's being hunted.'

'Did she answer you?'

'No.'

'Could you see anyone behind her?'

'Not a soul! The road was empty. No traffic, no people, all the houses shut up and sleeping. I tried again, but she just stood, hunched and waiting for me to go.' He sighed and said gloomily, 'So I left her. I went back to my car.'

'What time was that — do you know?'

'Just gone two. I rang your lot from the car five minutes later.'

'If you were worried, why did you wait five minutes?'

He looked taken aback at that, alarmed and a little offended. 'Well, I . . . I was concerned but, well, she clearly didn't want my help. I reckon I was torn between interfering

10

and, well, doing what I had to do. Then common sense won: I knew that girl was in trouble — and so was that baby. I rang 101.'

'Not 999?'

He shifted uncomfortably again. 'I wasn't sure it was an emergency. Oh God.' His expression darkened. 'You about to tell me it was?'

'Describe her to us,' Lola asked, ignoring his question. 'We know you gave a description to the call handler. But describe her for us. Everything you remember.'

He frowned and his eyes roved about the cluttered kitchen. 'She was tall for a lassie. Taller than me, though I'm no exactly towering.'

'What height are you, Rab?'

'Five-five. She'd have been two, maybe three inches taller. Erm . . . dark hair, tied back but sort of coming loose, maybe from running. She was all in black, black jacket, black bottoms — like runners wear — and black trainers. Oh, and she had a . . . one of those elasticated scarf things, you know, hill walkers keep 'em round their neck and you can pull it up over the lower part of your face when it's cold.'

'But it was pulled down when you spoke to her?'

He nodded.

'How would you describe her face?'

He winced. 'Oh, erm . . .'

'Was she chubby or gaunt?' Lola prompted.

'Neither. She looked normal. Fit, I suppose. Healthy. She had these big eyes. Can't tell you what colour. Kind of . . . reminded me of, well . . .' He looked sheepish for a moment.

'Reminded you of what, Rab?' Lola pressed him gently.

'Reminded me a wee bit of that dark-haired lassie out of ABBA — remember her? Not the blonde lassie, the other one.'

Lola sat very still. She liked Rab McCreedy. He seemed very genuine — an honest, hard-working, concerned citizen without a gram of malice in him. He'd reported his concern for a young woman — the action of a man with a clear

11

conscience — but Lola was also grimly aware the call might have been part of an act: the establishment of an alibi.

She watched him carefully as she said the next words: 'A young woman's body was found this morning at Darnley. She answers the description of the woman you spoke to.'

Blood visibly drained from his face.

'My God,' he managed. His bottom lip trembled. 'Oh dear God . . .' He put a hand to his mouth and asked, 'And the baby?'

'There was no baby with her,' Lola said. 'Nor any sign she'd been carrying one.'

'What you saying?' he asked. 'That someone took it?'

'We don't know,' she said honestly.

In the silence that followed, McCreedy became more and more distressed, groaning and pulling at his thinning hair. 'I should've done something,' he gasped. 'I should've rung 999 right away and said she was in danger. Or I should've gone after her, stayed with her, or at least followed her in my car.' He looked up. 'Darnley isn't far from there. What, another mile? Where did you find her?'

'Next left after the Sainsbury's,' she said. 'In woods by the new houses.'

He nodded. 'Waukglen Road?'

'That's the one. You ever have customers who live there?'

'Once or twice.' He didn't seem to see the implication in the question. 'That's the bottom way into Darnley Glen, isn't it?' He stopped and his eyes widened with sudden realisation. 'You're gonnae want me to identify her, aren't you?' Both hands went to his mouth. 'I don't know if I can.'

'We might want to show you a photograph,' Lola said. 'To confirm if she is the young woman you spoke to. But not now. Later today, perhaps. If not today, tomorrow.'

He swallowed. 'I can do that,' he said gruffly.

Lola glanced at Kirstie, who nodded to say she had everything noted.

'We'll leave you now,' Lola said, and got up from the table.

McCreedy rose unsteadily.

'You tried to help her,' Lola said kindly. 'She didn't want your help so there was nothing you could do — apart from report it, which you did.'

'Thanks,' he said, but looked unconvinced.

'We'll be in touch.'

Descending the stairs of the flats, she checked her personal phone and saw Sandy had tried to call her. He hadn't left a voice message but there was a text. *Ring me when you get a minute*, it said.

It was the first time she'd heard from him in two days — since the bombshell. She groaned aloud as the knot of anxiety tightened inside her.

Well, he'd have to wait. She dropped her phone back in her pocket.

She checked her work phone and saw Anna had emailed her the draft text of an appeal from Corporate Comms. She read through it:

WOMAN'S BODY FOUND AT DARNLEY GLEN — URGENT APPEAL FOR INFORMATION

We are appealing urgently for information about the identity of a woman found dead this morning in woodland in Darnley.

The woman is white, believed to be between 25 and 35, with a height of approximately 5 feet 8 inches (173 cm), and has dark, shoulder-length hair.

Anyone with any information relating to the woman's identity, or who may have seen suspicious activity in the vicinity of Waukglen Road during the early hours of 29 October, please contact . . .

It ended with the usual numbers and a note that callers weren't obliged to give a name. Lola replied to Anna's email saying it was good to go. Suddenly Anna was ringing her.

She put the phone to her ear.

'Boss, I just spoke to Command and Control. They've taken a 999 call from a man in Giffnock. Says a woman broke into his house at one this morning and kidnapped his ten-week-old son at gunpoint. Boss, she answers our woman's description.'

'Who's the caller?' she asked urgently, steeling herself, just in case . . .

'A Lawrence Dixon, of 19 Baslow Gardens in Giffnock.'

It was like being doused in iced water and for a moment she couldn't speak.

'Boss?'

She said quickly, 'If the child was taken from the house, then it's a crime scene.'

'I know. And they're out of there. They're at a neighbour's, next door — number seventeen, home of a Jean Quigley.'

Sorcha's Auntie Jeanie . . .

'The duty inspector is on her way there now with a constable to get a cordon in place, though Mr Dixon has asked us to attend in unmarked cars.'

'Kirstie and I will head there now. Sorry, Anna — did you say Command and Control took the call just now?'

'That's right, boss,' Anna said. 'Call came in at 9.48 a.m.'

'He waited *eight hours*?'

'I know,' Anna said darkly. 'You reckon they've been threatened?'

'Quite possibly,' Lola said, and rang off.

CHAPTER FOUR

10.21 a.m.

Lola parked at the end of the curving road and she and Kirstie walked the two hundred metres or so to 17 Baslow Gardens. The Dixons' house next door was as Sorcha had described it: a modern place that dominated the otherwise conservative suburban street. A high fence hid most of it from view, but the upper level was visible: it looked to be made of piled-up white boxes.

Lola led the way up the short garden path to Jeanie Quigley's door and rang the bell.

Seconds later it was opened by a seventy-something lady in a cashmere cardigan. Jeanie Quigley was pink and upset.

'Police Scotland,' Lola told her quietly. 'We're here to see Mr and Mrs Dixon.'

'Come in, please.' She pulled the door wider. 'No, no, Maxwell,' she said to an orange cat that had scrambled down the stairs and made a beeline for the open door. 'That's a good boy, in you come.' She closed the door over. 'This is so awful, isn't it?' she said. Tears were brimming in her eyes. 'That poor girl and that dear, dear little boy. Mr Dixon is in the kitchen. This way.'

15

But before they reached the kitchen door, Inspector Michelle Brown appeared through it and pulled it closed after her. She nodded a hello to Lola and Kirstie.

'I'll leave you to it,' Jeanie said awkwardly and disappeared into her living room. The orange cat went with her.

'I take it you know what this is about?' Michelle checked.

'A woman with a gun kidnapped a young child from next door in the early hours of the morning.'

'That sums it up,' the inspector said drily. 'Their solicitor was with them when my constable and I got there. Idiot should have told them to clear out at once. Anyway, they're all installed here for now. We've secured the house, but Mr Dixon is insisting on no visible cordon. The gates are locked, so no one can get in — so he says. The kidnapper got in no problem at all. No sign of a break-in. "Smart locks".' She rolled her eyes. 'Not that smart, apparently. Anyway, my constable's next door, keeping an eye on things.'

'Thanks, Michelle. You can go if you need to. Get an operational statement to us today, will you?'

'Will do. The pair of them are in a state,' she confided now. 'Mrs Dixon's got a friend with her. She gave her a sedative so the poor woman's out of it. She's upstairs in one of the bedrooms, "lying down".' She hesitated, as if unsure whether to say anything.

'What is it?' Lola prompted.

'Dixon's got a story,' Michelle said, 'but, if you ask me, something's not right.'

'Okay, thanks, Michelle.'

Michelle nodded a goodbye and headed for the front door.

Lola knocked once on the kitchen door and went in.

'Mr Dixon?' she said. 'I'm Detective Chief Inspector Lola Harris and this is Detective Constable Kirstie Campbell.'

A stocky man rose from the kitchen table, his red face a picture of wired anxiety.

'I'm Lawrence Dixon,' he said, his jaw tight. 'Did you come in a police car?'

'No, in my own car, Mr Dixon, and I parked further down the street.'

'Good.' He gave a grunt of relief.

A gaunt man in a grey pin-striped suit had risen too and was lingering at Dixon's shoulder.

'My solicitor, Jeremy Wilder,' Dixon said.

Lola nodded. 'Shall we sit down?' she asked.

They took their seats.

'Tell us exactly what happened, Mr Dixon,' Lola said. 'Don't leave anything out.'

Dixon peered at his solicitor as if for permission — or moral support — but Wilder gave nothing away. Dixon cleared his throat. 'Just after one o'clock this morning,' he said, 'a woman broke into our house, next door.' He stopped and cleared his throat again.

'Take your time,' Lola said.

He nodded and took a sip of water.

'She broke in somehow,' he went on. 'She appeared in our bedroom and threatened us — with a gun. She took my son Adam from his cot in our room and left with him. She took our boy—' his voice cracked — 'and she threatened to kill him if we went after her or reported it. I have a friend, a contact in Police Scotland — and no, I won't say who. I called him because I was desperate. I told him and asked for his advice. He tried to persuade me to report it, but . . . but I just couldn't. We talked a few times during the night, then he rang me about an hour ago.' He looked Lola hard in the eye. 'He told me a woman had been found dead in Darnley. He said she sounded like the woman I'd described to him. He . . . he also said there was a witness who'd seen her — running with a baby.' He burst out in sobs and pressed the heels of his hands against his eyes. 'He said — he said there was no sign of the baby with her when she was found. I panicked. I just couldn't keep quiet anymore. They've got my boy and I don't know what to do.' More sobs followed.

'You did the right thing in calling us,' Lola told him when he was calmer. 'Now, as you know, your house is a crime scene. That means it may contain evidence to show what happened and who did this. We have specialist colleagues who will examine the house in detail. I'll call them shortly and you can show us where all of this happened.'

'How will they get here?' he asked sharply. 'In a load of vans?'

'I'll tell them to be discreet,' Lola said. 'That might mean an unmarked vehicle. We can have them park inside your property, out of view from the road. Please don't worry about that. We'll need to make an urgent appeal for information.' His expression turned to one of terror. 'Mr Dixon, it's critical we call on the public to help us.'

'You can't!' he cried. 'They threatened to *kill* him, for God's sake! Don't you understand?'

The solicitor said, 'Mr Dixon has reason to believe these people are serious.'

'Oh? Meaning what?'

Dixon shot his solicitor a hard look and he seemed to back off.

'We will not put your son in danger, Mr Dixon,' Lola said. 'The fact is, he's in danger already and we must do what we can to get him back quickly. We've already lost several hours.'

Dixon was hunched with tension, his hands fists. He said something to his solicitor.

'My client has made his wishes very clear,' Jeremy Wilder said. 'There will no public appeal without his say-so.'

* * *

10.37 a.m.

Lola used Jeanie's dining room to call the Identification Bureau. A cat — a different one, this one black and white — emerged from under the table and curled itself round Lola's ankles while she spoke. She gave the Dixons' address and

18

stressed the urgency — and the need for as much discretion as possible. 'Ring me when you get here,' she said.

Back in the kitchen, she asked Dixon to describe the woman who took his son.

'She was . . . dark-haired, tall, quite athletic. She was dressed in black and I think she had running shoes on. Her face was half covered with one of those elasticated scarves.'

'But you could see her eyes?'

'Yes.'

'What colour were they?'

He closed his eyes. 'Blue maybe, or grey. We've got it all on film, you know. I've got digital CCTV cameras outside the house and one inside. You can see her coming into the garden and up to the side door, which is where she must have come in. Then you can see her in the hallway, going up the stairs and . . . and coming down again a minute or two later . . . with Adam. The film's stored in the cloud. Look, I'll show you.' He reached behind him for a laptop bag.

'Yes please, but in a minute,' Lola said. 'First tell us about the threats that have been made to you.'

Dixon put down his bag and looked at Lola miserably for several seconds, then turned sheepishly to his solicitor, who answered for him:

'Mr Dixon received a threat to his child's safety some weeks ago,' Wilder said. 'For what they believed to be good reasons, he and his wife chose to try to protect their son themselves.'

'What threat, Mr Dixon?' Lola asked.

Once again Wilder answered for his client: 'That the boy would be taken unless Mr Dixon undertook a . . . *certain* task on behalf of a *certain* organisation.'

'What task, Mr Dixon?' Lola demanded. 'What organisation?'

'I don't know what organisation,' Dixon said. His hands were clenched into fists on the kitchen table before him. He looked as if he was suppressing an explosion. 'They wouldn't say, but it seemed clear to me they represented another government. They approached me when I was in Germany and said they wanted access to an ethical hacking program my company has developed. They wanted to use it to hack into UK and US government defence intelligence.'

Lola studied him carefully. 'Did you believe they were serious?'

He glanced sharply up at her. 'Of course!'

'Tell us what happened.'

He took a moment before speaking. 'I was in Berlin a month ago. I was in the bar of my hotel and was approached by two men who said they wanted to discuss some potential business. We had a drink. A couple of drinks, actually. They took me to another hotel — they had a driver waiting and he drove us there. We met in a room. I don't remember which room and I don't know which hotel. We went in via a side door. They offered me a lot of money to "obtain data" for them. When they became specific, I declined. I tried to leave and . . . the tone changed. After that, two more men came along and they were more aggressive. Threatening.'

'What were they like, these men?' Lola said.

'Thugs. Well-dressed thugs. Russians, I think, though they denied the fact. White men, younger than me, apart from one who was older.' He paused, breathing hard through his nose. He cleared his throat. 'The older one had a gun inside his jacket. He made sure I'd seen it.'

'When was this?'

'Wednesday the twenty-fourth of September.'

'In Berlin, you say?'

'Yes. I was staying at the Hotel Maximillian in Mitte. The hotel they took me to was a few streets away, in the old eastern part of the city, I think. It was the kind of place where all sorts goes on.'

'How did the meeting end?'

'Without a deal,' he snarled. 'I didn't want anything to do with that kind of business.'

Lola said nothing and Dixon relaxed a little.

'I just wanted to get out of there. I said I'd forget the whole incident if they let me go. Then things got nasty. They said if I didn't want money then I should just hand the program over to them or expect . . . or expect harm to come to my wife and son.

'I started to panic but then there was a racket in the corridor outside the room. Shouting. It was enough of a distraction and I got the door open and ran out. There were police in the corridor, talking to a woman. The men saw the police and hung back, meaning I could get away. I ran down the fire stairs and hailed a cab. I got back to my hotel, gathered my things and got out of there. I moved to another hotel and got a train to Hamburg the next day. I flew from there to Amsterdam and back to Glasgow.

'For the next few days I was terrified. I kept expecting to hear from them, that they might turn up here. I was so scared. I worked from home, keeping an eye on Marta and Adam. But then days passed and I didn't hear a thing. It started to feel unreal, more like a nightmare. I decided to forget all about it.' He closed his eyes and looked despairing.

'Did you tell anyone about this?'

He nodded sheepishly. 'My friend in the police. But not because I wanted him to help. I made light of it, if I'm honest. I told Marta too, though I soon wished I hadn't. Again, I tried to make a joke. I said the Russians had tried to recruit me to spy on the government, only she didn't take it as a joke. A lot of Estonians are fearful of Moscow. A few days later she called me at work and said someone had been watching her in the woods.'

'Tell us about that.'

'It was Tuesday the seventh of October,' he said. 'Marta rang me at work, about three o'clock. Just before, actually. I had a meeting at three, and I cancelled it and came home at once.'

'So you believed her?'

'Yes,' he said. 'I . . . I'd been on the alert, you see? I panicked when she rang, but tried to sound sceptical. When I got home I made her tell me about it, at the same time pretending I didn't take it all *that* seriously. I didn't want her afraid. Even so, I made her take me to the woods. We went in the car, but when we got there she didn't want to get out. She stayed in the car and I took a look in the trees but I couldn't see anyone. Some kids, that was all. I worked from home for the next few days. I made her go there again with me the next day and the day after that, just sitting in the car, but we didn't see anyone. I started to think she maybe had imagined it after all. I *hoped* that was the case.

'Then, the following Monday — I'd gone back into the office that day — she called and said someone kept driving past the house. I said, try not to worry — but I was worried myself. Worried sick. She said she wanted to call the police. I thought about it, I really did. But I persuaded her not to. Basically I manipulated her, suggesting it was all in her mind. But I did act. I ordered new fencing. I found a company who agreed to shift their jobs around so they could do the work over the next couple of days. I had to pay them a lot, but it seemed worth it. I got cameras fitted too. And I asked an old colleague, a security expert, if he'd look after the house while I wasn't there. A man called Desmond Anderson.

'I started to feel better. I think Marta did too. But then . . .' He took a deep breath, straining as if he couldn't get enough air in his lungs. 'Then, two nights ago, a man came to see me. He came to my office — a unit at an office park near Coatbridge. It was late in the working day, after seven, and I was there on my own. He banged on the fire door at the back. I opened it a crack and he forced his way in. He wasn't one of the four I'd met in Berlin. He was English. He said I'd met with his colleagues in Germany and this was a courtesy visit. Some courtesy.'

'Did he threaten you?'

'He was very polite about it. He said he had people watching my wife and son. He knew where I lived. He showed me photographs on his phone, including — sorry . . .'

'It's okay. Take your time.'

'Including one of Marta and Adam in the woods. He said there'd be action if I didn't release my program to them within twenty-four hours. Then he left. I went straight home. I rang an estate agent to put the house on the market, except it was after hours, though I did leave a message. I decided we'd leave in the morning. We'd take a place somewhere in the middle of nowhere — in Argyll, maybe — and I'd think what to do from there. I asked the security man to stay overnight but he couldn't. His wife's mother's very ill and he needed to be with his wife in case anything happened. I was terrified. I even . . .' He paused and gave Lola a sheepish look. 'I even thought about trying to get a gun, or some other kind of weapon, though I wouldn't know where to start. We moved Adam's cot into our room — normally he's in his own room, but I wanted him with us. I set the alarm. But still . . . she got in, and without tripping the alarm. She took Adam and said, "Go to police and we kill him. Someone will contact you in the next few days." She took him from right under our noses and disappeared.' He shut his eyes. 'Marta was frantic. She screamed at me to call you, but I didn't dare. But now the bitch is dead . . . and whoever killed her has our boy.' He looked at her, his face bone pale, his jaw trembling.

'We'll do what we can, Mr Dixon,' she said. 'Now let's see the video footage you've got on your computer.'

He reached for his computer bag and took out an Apple MacBook, seeming pleased to be doing something practical. Lola rose to stand at his shoulder. Kirstie flanked him on the other side.

'I've already downloaded the relevant film,' he said. 'I'll transfer the file to you, but you can watch it here. I've edited the clips from the different cameras into a single one. It only took me a minute or two.'

He pressed play. A grainy, black-and-white image showed the Dixons' garden, but ill-defined in the darkness. There was a movement at the top of the image, then a figure appeared, running towards the house and the camera. It was impossible to make out any features. The image then cut to show a hall-way dominated by a curving, open-tread staircase, lit by a lamp on a console table. The figure, clearly a woman now, tall and lithe, emerged from a doorway and headed straight for the staircase — no stopping to look about, seeming for all the world to know exactly where she was heading. Up the stairs she went, returning only a minute later, a baby in her arms. Lola's breath caught at the chilling sight. The woman ducked back into the doorway through which she'd come, which looked to be into another room of the house. A second or two later, Dixon came racing down the stairs after her, then Marta Dixon appeared. She stopped halfway down the stairs and seemed to collapse, hanging onto the banister for dear life. The video cut to the camera at the rear of the property and showed the woman heading back down the garden. She van-ished into the gloom as Dixon came onto the lawn, stumbling as he went before stopping and looking desperately about, his whole body sagging as if he knew he'd lost her.

'We'll need the raw footage,' Lola said. 'Can you give us access to that?'

'Yes, fine.'

'DC Campbell will explain what you need to do.'

She broke off when her phone buzzed into life.

'Yes,' she said to the caller — an IB officer. 'Yes, fine. Pull up by the gates. I'll be right out.'

* * *

11.10 a.m.

Dixon and his solicitor followed Lola and Kirstie from Jeanie's house. Dixon seemed relieved when he saw the van was an unmarked white Transit. He opened the gate of his property by scanning his palm on a screen — not quite touching it — and they followed the van into the enclosed driveway. Lola got her first full view of the house. It really did resemble a pile

24

of boxes, with windows everywhere and flat roofs and balconies. The front garden was manicured to the point of looking unreal, as if the grass might be fake and the trees plastic. There was a big black Mercedes parked at the side.

Three IB officers got out of the van. Lola took the most senior aside and explained the situation while the other two put on white forensic suits.

'Who's coming into the house?' the lead officer asked.

'Mr Dixon, myself and my constable,' Lola said. 'I expect Mr Dixon will want his solicitor there too.'

'I'll ask one of the boys to organise suits for you.'

While they waited, Lola took the opportunity to have a word with Kirstie.

'Do you believe it?' she asked quietly.

'I'm not sure. It's improbable, but at the same time . . .'

'At the same time, we've got a dead woman and a missing baby — plus CCTV footage of the woman taking the child from the house.'

'But who killed her?' Kirstie asked. 'And where's the child now?'

'Good questions.'

Lola thought about the story Sorcha had told her that night in the restaurant. If she was honest, she hadn't placed a lot of store on the young woman's tale of being followed in woodland, of someone driving by her house with sinister intent. She'd imagined a lonely young woman in an unhappy, possibly controlling, relationship. She'd requested her colleague run checks on Lawrie Dixon, just in case he had form for abuse. Now it seemed she should have taken Marta's story more seriously. Should she have offered to meet her, at least? If she had, would she have recognised the threat as real? Might the child still be here, safe and well?

'If the story about the Russians is true,' Kirstie said quietly, 'then the threat to kill the child must be true as well. But how do we even begin to try to get the child back if Dixon won't let us go public?'

'Alerts at every port,' Lola said, considering all the agencies that might need to be involved, 'warnings sent to every police force . . . Hope someone, somewhere spots *something*.' Their eyes met. 'I agree, Kirstie. It would be next to impossible to find the child without a wide appeal.'

She felt shaken by the enormity of the task. Once she had more facts, she'd talk to her superintendent, Elaine Walsh. Elaine was expert at asking the right questions.

'We'll take a look inside the house, then talk to Marta Dixon,' she said to Kirstie. 'See how well her story matches her husband's and find out what else she knows.'

One of the IB officers came over with suits.

'You stick by me,' Lola said to Dixon once they were kitted out. 'If anything needs to be touched — doors opening, that kind of thing — I'll do it.' She showed him a gloved hand.

They went to the front door.

'It recognises my palm,' Dixon said through the forensic mask, eyes on the scanning device by the door. 'Or you can put in a code.'

Lola saw there was a keypad.

'What's the code?' she asked.

He recited a ten-digit string of numbers. Lola punched them in and heard a mechanism whirr.

'That's it unlocked,' Dixon said.

Lola turned the handle, pushed open the door and stepped inside.

The house, for all its windows, was oppressively dark inside, and freezing cold, as if refrigerated. Her eyes quickly accustomed themselves to the shade and she made out the staircase she'd seen on the video. It curved up to a gallery. She spied the camera, fixed into a corner of the architrave. There were framed photographs on the walls, including one of an older man holding a baby — Adam, Lola assumed. She wondered who the man was. Marta's father, perhaps?

'Is that the door she came through?' she asked Dixon.

'Yes. It's goes into the utility room.'

Lola went to it, and pushed it open to reveal a narrow space. A washing machine, dryer and cupboards stood against the right-hand wall. A door in the far wall showed daylight through an opaque glass panel. Beside it was another palm scanner and keypad. Dixon went to it, then turned and eyed Lola, waiting for an instruction.

'A different code?' she asked him.

'Same.' He reminded her of the numbers and she typed them in. The door's lock whirred within the wood. She turned the handle, opened it and stepped back out into the overcast morning, to find herself on narrow, fenced-in decking that ran towards the back of the property. She turned to examine the door. There was the familiar palm scanner and keypad on the brickwork to one side.

'Come outside, would you?' she said to Dixon.

Dixon came to stand beside her, his solicitor staying close. Lola pulled the door shut. Locks whirred quietly back into place. She examined the closed door. There wasn't a scratch on it or the frame it fitted snugly into.

'So she knew the code?' she asked Dixon.

'Clearly.'

Lola followed the decking to the back of the property, Dixon at her heels. Here a flight of wooden steps led down to a long sloping garden. Fencing surrounded the garden to a height of at least six feet, including at the farthest point, where it separated the garden from dense-looking woodland.

'You think she came over the fence at the end?' she asked Dixon.

'She must have done.'

'Are those the same woods where your wife says someone was watching her?'

'Yes. They extend that way.' He pointed left. 'The short-cut is over there, but yes, it's all the same woodland.'

She led the way back inside and stopped in the hallway, then looked from the utility room door to the staircase.

'On the video she comes out of the utility room and heads straight for the stairs,' she said to Dixon.

'That's right.'

'Almost as if she knew where she was going.' She looked at him for a reaction.

He shrugged and shook his head. 'She'd have assumed we slept upstairs, I guess . . .'

'Shall we go up?' Lola asked.

He led the way up the curving staircase. There were gaps between the treads that triggered Lola's vertigo, but she made it to the top without having to hold the banister to steady herself.

Dixon took them into a bedroom at the back of the house: a vast room with floor-to-ceiling windows on two sides and a wrap-around balcony. A child's cot stood in a corner, made of wood with a bright-painted mobile dangling over it. Dixon's eyes seemed locked on it.

'Where were you when she came in?' Lola asked.

'In bed,' he said. 'Marta was asleep. I was awake. I'd been to sleep but I woke up and was dozing. That's normal for me.'

'And she came through the door we just used?'

He nodded, eyes still on the cot. He looked to sway a little.

'Are you okay?'

'Not really,' he managed. 'I'll be all right.'

'Take your time. Tell us what happened.'

He moved his eyes to the door and pointed. 'She opened the door and put the light on. I jumped out of bed. I could only see her eyes because of the mask. She said, "Stay where you are," and I saw she had a gun. I . . . I thought it was a nightmare. I hadn't heard anything until she burst in. But it wasn't a nightmare. I said, "What do you want?" She said, "I'll shoot you both if you move again. I've come for your child." I screamed at her to get out, then I ran at her in a blind panic, but she pointed the gun at the cot — and I froze!' His voice was shaking. 'By this time Marta was up, kneeling on the

28

bed, terror-stricken. Adam was crying too. Marta screamed at the woman to get out, to leave Adam alone — only then the woman pointed the gun at Marta.' He shut his eyes for a moment. 'Then she pointed the gun back at me and went to the cot. She positioned herself at that end—' he pointed — 'and reached down and scooped Adam up in one arm, all the time keeping the gun pointed at one of us. Adam was wriggling and Marta was beside herself. "Come after us and we'll kill him," she said. "You'll hear from us, then you'll know what to do." Then she started backing out of the room, still waving that bloody gun about. And she was gone. Down the stairs and out of the house. I went after her — I couldn't help myself — but she was so quick. Like an athlete.'

He stopped, eyes squeezed tight now, near to tears.

'What did you do then?'

He sighed. 'I saw to Marta. I found her clinging onto the banister at the bottom of the stairs, having a sort of panic attack, asking me over and over, "What do we do? What do we do?" She said we should call the police but I said, "We can't. Don't you understand? They'll hurt him if we do."

'I called Desmond and he came within fifteen minutes. We gave Marta whisky and a sleeping tablet. Desmond stayed at the house while I went out.'

'Out where?'

'Driving around the streets like a madman. I thought, if I could find her — the woman — I might be able reason with her, or — I don't know — offer her money.'

'What time did you go out?'

He frowned. 'Erm . . . I'd have left about ten minutes after Desmond arrived. So, one forty-five?'

'Where did you go exactly?'

'Round the local streets. Round Giffnock, through Newlands, Clarkston, Whitecraigs. It wasn't systematic. I was panicking. I called home about ten minutes after I'd left. Desmond said Marta was asleep.'

'Did you go to Darnley?'

'Darnley? No, I didn't go that far.' He looked at her and his expression darkened. 'You mean, because that's where you found her?'

Lola ignored the question and asked smoothly, 'Or near Rouken Glen Park? Did you pass by there?'

He took a moment. 'I'd have passed it on the way back from Whitecraigs.'

'What time did you come back to the house?'

Something seemed to occur to him. 'It'll be on the dash-cam. The whole drive will be on there. That's the last time I drove anywhere, so it won't have recorded over. I'll give you the SD card. It'll have the times on it too.'

'And after you came home?'

'Marta was asleep in the living room. Desmond was in the hallway waiting for me. I made coffee for the two of us and we talked about what to do. I called my . . . my police contact about three — and no,' he said with challenge in his eyes, 'I still won't tell you his name. He's helped me. I won't betray his trust.'

Lola nodded, acknowledging his position while not approving.

'He offered to come round. He said I should phone 999 at once, or he could do it. I said no. We spoke again around six, then he rang me at nine thirty to tell me a woman had been found dead at Darnley Glen. She matched the description I'd given him — and a witness had seen her with a child. I knew then I had no choice, so I reported it.' He sighed dismally. 'That's it. Now you know everything.'

'That's all very helpful,' Lola said. 'Of course, we'll need you to give a full statement in due course.'

He nodded.

'Okay, let's go back next door,' she said. 'Time for me to talk to your wife.'

CHAPTER FIVE

11.54 a.m.

She found Marta Dixon sitting on the floor of Jeanie's back bedroom, wearing a pink tracksuit. She was holding a teddy bear — her son's, Lola assumed — and resembled an over-grown toddler. She was pale, and her ash-blonde hair was tied back but coming loose. She looked exhausted and seemed barely to register Lola's arrival. An older woman — the friend Michelle had mentioned — rose from a wicker armchair beside the bed.

'Are you the police?' the woman asked. She was for-ty-something and low-key glamorous in a corporate way, in a red jacket, black skirt and heels.

Lola introduced herself.

'She's petrified. Don't bully her.'

'Why would I do that, Ms . . . ?'

'Sarah Finnie.' She looked down her rather sharp nose. 'People make mistakes when they're frightened.'

'Mistakes?'

'They would have called you, but fear got the better of them. They're human and vulnerable. Please try to remember that.'

31

'I'll make sure to,' Lola said smoothly. She turned and spoke to the woman on the floor: 'Hello, Mrs Dixon. Is it all right if I call you Marta?'

The young woman peered up and nodded.

'I'm DCI Harris of Police Scotland. Marta, your husband has told us what happened. He's shown us the house as well and some of my forensics colleagues are currently going over it. I'd like to ask you some questions, if that's okay? It would be easiest to do it downstairs, but we can talk up here if you prefer.'

Marta Dixon nodded. 'Downstairs is fine.' She started to get up.

'I assume I can come too,' Sarah said.

'You can come downstairs,' Lola said. 'But I'll be talking to Marta on her own — or with her solicitor, if she likes. Perhaps you'd like to keep Mr Dixon company.'

'Very well,' Sarah Finnie said, then seemed to hesitate before saying, somewhat sheepishly, 'I gave Marta a sedative, by the way.'

'So my colleague said.'

The woman's eyes narrowed. 'The poor girl has hardly slept,' she snapped. 'I couldn't bear to see her like that. I'm sure you'd rather I hadn't, but there we are.'

'What did you give her exactly?' Lola asked, looking at Marta, at her barely focused eyes.

'Diazepam,' she said. 'One of mine, as it happens.' She looked at Lola with challenge in her eyes.

'I see.'

Lola turned and left the bedroom.

* * *

12.02 p.m.

Lawrie Dixon was in the dining room, tapping irritably at his phone. Sarah Finnie went in and spoke quietly to him. He reacted by turning to glower through the doorway at Lola.

Lola nodded in acknowledgement, then turned and went into the kitchen.

Marta sat down at the table and the solicitor took the place beside her. She looked hunched and small and not very present. Her eyes were on the table before her, but unfocused.

'How are you, Marta?' Lola asked.

Marta blinked at the question and frowned. 'Okay,' she said unconvincingly.

'Marta, did you see the person who took Adam?'

Marta nodded, then closed her eyes with a wince of pain. 'She came into our bedroom,' she said. 'She put the light on. She had a gun.'

Her English was perfect and nuanced. Only some of her vowels gave her away as a non-native speaker.

'Did you recognise her?'

'Did I . . . ? How would I?'

'I understand you thought someone had been spying on you. That someone had been watching you in the woods then driven past the house.'

Her lips parted as she processed the words. 'Yes, but . . .' She stopped and frowned.

'I wondered if it was the same person.'

Marta's eyes moved as if she was examining her memories but struggling to make sense of them. 'Well, it must be. It *must* be . . .'

'Your husband told you about the approach he'd had in Germany a few weeks ago?'

Marta eyed Lola carefully. 'I didn't realise how serious it was. Then someone came to see him at his work last night. Did he tell you? He was very frightened, saying we needed to move house.' She shut her eyes and groaned. 'I begged him to call the police but he wouldn't have it. These people had warned him not to. He said we'd go away for a few days, the three of us, until we worked out what to do.'

'Tell us what happened last night in your own words,' Lola said. 'Tell us everything you remember and in as much detail as you can.'

33

Marta nodded unhappily, then told her tale haltingly. It matched Lawrie's in all the important ways, though with enough diversion that Lola tended to believe her.

'We should have left last night, as soon as he came home,' Marta said in a whisper. 'Just got in the car and gone. Anywhere!' She shut her eyes, then began to shake as she sobbed. 'We're going to lose him, aren't we?' she asked quietly, of no one in particular. 'We're going to lose our beautiful boy.'

* * *

12.25 p.m.

Kirstie went to find Lawrie Dixon and brought him to the kitchen. Sarah Finnie came too. There weren't enough chairs, so Lola stood, bidding Dixon to take hers. Kirstie offered Sarah her chair, but she refused.

'You believe us now?' Dixon asked her grimly.

'We need to find your son, Mr Dixon. That's all I'm concerned with. We'll act fast, but we'll need your help. We'll need all your devices and access to your accounts: email, social media, home, work.'

'What?' That clearly horrified him.

'And we need to make a public appeal. It's imperative.'

'I've already told you — *no!*'

Marta flinched at his tone.

'Such threats are made for a reason, Mr Dixon,' Lola went on. 'To frighten off any attempt of recovery. In fact, time is critical.'

Dixon looked sick.

'Not yet,' he said, his voice breaking. 'Please, not yet.'

'Very well. We will make it known a baby has been taken and that we believe the dead woman at Darnley Glen is the one who took him. We will keep your names out of it.'

He thought about it then gave a grudging, 'Okay.'

'As for your devices and accounts—'

34

'You can't have them,' he said abruptly. 'I'm sorry. These people are going to contact me. I want them to be able to reach me. I'll tell you if I hear anything.'

'Mr Dixon—'

'I said *no*.'

Lola breathed. 'Very well, for now, but we will discuss it again. Keep your phones on and charged and let us know the minute you hear from anyone. In the meantime, we'll set about finding you both somewhere to stay in Glasgow.'

Dixon nodded.

'If you could give us Desmond Anderson's contact details, that would be helpful, as we'll need to speak to him. DC Campbell will stay here until we can arrange for a family liaison officer to be with you. I believe Mrs Quigley is happy for you to be here for now, and we'll hopefully have a place for you to go later this afternoon. In the meantime, I'll need photographs of Adam, taken as recently as possible, please, clearly showing his face — not for public broadcast,' she added, seeing Dixon's alarm, 'but so we can ask the Home Office to alert all ports.'

'All ports?' Sarah Finnie asked. 'You mean—'

'A precaution,' Lola said. 'We have to do everything we can.'

'I see,' Sarah said. She looked unsettled for the first time. Lola studied her for a moment.

'I wonder if you and I could have a chat, Ms Finnie,' she said. 'In the dining room, perhaps?'

'Of course.' Sarah Finnie bent and murmured something to Marta. Then she stood upright, looked Lola in the eye and said, 'After you.'

* * *

12.39 p.m.

'I'm not sure there's anything I can tell you that you don't already know,' Sarah said. She'd pulled out a chair and made herself comfortable at the dining table.

35

Lola sat down opposite her.

'How well do you know Marta?' she asked.

'She's my friend,' Sarah said. 'I'd say I know her very well.'

Lola nodded, considering. How old was Sarah Finnie? Forty at least, maybe forty-five. Marta was in her mid-twenties.

'She doesn't have many friends, does she?'

'Not in this country, not yet. She's only been here a couple of years. It takes time.'

'How did you two meet?'

'Through Lawrie, of course. I used to work for him, some time ago now, in his first business — the one he sold.'

'Doing what?'

'Head of sales.' She smiled. 'Now I have my own company, dealing with property, but Lawrie and I have remained in touch. When he moved back from Estonia with Marta in tow, Lawrie asked me to take her out shopping and for a meal. As it happened we got on very well. We see each other once a month or so. I like her.'

'Do you have much in common?' Lola asked.

'We have Lawrie in common,' Sarah said, a little archly.

'Did Marta tell you she'd been worried lately?'

'About the person who was following her, you mean? Yes, she did — after she'd told Lawrie. She called me and I tried to reassure her.'

'What did she say to you?'

'That someone had been watching her and the baby as they came through the woods near the house. She said she'd told Lawrie but he'd refused to call the police. I offered to come over. She said no. Then . . .' She paused and looked at her hands.

'Then what, Ms Finnie?'

'Then she asked me not to tell Lawrie she'd called me.'

Lola frowned. 'And what did you make of that?'

She took her time before answering. 'I took it as a sign, if I'm honest. I know Lawrie very well. He's one of the most rational people I know. I'm afraid I read between the lines and took it that he didn't believe her, that he thought she was imagining things. So I didn't go round and I didn't tell Lawrie she'd called me. I did, however, call Marta a couple of days later. I asked if she'd like to go to a vintage clothing market with me on the Sunday. She said she'd like to but that she wasn't feeling very well and planned to stay in for a few days. I'm afraid I didn't call again. Then, this morning,' she said, her tone darkening, 'Lawrie called me and told me everything that had happened. I came straight over. It seems they've got themselves into something of a mess, doesn't it?'

'Where do you live, Ms Finnie?'

'Outside Milngavie,' she said. 'I have a big house there and plenty of room for them to stay, but I understand you have other plans.'

'Yes, we'll find them accommodation,' Lola said. 'Can I have your contact number?'

'Of course,' she said. 'I'll give you a business card.'

* * *

12.56 p.m.

Lola called Anna from the car.

'Are you still at Darnley?'

'Yes, but not for much longer. We're about to move the body. I've had Aidan Pierce and Marcus McVittie on house-to-house for the past hour, but nothing so far — not that I'm aware of anyway. How did you get on in Giffnock?'

'A baby was taken — from his parents' bedroom. I've seen CCTV footage and it looks like our victim. The parents say she had a gun. Just came into the house, waved the gun about, grabbed the baby, told them they'd be hearing from someone, then took off.'

'My God, boss. We'll need to make an appeal — and fast.'

'Not without the parents' permission,' Lola said, 'and they're not giving it. They're terrified. I didn't push it but I think I'll have to. There's something very strange about their story, and yet so much of it is already evidenced. It looks like a very slick, professional job — or at least it was to start with. Not long after that, the same woman was running with the child, apparently in distress; within an hour or two she was dead and the child gone again. Has Jonno had any luck getting CCTV footage from the local authority?'

'Yes, quite a bit. Good images of a young woman running westward along Rouken Glen Road at the right time, he says. He says she disappears into an industrial estate just before the motorway, not far from here. He's on to businesses to see what their security cameras might have picked up.'

'Excellent. I'd like him to present the footage to the team later today at Helen Street. Shall we aim for three o'clock? Meantime, I'll talk to someone in Organised Crime. We'll plan next steps then. Any attention from the media since the appeal?'

'Sky TV are here but they're keeping their distance. Apparently the papers are itching for comment, but I've referred them to Deborah Truebig in Corporate Comms. Oh, there was a funny thing, boss. A young lad — well, in his early twenties, by the sound of it — came by on a bike. A pedal bike, I mean. I didn't see him but he talked to one of the lads guarding the cordon. Asked all sorts of questions and seemed agitated. Gary — the officer — asked him for his name and he took fright and rode off. But not before he'd pulled one of those elastic bandanas up from his neck to cover his face. Just the same kind the dead woman had on. Gary alerted Marcus and Marcus tried to go after him in a car, but no luck.'

'What sort of questions was he asking?' Lola asked.

'Was someone dead? Do we know who? Is it a woman? Gary's written out a description of the lad and the bike. It might be nothing. But then again . . .'

Next, Lola rang Superintendent Elaine Walsh and gave her a quick update. 'The husband's Lawrence Dixon,' she said. 'A cyber security expert. His name seems familiar.'

'So it should,' Elaine said sharply. 'He's Police Scotland's new cyber forensics "tsar".'

'Is he?' Lola's skin crept a little. 'You mean he's a colleague?'

'I think he's been given some kind of advisory role by the new assistant chief constable.' Lola heard Elaine tapping at the keyboard. 'Yes,' she said after a few moments, 'that's him. I'm looking at the press announcement that went out a few months ago. *Lawrence Dixon, founder of Cyber Forager Ltd and a global leader in the procurement and protection of digital forensic evidence, is to lead ACC Thompson's new cyber taskforce, it was announced today.*'

'He didn't mention that to me,' Lola said.

'Well, he does have other things on his mind,' Elaine pointed out.

'Of course, boss.'

'I was at an event he spoke at,' Elaine said now. 'Let me have a look and see if I've still got the programme.'

Lola heard papers being shuffled.

'If I remember rightly,' Elaine said, 'he was on a panel at a cybercrime conference in Glasgow back in August. I remember now. I didn't particularly take to him. He was . . . very smooth, shall we say? Yes, I've got the programme for the event here.' A pause. 'There are speakers' biographies at the end, including his. Remind me to give it to you.'

'Thanks, boss.'

* * *

2.16 p.m.

Lola phoned the Organised Crime Unit and was pleased when an old pal, Inspector Cath McKay, answered. Even more pleased when Cath said she had ten minutes right now.

'Russians?' Cath said when Lola had finished telling her story. 'Blimey. Do you believe him?'

'I'm not sure, but the Dixons' baby was taken in the night. I've seen CCTV footage.'

'And they're refusing to let you name him or publish photos?' Cath said. 'Sounds like their fear's genuine — or they're afraid of something they don't want you sticking your nose into.'

'They've given us a couple of photos we can share with other agencies,' Lola said. Dixon had supplied two good photos of his son's face, a bright-eyed little boy with Marta's fair colouring, each clear but taken in different lights and contexts. 'He's a bonnie wee thing,' she said.

'Any distinguishing marks?'

'I'm afraid not. So, what do you think we can do, given the constraints?'

Cath took a moment to think. 'Alert all ports,' she said. 'We can do that for you. I'll let the Kidnapping and Extortion people at the NCA know as well.' This was the National Crime Agency, based in London but with a UK-wide remit. 'Apart from that, I'm not sure you can do much more than make it public and see what comes in — a neighbour who suddenly has a kid they didn't have before, the sound of a baby crying from a flat, that sort of thing. Of course, you know you'll be deluged with calls — well-meant and otherwise.'

'Thanks, Cath. I'll email scans of the photos of Adam Dixon across to you now.'

'I'll do what I can, but I don't hold out much hope, Lola. I've got to be honest.'

'I understand,' Lola said.

CHAPTER SIX

3.05 p.m.

DC Jonno Gillies had made a montage of CCTV footage obtained from a number of sources. Lola's team watched it together in a meeting room at Helen Street on a wall-mounted screen. Jonno seemed as giddy as a schoolboy giving a particularly exciting holiday report.

'Everything you're going to see is from cameras along the A727,' he said, 'taken over a period of twenty-two minutes between 1.47 a.m. and 2.09 a.m.' He had a clicker in his hand and pressed a button. 'This first clip is from one of the cameras at Eastwood Toll, looking west along Rouken Glen Road.'

The video was grainy because of the poor light. A car passed in one direction and another came in the opposite direction, then a dark figure crept out from what looked like a side road.

'That's one of two road entrances to Eastwood Park,' Jonno said.

The tall but slight figure, which seemed to be holding something at chest height, hurried away from the camera along the main road, keeping close to a wall. The clip ended.

'Now we cut to a second camera, this one about three hundred metres west of the roundabout but pointing back the way, so the individual is now coming towards us.'

The video showed a still street, the only movement a flicker on the left-hand side as the figure came along the side of the wall, walking quickly, but not running. A car passed, heading away from the camera; a second came towards it. Its headlights flared, briefly distorting the image.

'Now we're onto the third clip,' Jonno said. 'We're looking east again, but from Spiersbridge Roundabout, about three minutes later.'

The same figure was moving quickly now, legs kicking in a light jog. A car approached in the opposite direction, then slowed as it passed the figure, before speeding up, then making a quick U-turn at a gap in the central reservation.

'The car's registration is a match for McCreedy's Skoda Octavia,' Jonno said.

They watched as the car came back past the running figure and halted. A man got out and crossed to the middle of the road. They watched the scene play out just as the cab driver had described it.

'Are these images digital?' Lola asked Jonno.

'They certainly are.'

'Zoom in on the woman,' she said.

Jonno did as he was asked. The image was fuzzy at first then crystallised to show a dark-haired woman, dressed all in black and holding a bundle — seemingly wrapped in some kind of blanket — at chest height.

'Can you get any closer?'

'Not without it distorting, boss.'

'Try.'

Jonno tried, but the image grew blurred.

'There's a clearer shot of her face on a later clip,' Anna said.

'Okay,' Lola told Jonno. 'Zoom out and let it play on.'

The scene unfolded, showing McCreedy returning to his car and driving off. The woman remained where she was for several seconds, then began to walk on before breaking once more into a run.

Jonno's next clip showed the figure passing the edge of an industrial estate, keeping close to the buildings, then slowing to a walk, before slipping down the side of a building.

'There's one final clip,' Jonno said, moving the video on. 'This is from inside the industrial estate, courtesy of one of the businesses. We're chasing recordings from others.'

The clip was crisp and showed the woman coming along the side of a building, not hurrying but taking her time, occasionally pausing to peer back the way she'd come. Then she whirled completely around. In that moment, there was a glimpse of something. Jonno stopped the video and zoomed in. Lola saw something pale amid the bundle in her arms.

'A baby's face?' Lola asked, her mouth suddenly dry.

'Could be,' Anna said grimly.

No one in the room dared breathe.

'Let it play on,' Lola said quietly, aware how tense her muscles were.

The woman on the screen reached a doorway and stepped into it. She adjusted the bundle in her arms to free a hand then held something to her ear. A phone. A second later, she became animated, as if she was in conversation. She leaned out from the doorway and peered about.

Jonno pressed pause. 'That's the best image of her face, we reckon.'

Lola leaned in forward.

The face on the screen was distinct, clearly showing her jawline, her nose, even the shape of her brow. Her hair was distinct too, dark but pulled back from her high forehead and knotted or pinned somehow. Lola was as sure as she could be that this was the woman they'd found dead at Darnley Glen.

'Have we taken screenshots from this?' she asked.

'Three decent ones,' Jonno said, 'at quarter-second intervals.'

'Where are we with the appeal for information about the woman?' Lola asked.

'Thin pickings so far.' Anna consulted a couple of stapled sheets of A4. 'A German woman thinks she might be her daughter who went missing three years ago, but the age seems wrong. The daughter would be thirty-five now.'

Lola recalled the victim's face and would have put her at no older than thirty. 'Get a photo of the daughter anyway. Have we spoken to Interpol?'

'I have,' Kirstie said. 'I registered that we'd found a woman along with a description. They'll check their database and send through results.'

Lola thought for a moment, weighing risk.

'I think we need to go public with the screenshots,' she said. 'We'll say she may have had a baby with her.'

No one spoke. Anna looked understandably alarmed. It was horrible to think of a family member seeing their loved one's image in a police appeal relating to a murder.

'I'll talk to Superintendent Walsh,' she said. 'Get her okay. Can you email the images to me now, Jonno?'

He nodded and clattered at his keyboard.

'Right, let it play to the end,' Lola said.

The woman on the screen turned her head sharply to the right, as if she'd seen something. She put the phone away, then darted back the way she'd come and out of range of the camera.

'That's everything we have so far,' Jonno told the silent room. 'We've checked cameras further west along the A727, covering the next hour, including under the motorway — she must have passed that way, but if she did, it wasn't on foot.'

'Someone got her,' Anna said quietly. 'Someone with transport.'

'We need the registration of every vehicle passing under the motorway heading west for the next hour,' Lola said.

'We're already on it,' Anna said. 'We've got ninety-seven registrations to go through.'

'That many, at that time of night?'

44

Anna nodded. 'Lawrie Dixon's Land Rover wasn't one of them,' she said. 'Which tallies with the dashcam footage he gave us. That shows him tearing round the suburbs for just over an hour. He didn't go anywhere near the M77. A good number of the cars going under the bridge were taxis,' Anna said now, and added pointedly, 'including one belonging to Murphy Cars. It's a black Skoda Octavia, registered to a Robert McCreedy of Thornliebank. It passed under the motorway about twenty minutes after that last bit of footage.'

Lola felt all eyes on her.

'We don't have any other evidence pointing his way,' she said. 'Not enough to search his car, not yet.' She thought for a moment. 'There's nothing to stop us running a few checks on him, though. See what comes back.' She looked to Anna, who nodded to say she'd get onto it. 'Have we no film behind Sainsbury's?' Lola asked now. 'Nothing from any doorbell cameras?'

Jonno shook his head.

'What about the lad on the bike?' she asked Anna. 'The one the uniformed officer spoke to?'

Anna looked to Marcus to answer.

'No luck, boss,' Marcus said. 'I never even got a look at him. Jonno's checked the CCTV but no luck there either.'

'I've got the officer's description of him,' Anna said, leafing through her notes. 'Six feet tall or thereabouts, skinny build, scruffy sandy-blond hair, freckles, sharp features, blue eyes. The bike was black, a mountain bike. He wasn't wearing a helmet. He had on outdoor wear, a zip-up black top, black outdoor trousers, possibly black boots too. He was English, Gary thinks, possibly northern. Well spoken. That's all.'

Lola sat for a moment, thinking about the baby, taken and apparently untraceable. Adam Dixon's photographs had gone out to all ports, Cath McKay had confirmed as much. Now it was a case of waiting — and hoping.

'Any news on a post-mortem on our victim?' Lola asked Anna.

'Tomorrow morning, hopefully,' Anna said. 'I've asked for a verbal account ahead of a written report.'

Lola got wearily to her feet.

'Good work so far,' she told the team. 'Jonno, are you free to come and see the super with me now? I'd like her to see some of that CCTV footage.'

* * *

3.52 p.m.

'My God,' Elaine Walsh said when Jonno paused the clip. 'That's the baby's face, isn't it?'

'We think so, boss,' Lola said.

'Why would any young woman do such a thing?' Elaine asked. 'And if she did, where's the child now?'

'Excellent questions, boss,' Lola said.

'The call for information has gone out, hasn't it? Anything come back yet?'

'Nothing significant.'

'And no one's been reported missing who fits the woman's description?'

'Not in the UK, not yet. Kirstie Campbell is speaking to Interpol, focusing on Northern European countries initially.' Lola turned to Jonno. 'Thank you, DC Gillies.' The constable nodded, shut his laptop and left the room.

Elaine rubbed her mouth, thinking. Lola said nothing, just waited.

'Your cab driver witness said the woman seemed in distress,' she said. 'Why would she be in distress, unless something had gone wrong with her plan?'

'Good question, boss.'

'And if she threatened the Dixons with a gun, what happened to it? Why didn't she use it to defend herself from her attacker?'

'We only have the Dixons' word she had a gun,' Lola pointed out.

'That's true. As for his story about the Russian gangsters . . . it's incredible.'

'I know,' Lola agreed. 'But why would he make it up?'

'Let's say he is lying,' Elaine said, 'then who was following his wife? Or is she lying too? If so, why?'

'I don't think she's lying, boss. I think Marta Dixon is very frightened.'

'Distressed or just frightened?'

She started to answer then stopped herself. 'Frightened, definitely. I'm not sure about the distress. She was sedated when we spoke to her earlier. We will speak to her again, of course.'

'Lawrie Dixon said a man visited him at his office,' Elaine said now. 'Is there any proof?'

'We're trying to get some,' Lola said.

Elaine fell quiet, thinking. Lola waited a few seconds, then took her chance: 'Boss, it's essential we learn the woman's identity. That might lead us to the child. I think we should publish the woman's photo — a still from the footage at the industrial estate. And . . . I'd like to make it known she had a child with her — and that a child was taken from a home in Glasgow. But we won't name the child or the family.'

Elaine eyed her for several seconds.

'It's a gamble, I know,' Lola went on. 'For one thing, we could end up with a media circus — plus a thousand and one well-meant but unhelpful calls from the public. But maybe that's what we need. I was wondering . . . about holding a press conference.'

Elaine considered it. 'Okay. It'll get people's attention for sure. Did you get the Dixons a safe house, by the way?'

'Yes. Anna managed to get one of our flats in Garnethill. They should be there now.'

'Okay, Lola. Tell Corporate Comms you need a press conference for this evening. Say you've agreed the approach with me. Let me know the time and I'll be there. Oh — and Lola?' The super's expression changed. 'I think I need to tell the assistant chief constable it's Lawrie Dixon's boy who's been taken.

He'd want to know. Partly because he might want Dixon to step aside from the cyber tsar role while this is going on.'

'Probably sensible,' Lola said, then caught herself.

'What is it?' Elaine asked.

'Dixon spoke to a "friend" in the police during the night, wanting advice. This friend urged him to report the boy missing but he didn't — not until the same friend gave him intel about the dead woman at Darnley Glen. Dixon doesn't want to tell us who his contact is.'

'Not a lot we can do about that,' Elaine murmured grimly.

Lola chewed her lip before saying tentatively. 'It couldn't . . . You don't think it could be ACC Thompson, do you?'

Elaine's expression told her what she thought of that suggestion.

'No,' Lola said, and smiled. 'Silly me.'

'I'll call the ACC right now,' Elaine said, lifting her phone receiver. 'It's up to him if he wants to offload Dixon temporarily. Oh, and I nearly forgot—' she lifted papers from a pile on her desk and pulled out a glossy brochure — 'the programme for that cyber conference I was at in August. Lawrie Dixon's biography is at the back.'

'Thanks, boss.'

* * *

4.14 p.m.

Back at her desk, Lola looked over the conference brochure. The event had taken place at a big hotel in Edinburgh and was titled, *Unlocking the Future of Cyber Forensics in Policing*. The programme for the day was on the second page, after a foreword from a government minister. Lawrence Dixon, of Cyber Forager Ltd, had appeared as one of a panel of expert speakers immediately after the keynote speech from a UK-based FBI official.

She flicked to the back and found the 'speaker biographies'. Dixon's photograph was arresting. He posed side on, smiling unpleasantly over his left shoulder, his eyes dark and dead like a shark's. A string of academic qualifications and professional certifications followed his name, and a potted CV of his career in cyber security, including a senior role at one of the banks, before he set up his own business. He'd served as an expert witness in a number of court cases, presenting digital evidence for both prosecution and defence. He was married with one child, the biography concluded, and lived in Glasgow.

What are you hiding? she asked that smiling, dead-eyed face. *What are you lying about and what's the truth?*

On her computer she went onto the Police Scotland website and found the pages dedicated to combating cybercrime. There was a page outlining Dixon's new role. The same photograph leered out of the screen at her and beneath it was some text spelling out Dixon's focus during his appointment, including various projects. One of these was to create a 'band' of cyber champions within Police Scotland, with officers and staff members drawn from all areas.

Something stirred in her memory. She glanced up and across the open-plan office to DS Aidan Pierce's desk. He wasn't there. She peered about the office, then reached into her pocket for her work mobile.

'Hi, Anna, it's me,' she said. 'Did Aidan apply for that cyber champions thing? I remember you mentioning it.'

'He did, boss, and he got accepted.'

'What does it involve?'

'As I understand it, it's to do with communicating the importance of cyber security, recognising a cybercrime, and gathering and protecting digital evidence,' Anna said. 'He's done some online training and there's a network been set up. I think there was talk of an away day one weekend. Why, boss?'

'Has he met Dixon, do you know?'

'Hmm. Not sure. I can ask if you like.'

'No, don't,' Lola said. 'I'll talk to him myself.'

She hung up then wandered to Pierce's desk. Pierce was obsessively tidy, and his papers were squarely piled in a plastic tray. With another surreptitious glance about the office, she began to leaf through them — and found a shiny Police Scotland–branded brochure entitled *Cyber Forensics for the 2020s*. Lawrie Dixon grinned at her in close-up — this a different photograph, but no more appealing. She put it back where she'd found it, then stood, mulling it over grimly. Dixon would be training a number of officers and staff across the Force. There was no reason to think Pierce was his contact — other than the fact Dixon was exactly the kind of man Pierce looked up to and wished to emulate: the 'strong man' leader who always got his way.

Back at her own desk her personal phone was buzzing.

Her heart sank when she saw it was Sandy. She remembered he'd messaged her earlier, asking her to call. While she'd been busy it had been easy to put him, and the news he'd broken on Sunday evening, out of her mind.

Her first instinct was to ignore the call, to let it ring out, to let him leave a message if he chose to. But she chided herself and picked up.

'Hiya,' she said, determinedly breezy.

'Hi. Erm . . . you didn't call me back. You snowed?'

'It's been pretty full on.' She took a breath. 'You okay?'

'Aye, I'm fine.' He sounded tense and strained. 'Just . . . wondered what you were doing later. I thought we could get something to eat maybe. It might be good to go somewhere new.'

Somewhere new? Because their relationship had entered new territory? Or because it was a neutral place where neither of them had the advantage?

'But if you're too busy . . .'

'No,' she said quickly. 'No, it's not that. I'm planning to do a press conference but that shouldn't be too late. I can get away after that. Maybe after eight?'

'Okay.'

They listened to each other's silence for several seconds.

'So,' he began tentatively, 'how are you feeling about . . . things?'

'I'm not sure, if I'm honest, Sand. But, like I said at the weekend, it's for me to deal with.'

'I'm looking forward to seeing you.'

'All right,' she said, trying to put a smile in her voice. 'Book somewhere for eight or after, and let me know. I'll see you there.'

* * *

5.01 p.m.

Lola spoke to Deborah Truebig from Corporate Comms and they agreed to hold a press conference at six thirty. She left Deborah to send an urgent message out to all her media contacts, then drove to Garnethill to visit the Dixons at the safe house. It wasn't a house but a flat in one of the new-builds overlooking the motorway where it cut through Charing Cross. A family liaison officer was with them and set about making coffee while Lola talked to Lawrie and Marta in the living room. Marta seemed barely conscious, her eyelids drooping.

'I would feel happier if you saw a doctor,' Lola said gently.

'She doesn't want to,' Dixon answered for her.

'Is that right, Marta?' Lola asked.

Marta managed a nod.

The FLO came in with a tray of steaming mugs and put it down on a low coffee table.

Lola explained what steps she and her team had taken so far to find Adam.

'We're planning to hold a press conference at six thirty,' she said. 'We're telling our media contacts that it relates to the woman we found dead at Darnley Glen — *and* that we'll

51

be announcing a development. We're going to tell them we believe the woman had a young child with her.'

'You're what?' Dixon demanded in alarm. Beside him, Marta's hands fluttered to her mouth.

Lola went calmly on: 'We'll say we believe it's the same child who was taken from a house in Glasgow's Southside in the early hours of the morning. We don't plan to name the child, or you or your wife, and we won't say which area of the Southside.'

'Is it really necessary?' Dixon asked shakily.

'The media will cover the news extensively and it will get the attention of the public. It should prompt more calls and hopefully give us the lead we need to find Adam.'

Dixon's face was pale, his mouth drawn, but he nodded, seeming to accept the argument. Marta said nothing, staring at a spot on the floor and hunching lower in her seat.

On her way out of the building, Lola listened to a voicemail from Elaine saying she'd spoken to ACC Thompson, as they'd discussed, and that the ACC was keen to talk to Lola. She'd given him Lola's number — so she should expect a call.

It wasn't until she was back at Helen Street and parking up that he called.

'Please tell me Lawrie's not compromised,' he said. 'Any suggestion of links with organised crime would be most problematic. We'll have to offload him temporarily.'

'Might be wise, sir. We won't tell the media the identity of the parents, but I reckon it's only a matter of time before word gets out. We'll prepare a briefing for you with lines to take.'

'Very well. I'll speak to Lawrie myself,' ACC Thompson said. 'Assure him our best people are on the case.'

Lola hesitated for a moment, not exactly relishing the idea of Dixon telling the ACC what he thought of Lola's investigation thus far.

'The Dixons are in a safe house in the city. He has his devices with him. He . . . He didn't give us permission to monitor his calls, sir. You might mention to him how helpful it would be if he did.'

'I'll do that, DCI Harris.'

'And, sir, if you could persuade him to go public . . . I know they're frightened, but it could make all the difference.'

'I'll try,' he said grimly, and rang off.

* * *

5.40 p.m.

'DS Pierce?' Lola called, steeling herself.

He'd sauntered past her desk, whistling to himself. Now he stopped, made a slow pirouette and gazed insolently at her.

'A word, please,' she said, then got up and led the way to one of the small meeting rooms that lined the open-plan floor.

Her heart raced and she forced herself to slow her breathing. She and Pierce had a rocky history. In the past he'd tried repeatedly to undermine her, leading to a showdown that resulted in his being put on an 'improvement plan', to his disgust. He'd calmed down since then but a current of spite was always there, just below the too-smooth surface.

Inside the cubicle, Pierce sat, his expression neutral and disinterested.

'How is the cyber forensics training going?' she asked.

He made a face of mild surprise then shrugged lightly. 'Fine.'

'How many sessions have you attended?'

'Five.' He looked and sounded wary now. 'Why?'

'They're online, these sessions, aren't they?'

'Most of them. There was an in-person day event at Gartcosh.'

'When was that?'

'Three weekends ago.'

'And Lawrence Dixon was there, was he?'

53

His chin lifted a millimetre or two. She saw his Adam's apple bob. 'Yes,' he said gruffly.

'I have to ask you, DS Pierce,' she said, her heart racing now, 'are you in direct contact with Lawrence Dixon?'

A look of mild surprise. 'No. Well, we're in email contact. All of the cyber champions are.'

'And outside work?'

He frowned and began to look annoyed. 'No.'

'Lawrence Dixon has a contact inside Police Scotland,' she said. 'Someone who gave him informal advice throughout the night, following his son's kidnap.'

'It wasn't me.' The points of his cheekbones were pink with anger.

She waited a beat. 'Then I'll take you at your word.'

He shrugged and got up. 'Is that all?'

'Yes,' Lola said, still sitting.

He reached for the door handle and stalked away from the little room.

Did she believe him? She wasn't sure. But if he was Dixon's contact then he'd be careful from now on. He was too mindful of his own skin to risk helping Dixon anymore.

* * *

6.30 p.m.

The crowd of journalists quietened as Lola came into the room and approached the blue cloth-covered table. She looked about, seeing expectant if jaded faces. She recognised several. Her old nemesis and sparring partner, Shuna Frain of the *Glasgow Chronicle*, sat on the front row, one plucked eyebrow arched, cynical as ever. Lola saw Elaine standing at the back of the throng. Anna Vaughan was beside her. There was no sign of Aidan Pierce.

'Thank you, everyone, for attending at such short notice,' she said. 'My name is Detective Chief Inspector Lola Harris. This morning, a young woman's body was found at the entrance to Darnley Glen country park, off Waukglen Road. We have already made an appeal for information in relation to this woman's identity but have yet to confirm her name.'

She shared again the description of the woman that had already appeared in the appeal.

'What we're showing you on the screens behind me now are two images showing that woman, captured by CCTV shortly before she was killed.'

She paused while the audience goggled at the screens.

'We will provide you with copies of these images immediately after this meeting,' she said.

The room hummed with excited murmurs. She allowed them a minute before continuing: 'We have received information from a witness who we believe spoke to the young woman on Rouken Glen Road just after two o'clock this morning in a state of some distress.'

She paused and looked about the room, signalling that the next piece of information was going to be important. She caught an expectant gleam in Shuna's eye.

'That witness,' Lola said, 'was under the impression the young woman was carrying a baby in her arms, though he did not see a child himself.'

Going by their sudden alertness, it was news to the majority of the reporters in the room, but not to Shuna. Her eyes had narrowed and she was smirking to herself as she wrote.

'CCTV footage we have obtained shows she was indeed carrying a bundle in her arms. A number of frames show what appears to be a baby's face, wrapped in a blanket or shawl. No baby, and no evidence of a baby, was found at the scene of the crime.

'At 9.48 this morning, we received a 999 call from the father of a two-month-old baby boy, saying a woman had broken into his and his wife's home in the Southside of Glasgow and taken their son at gunpoint.'

That shocked them. The room went deathly silent. Eyes were wide, mouths open in horror.

'We believe the woman who took the child is the same one who was found dead this morning. We have reason to believe she was a foreign national, possibly of Northern European origin. The parents of the baby report being threatened before the kidnap by individuals who could be involved in organised crime. We will not be naming the family or the child at this time. All ports have been alerted and the National Crime Agency are ready to support us in our efforts to find the child.

'We would like to appeal for any information about who this young woman was, why she would take a child, and where that child is now. We are appealing for anyone who might have seen her before or after she took the child, and anyone who might have seen activity around Waukglen Road around two or two thirty this morning.'

She gave a number to call.

'Now, I'll take any questions.' She looked about. 'Shuna?'

'Wouldn't naming the family help you find the child? It seems odd to keep that information under wraps.'

'We and the family have good reasons for doing so,' she said, regarding Shuna carefully.

The journalist narrowed her eyes. 'Is it true the parents of the child waited nearly *eight hours* before calling for help?'

Lola met the journalist's penetrating gaze calmly. 'As I said, the parents had received a threat. They feared reprisals for reporting the kidnap. By the morning, I'm pleased to say they decided to seek our assistance.'

Shuna, looking profoundly sceptical, scribbled on her pad.

Lola took three more questions, each focusing on what action would be taken to try to find the missing child, then closed the conference to mild protest.

She found Shuna in the corridor outside.

Shuna whirled round, all smiles. 'You're going to be busy, Lola.'

'Yes.' Lola took her elbow and drew her aside. 'Go on then,' she said quietly, 'what have you heard?'

'Oh, pretty much everything you just told us. Good to have it confirmed, though.'

'Who did you hear it from?'

'Oh, Lola.' Shuna shook her head.

'A police source?'

Shuna seemed to be considering her answer. 'No, as it happens. So, go on then, what are these so-called "good reasons" for not naming the family?'

'Sensitivities,' Lola said.

Shuna rolled her eyes. 'It's Lawrence Dixon, isn't it?'

Lola shrugged. 'Is it?'

'The new assistant chief constable's pet cyber expert. So, what's happened? The cyberman get cyber hacked? An elaborate blackmail effort?'

Lola said nothing.

Shuna gave a small, knowing smile. 'Well, you know where I am when you need a friendly reporter to help.'

And with that Shuna turned on her heel and strode away.

CHAPTER SEVEN

7.10 p.m.

'Oh, it's you!' Jeanie Quigley said, peeking through the gap in her door. She had the security chain on and scrabbled to take it off, then pulled the door wide.

'I should have called ahead,' Lola said, 'but I didn't have your number to hand. I was on my way to Newton Mearns and thought I'd pop in.'

'Of course, of course!' Sorcha's aunt closed the door. The black-and-white cat Lola had seen earlier came tiptoeing down the stairs to greet her. 'Come through to the living room,' Jeanie said. 'I'll turn the TV off. Would you like a cup of something?'

'No, I won't stay long.'

Jeanie stopped in the doorway of the living room, unable to wait to ask: 'How are they?'

'They're okay.'

'No news?'

'No news.'

Jeanie went into the room and gestured to a sofa. She resumed what was clearly her favourite armchair by the electric fire. She lifted a remote control and turned the television off. The black-and-white cat leaped onto her lap and she began stroking it while it stretched luxuriantly.

'I wanted to learn a bit more about your neighbours,' Lola said, settling down. 'How well you know them. What they're like. And . . . I'd also like to hear about what Marta told you — about the time she thought she was being followed, and about the person she saw driving by the house.'

Jeanie nodded. 'It's awful to think about it now,' she said after a moment's recollection, 'but the first time she mentioned it to me, I'm afraid I didn't really believe her. I didn't. I thought she might be depressed or anxious. But then the more we spoke, the more I realised she *wasn't* depressed or anxious. But she was frightened.'

'How long have you known her?' Lola asked.

'Two years,' Jeanie said. 'Since the house was finished and they moved in. Well, I'd met them before, but only briefly. It was a bit of a strain living next door to all that building work, but I understood: they were making a nice home for themselves. When they finally came to live here, I invited them round for coffee. He didn't come. He was "busy".' She made a face. 'But Marta did. I found her shy and unhappy.'

'Why was she unhappy, do you think?' Lola asked.

'I don't think she was very happy with her husband. I asked about her family, and she told me about her brother and her father — her mother had died some years ago. I asked about friends. She said she didn't really have any. She'd met Lawrie in Estonia when he was working there, you see. She'd fallen for him, even though he was much older than her, and they moved here together.'

'You don't like him, do you?'

'No.' Her expression darkened. 'I find him insincere. And I think he's used to getting his way. That house was specially designed by quite a well-known architect, you know. Marta told me Lawrie chose everything — even designed the kitchen and picked the curtains.'

'Has Marta ever said he's mistreated her in any way?'

'Not that she's said. But this thing with the security guard — that's not normal, is it? Keeping her there, locked up like a princess in a fairy tale. You know,' she said, lowering her voice to a near-whisper, 'he put a *tag* on Adam's ankle.'

Lola stared at her, barely believing what she'd just heard. 'I'm sorry, Jeanie — a "tag"?'

'Yes,' Jeanie said, eyebrows up. 'I saw it. A sort of bracelet that locked. And it meant Lawrie would know where the baby — and I'd assume therefore Marta too — was at any time. Like a tiny prisoner who's been released on bail, or probation, or whatever it's called. Oh!' She put a hand to her mouth. 'Oh, but surely — why wouldn't he just track it now? He wouldn't have forgotten, would he?'

'I wouldn't have thought so,' Lola said carefully. She put the information to one side for now, intending to act on it as soon as she was out of here. 'Does Lawrie love Marta?' she asked, almost casually.

'I suppose he must do.'

'Tell me more about Marta,' Lola said. 'Anything you say is between you and me — it will help me to understand more about her and their relationship.'

Jeanie took a moment to think.

'I know her father has a business,' she said. 'I haven't met him, but he did visit when Adam was born. Oh—' she put a hand to her mouth — 'oh gosh, it's so awful.'

She squeezed her eyes tight shut. When she opened them, tears were welling. Jeanie snatched a tissue from a box beside her chair and wiped fiercely.

'I'm sorry. I'm just remembering Marta saying how her father doted on the boy. A "little miracle" — that's what her father called Adam. And it was true. Apparently he started talking about changing his will so the business came to him! Marta's brother is a bit of a wastrel, I'm afraid. A lot of problems. Mental problems. I don't think their mother was very well with that kind of thing either. Oh, listen to me gossiping . . .'

'It's not gossip,' Lola said, and smiled. 'What does Marta's father do, do you know?'

Jeanie frowned. 'Computers, I think. Yes. Internet security. It's the same line of business Lawrie is in. Marta worked for her father, though not doing anything technical as far as I'm aware. It was through her job she came to meet Lawrie while he was working over there.'

'I see.' Lola checked the time on her phone. 'I have to go.'

'Well, thank you for coming to see me,' Jeanie said, beaming now. She began to get up and the cat jumped clear.

'That's quite all right. If you think of anything I should know, do call me, won't you, Jeanie?' She handed over her card. 'If I don't answer, leave me a message and I'll call you back or come and see you.'

'You're very kind,' Jeanie said, and smiled. 'Sorcha said you were and she was right.'

She led Lola out into the hallway, the black-and-white cat at her heels.

* * *

7.35 p.m.

'Mr Dixon, it's DCI Harris here,' she said, back in her car.

'What's happened?' he asked warily.

'No updates, I'm afraid,' she said, then paused before asking, 'Mr Dixon, does your son wear an ankle tag?'

Silence. Lola waited.

'An ankle tag?'

'So you can track him, using GPS presumably.'

He gave a weak laugh. 'No! Of course not.' He cleared his throat and sounded thoroughly shifty. 'Who told you that?'

'So you're telling me you've never tagged your son to track his location?'

'No! If I had, we wouldn't be in this mess, would we? Was it that stupid cow next door who told you that? She

61

imagines things.' His voice was savage now. 'I told Marta to keep away from her.'

'Mr Dixon—'

'Find my son,' he railed. 'Find Adam, and don't waste any more of my time.'

And he hung up.

***

7.56 p.m.

The 'somewhere new' Sandy had chosen was a Chinese buffet place beside the Waitrose in Newton Mearns. Lola was a few minutes early so sat in the car and took time to brace herself for what might turn into another emotional wrangle.

The situation was no one's fault, which was irritating in itself because there was no one to blame. No one at whom to direct all these unexpected and knotty feelings.

Sandy had got the email from an ex-girlfriend called Julia a month ago. He and Julia had been together for six weeks, long before he was married to Geraldine — and that marriage had been over a few years now. In it, Julia told him she'd recently got divorced and decided it was time for him to know the truth: that her daughter, Maisie, wasn't her ex-husband's but Sandy's.

'A *month* ago?' Lola had cried when he told her on Sunday evening. She was up and pacing about her living room while he shrank deeper into his corner of the sofa. 'And you didn't think to tell me?'

'Because I didn't know it was true,' he'd replied. 'I talked to Ritchie and we decided it was best to wait till I knew one way or the other.'

'So *Ritchie* knew and I didn't?'

'Aye, well, he helped me look into it. He got hold of a copy of Maisie's birth certificate and everything. And he found photos of her online.'

She raised her eyebrows at that. 'Photos of a thirteen-year-old lassie online?'

'Not like that, Lola. On her mum's social media, on friends' accounts, and one at a school event. The photos are how I knew. Lola, she's the spitting image of my mum when she was a girl.'

She stopped pacing. 'Is she . . . ?'

Sandy's mum had died years ago, but Lola had seen photos, including ones of her when she was young and in Ireland. She pictured the dark hair, pale skin, fine bones and huge eyes. A slighter, female version of Sandy.

'So I went to see her this weekend,' he told her. 'Julia, I mean, not Maisie. I haven't met her yet.'

Lola went to stand in the bay window but the sight of a child's tricycle on a neighbour's lawn turned her stomach and she had to look away.

'Julia's told Maisie about me,' he went on. 'She's a level-headed kid, Julia says. She was confused but rationalised things quickly. She doesn't get on with her dad — Julia's ex, that is — which I guess helps a bit.'

At that Lola was consumed by a sudden anger — an irrational rage that made her want to yell at him and cry. But she kept a lid on it.

'Why now?' she asked him quietly. 'This Julia has kept this quiet all this time, then she decides to start telling people — you, her daughter. Does she want money?'

'No. At least, she says not. But . . . if she is my daughter, then I should make sure she's all right, shouldn't I?'

It was reasonable — of course it was.

'Money makes things formal, Sandy,' she said in a tight voice. 'It changes things.'

'I knew you'd be angry,' he said.

'I'm not angry!' She stopped herself. 'All right. Maybe I am. But because you didn't tell me! Didn't you trust me?'

'I know it's a shock,' he said weakly. 'Imagine how I felt.'

She tried to imagine, though in that moment it was an impossible task. But when she looked at him he was so hang-dog, peering up at her from under his nice dark eyebrows, that she softened.

'So, when will you meet her — Maisie?'

'Soon, I hope.'

They'd talked about it for an hour or more until she'd calmed down and they were able to discuss things rationally. She was even able to articulate her fears.

'It's threatening to me,' she told him as gently as she could. 'You've got a child from a woman you were with years ago, and you're seeing that woman and soon you'll meet your daughter . . . where do I fit in? At the same time, I'm asking myself if I'm being unreasonable and self-centred.'

'Lola,' he said very gently, 'you're the least self-centred person I know.'

And he'd taken her in his arms and it had felt better.

But before he left, just before midnight, she'd told him she needed a couple of days on her own, just to get used to the idea.

'If you like,' he'd said, though sounding dismayed.

Had she got used to the idea? Not exactly, but she'd accepted it as a fact. She'd told her sister, Frankie, and Elaine Walsh, but no one else. Today, thanks to work, she'd hardly thought about it at all. But now it was time to face things once more.

She got out of her car.

* * *

8.02 p.m.

Sandy was already there, in a booth at the back of the Lee's Royal Garden Buffet. He waved and sent her an awkward smile.

'Hiya,' she said, sliding into the seat.

'Sparkling water, please,' she said to the waitress. Sandy already had an Irn Bru. Condensation squeezed between his fingers as he gripped the glass.

'How you doing?' he asked.

'I'm fine, Sandy. Work's full on.' She looked briefly at the menu then gazed about the half-full restaurant. 'You know, I'm not all that hungry, but you go ahead.'

'You no well, or . . . ?'

'My stomach's in knots,' she said. 'What do you expect? Remember you've had weeks to get used to this.' She sighed but it sounded more like a groan.

Lola's water arrived.

'So, how's things?' she asked him when he didn't volunteer anything.

'Okay, aye.' He was apprehensive about something, she could tell.

'You got more to tell me?'

'I wanted to apologise,' he said, eyeing her warily. 'I've thought long and hard about it and I should have told you about the email when I got it. I'm sorry.' He sat back and puffed out a small sigh of relief.

'Been building up to that, have you?'

'You could say so.'

'It's okay,' she told him gently. 'I understand why you didn't tell me. It could have been a pack of lies. But it isn't, so you told me, and that's that.'

'Thanks,' he said, all the more relieved. Then the wariness was back. 'And . . . I do have something to tell you. Something to ask too.'

'Oh?'

'Only . . . I'm going to meet Maisie this Saturday.' A pleased little smile played on his lips though he was clearly trying to suppress it. 'I'm going to meet her, along with her mum, of course. We haven't agreed a time or place yet. Julia's going to let me know.'

'Right.'

A new waitress appeared. 'Are you wanting the buffet,' she asked, 'or would you like to order something off the menu?'

'Not right now, thanks,' Lola said.

The girl went away.

'Well, I hope it goes okay,' Lola said now, unsure what else she was supposed to say.

'The thing is . . . well, I was wondering . . . would you want to come too?'

She stared, feeling her muscles tightening again.

'Erm . . . I'm not sure.'

'It was Julia's idea. Her suggestion, I mean.'

'Was it?' she asked, frowning.

'She knew I was nervous and I'd told her about you already — not in any detail, of course — and she said, ask you to come. You don't have to,' he added quickly. 'But I'd like you to. It would be a help — for me, I mean.'

'Like an emotional support animal?' she asked before she could stop herself.

'What?' He looked shocked.

'Sorry,' she said quickly. 'That wasn't fair.' She took a moment to breathe. 'Look, I don't know how I'd feel about being there. I also . . . Look, if I'm honest, I find it a bit strange that Julia suggested it, that she's looking out for my feelings. Also, who would I be? What role would I have? I mean, are you "Dad"? What does that make me? Step-mum?'

'Don't decide now.' He reached across the table and took one of her hands. 'It'd mean a lot to me. I'd want you two to get on, in any case. Like you said on Sunday, it's a huge change for all of us — a new life, really. It'll be easier if you're beside me.'

He smiled one of his little-boy smiles.

'Okay. I'll think about it. But no promises, eh?' And she managed a smile in return, pretending her heart wasn't sinking into an abyss.

CHAPTER EIGHT

Thursday 30 October
8.09 a.m.

'We've had 108 calls in response to last night's appeal,' Anna said when she and Lola met in a room at Helen Street. 'I've scanned through them and identified a number for the DCs to prioritise. The list doesn't include any that have come in since seven o'clock this morning.'

'Any you want to tell me about now?' Lola asked.

'A couple.' Anna looked quickly down the page. 'A second witness saw the woman running beside the industrial estate,' she said. 'Another cab driver, on his way back taking members of a hen party home to Greenock. He saw her head into the industrial estate, but didn't think much of it till he heard the appeal last night.' She turned to another page. 'Oh, and a man out walking his dog late — said he's an insomniac and so's the dog apparently — thinks he saw a van parked in Waukglen Road about the right time. "A small, dark-coloured Transit van parked by the woods."'

'We need to find video evidence of it,' Lola said.

'Agree, boss. We're still contacting drivers and asking for dashcam footage, but Waukglen Road goes off from the main road at ninety degrees. I'm not very hopeful.'

'You never know,' Lola said. 'The story's all over the media.'

She'd woken to a flurry of notifications on her phone. All the Scottish newspapers had covered the story, the majority with a headline on the front page. *BABY SNATCHER FOUND DEAD IN WOODLAND*, the *Glasgow Chronicle* had announced. It was on the BBC and STV news websites too, and BBC Scotland were discussing it when Lola tuned in as she made her morning coffee.

'Some more things to tell you,' Anna said, and turned over a page. 'A chap in a café in Dennistoun reckons he served the woman coffee the day before yesterday. Said she was quiet, paid with cash. I'll send someone out to talk to him and to pop into other local businesses. She might have been staying out that way.

'Remember the German woman who contacted us thinking the dead woman could be her daughter? She's sent a couple of photos. It can't be her. Different build, different colouring, and the age isn't right.'

Anna turned another page. 'Oh, and Marcus ran checks on Rab McCreedy, the cab driver. Nothing came up.'

Lola nodded, oddly relieved. She'd liked the man.

'DS Pierce is due to interview Dixon's security chap, Desmond Anderson, this morning with Jonno. They'll update us later.'

Anna's phone lit up on the table by her elbow. 'That's DS Pierce now,' she said and answered. Lola started to get her things together.

'Is that so?' Anna said into the phone. Her tone alerted Lola that Pierce was telling her something significant. 'Right,' she said, and picked up her pen to write. 'Right, okay. Yes, I think she is. What's the name?' She scribbled some more. 'Thanks. Yeah, I'll call her back myself.'

She put her phone down and turned to Lola.

'Control just took a call from a Wendy Baker, who's the registrar at Clyde University — you know, the one with the new campus at St George's Cross? She reckons she can identify our dead woman. Her name's Tiina Valk — Tiina with two "i"s. She says Tiina was an Estonian national . . .'

Estonian, like Marta . . .

'I've got her number here,' Anna said. 'I'll ring her back and tell her we'll go see her ASAP, shall I?'

* * *

9.05 a.m.

Clyde University's brand-new campus was a multi-storey glass-and-metal construction beside the motorway. There was parking in the basement, so the registrar had told Anna, but they parked instead on Garscube Road.

The reception was in a vast atrium which also contained a café with a seating area beyond a glass security barrier. Students sat about glued to their phones or laptops.

'Excuse me. Are you the police?' a quiet voice asked.

'That's right,' Lola said and turned to find a small woman in her late fifties, with short greying hair and a chintzy blouse, eyeing her nervously.

'I'm Wendy Baker,' the woman said, attempting a smile. 'I'm the registrar. Thank you so much for coming.'

She got them to sign a register and equipped them with visitors' badges on red lanyards, then led them into a waiting lift.

Wendy Baker seemed consumed by nerves, breathing fast and clenching and unclenching her hands. Lola made soothing noises about the impressiveness of the building, and Wendy began almost manically to recite facts about the floor space and the cost of the building, and mentioned an architectural award they hoped to win.

The lift reached the fourth floor and Wendy beetled out ahead of them and hurried along one side of an open-plan area to a suite of offices. Lola saw heads turn their way and felt curious eyes on them.

Wendy Baker was panting by the time they arrived at an air-conditioned meeting room along the corridor from the open-plan area.

'Do come in,' she said. 'I can order coffee or tea if you'd like some.' She began pulling out chairs. 'Our principal, Ms Carstairs, will join us very shortly,' she added fretfully.

'Oh?'

'She'll have a few questions for you, I'm sure.'

Suddenly the door flew open, making Wendy yelp, and in thundered a heavy-set older woman with a dyed-blonde helmet of hair, wearing a bright fuchsia jacket and black trousers.

'Oh, Ms Carstairs,' Wendy said. 'This is DCI Harris and her colleague, DI — oh, I've forgotten already—'

'Anna Vaughan,' Anna said.

'This is our principal, Ms Prue Carstairs,' Wendy said.

Lola put out her hand.

'Principal *and* chief executive,' the fierce woman said, shaking it.

She had a pure 'Kelvinside' accent, superior and hard-edged with entitlement.

'I haven't got all day,' she said unpleasantly, reaching for a chair. 'I'd rather we got this business done and dusted.'

'Ms Carstairs—' Lola began.

'Let me be clear up front,' Carstairs interrupted, hand still on the back of the chair. 'As a condition of our assistance, no mention of this institution must be made. It's actually *nothing* to do with us or what we do here. We'll help you now, but in confidence. Is that clear?'

Wendy Baker looked to be folding into herself, her head going down and her shoulders up.

'A young woman was murdered, Ms Carstairs,' Lola said coldly. 'As you will know by now, we believe she had a baby with her. You have a duty to help us as much as you can.'

Prue Carstairs' face became as pink as her jacket. She scowled, but seemed chastened, and sat, lips bunched and cross.

'Now,' Lola said, turning determinedly to Wendy to her right. 'Perhaps you'd tell us what you know.'

'Very well,' Wendy said while Carstairs seethed. 'I saw the young woman's picture on the news this morning while I was having my breakfast. I couldn't believe it. I said to myself, "I know her!" So I called the number and explained. And then—' she peeked nervously at the principal — 'and then I rang Ms Carstairs—'

'And now we're about to tell you,' Carstairs said tightly. There was a nasty curl to her lip. Lola considered asking her to leave the room, but at the same time the woman's hostile demeanour intrigued her. She wondered what was behind it.

'So, was Tiina Valk a student here?' Lola asked Wendy.

'Oh no! No, she wasn't. But her sister Ingrid had been, though Ingrid had left her course. Tiina came to see me, trying to trace her, you see.'

'Had they lost touch?'

'Yes. There'd been some sort of rift but it had been so long . . . now they were worried.'

'What day and time did Tiina Valk come here?'

'Thursday the sixteenth,' she said after a quick glance at her pad. 'About three in the afternoon. I took a call from reception saying a young woman was here to see me — well, to see the registrar. She hadn't asked for me by name. I happened to be free, so said I'd come down and meet her. One of the meeting rooms on the ground floor was available, so I took her in there.'

'What was she like?' Lola asked.

'A self-possessed young woman — in her mid-twenties, I'd say. Very upright, if you know what I mean.' Wendy straightened her back and lifted her chin, as if to demonstrate. 'She was quiet and when she spoke she didn't waste any words. She seemed . . . anxious but in control. She thanked me for seeing her. She said, "I'm Tiina and I'm here about my sister Ingrid Valk." She explained her sister had been studying with

71

us. They'd lost touch, having argued. Tiina had been living in Australia, but she'd gone home to Estonia when she found out her father was very ill. He'd become estranged from Ingrid too but now wanted to see her. Tiina had tried to contact Ingrid, but no one knew where she was. Then she learned she'd left her course here. She hoped I could tell her where Ingrid was now.'

'And could you?'

'No.' She looked nervously down at her hands. 'No, I'm afraid not.'

'Did Tiina tell you where she was staying, or give you contact details, anything like that?'

Wendy shook her head. 'I suggested she might leave her details with me but she declined to do so.'

'Did she say why?'

'No. I'm sorry.'

'Did she say why she and her sister had fallen out?'

'No.'

'And could you tell her anything at all about Ingrid?'

'Not very much, and of course we have to be mindful of people's personal data, but in this case, we had no notes of where she'd gone to. It seemed she had indeed left her course and . . . and disappeared. I was sympathetic and suggested a couple of organisations she might like to contact, and then she left. The whole meeting lasted no more than ten minutes.'

'Is it common that students just disappear?' Lola asked.

'It is not,' Prue Carstairs snapped, making Wendy start a little.

'People do leave courses from time to time,' the registrar said in a panicky voice. 'For all sorts of reasons. They often tell us why, but sometimes they don't. They are adults, after all.'

'Would you have any CCTV footage from the time and day Tiina came here?'

'We have security cameras throughout the building,' Carstairs said, 'but footage is overwritten every seven days, so no.' She sounded pleased about the fact.

'What was Ingrid Valk studying?' Anna asked.

'Erm . . .' Wendy consulted her notes. 'Business finance. She'd done two years and had two years more to do. She sat the first of her three assessments at the end of May this year, but didn't turn up for the rest. When the university tried to contact her, we learned that Ingrid had apparently left her accommodation. One of her housemates mentioned a boyfriend, but didn't know a name. Now, that was a problem for us.'

'Because she was an international student?' Lola asked.

'That's right. Since the United Kingdom left the European Union, EU students need a study visa to do any course over six months. The university is responsible for monitoring their attendance at classes and assessments and generally making sure they're abiding by the visa's terms. We have to report any transgressions to the Visas and Immigration department of the Home Office. Our Student Services colleagues did their best to try to find Ingrid and to identify the boyfriend. They didn't find her—' she winced — 'so I'm afraid we had to report her.'

'And she hasn't been in touch since?'

She shook her head. 'She certainly didn't attempt to enrol for her third year.'

'Did you report Ingrid missing to the police?'

Wendy shifted uncomfortably in her seat. Lola saw her glance at the stony-faced principal. 'Well, you see,' she began, 'there was no suggestion she'd come to any *harm*. She is an adult, so . . .' She sounded, Lola thought, as if she was trying to convince herself.

'And you told Tiina all of this?'

Wendy nodded.

Carstairs said stiffly, 'In spite of our duty to protect data.'

Lola saw Wendy's shoulders tense. 'Tiina was so worried,' she said meekly.

Carstairs narrowed her eyes.

Lola said, 'How did Tiina take it?'

'She was angry,' Wendy said, provoking a loud dismissive tut from the principal. 'With her sister, but also with us. She accused us of failing in our duty of care—'

'That's quite irrelevant,' Prue Carstairs came in.

Lola ignored her. 'This is all very helpful,' she said encouragingly to Wendy. 'Please, go on.'

Wendy said, 'Tiina pointed out how quick we'd been to accept what she called her sister's "enormous international fees".'

Carstairs made to intervene but Lola shut her up with a look.

'She — she also said she'd tried to phone us but been ignored. Well, I knew nothing about that and I promised I'd look into it. I asked her for a way to contact her, but she said she would contact me. I also asked her if she was staying in Glasgow very long. She said she didn't know but I got the impression she just didn't want to say. Of course, I was aware of the possibility Ingrid might be avoiding her sister deliberately. I provided facts: dates, that's all. She asked me for her sister's last address — for the flat she shared with two other girls in Dowanhill. She wanted me to tell her the names of the flatmates too. I said I couldn't tell her but I did offer to contact them myself. She grew rather angry again. I suggested she might speak to the police because they have a way to check where and when a passport has been used. She didn't seem to think much of that suggestion. And with that, she left.'

Anna asked, 'Do you still have Ingrid Valk's details on your system?'

'Yes, of course.'

'Including an emergency contact?'

'Yes . . .' she began, but it was clear something about the question had touched a nerve.

'Did you try that number when you lost touch with Ingrid?'

'Well, that's just it, you see.' Wendy bit her lip. 'It had been changed — to the name of a Scottish man, sometime in the summer term. A Ewan-somebody. Ingrid herself had updated it, and that wipes the previous contact. The fields in the online form are static, you see, so previous data gets overwritten.'

'Did you call that number?'

A nervous nod. 'It rang but no one answered. I tried it myself, several times. It didn't go to voicemail or I'd have left a message.'

'I'd like the new emergency contact's name, please.'

'Yes, I can give you that. We'll have Ingrid's photograph on file as well, if you'd like it.'

Wendy looked at the principal as if to check she hadn't overstepped any mark, but Prue Carstairs gave a grim nod of assent.

Carstairs said to Lola now, 'If it turns out that your murder victim is indeed Tiina Valk, then we consider the university's role to be complete: we have provided you with a most helpful lead as to her identity. The fact her sister studied here is irrelevant — as is the fact she left her course. We ask that you do not mention the university in any press statement or in answer to any questions that arise.' She folded her hands on the table before her, then pursed her lips. 'Is that understood?' she asked primly.

Lola stared, astonished.

'This is a world-class institution of learning, with a world-class reputation,' the principal went haughtily on. 'Students come to study here from *across the globe*. Any link to a sordid business like this could be *devastating* to our reputation. My board would not take lightly to that under any circumstance.'

'Ms Carstairs,' Lola said coldly, 'a young woman has been murdered in this city. We expect any institution, no matter how glowing its "global reputation", to give us all the information and help we need to catch her killer. We need to know everything about our victim's movements in the days before she died, and to understand what she was doing here in the city. It sounds as though she was here to find her sister. Her sister studied at this university and, apparently, disappeared from it. Ingrid Valk may be safe and perfectly well. But equally she may not. You and your institution are involved already, and if we need to make your involvement publicly known, then we will do so. Now, is *that* understood?'

Prue Carstairs reared back from the table. Now it was her turn to look astonished.

Lola turned to Wendy, who looked as if she was about to burst out in a fit of nervous giggles. 'Now, if you could furnish us with any information you hold about Ingrid,' she said, 'we'd be most grateful.'

* * *

10.10 a.m.

Wendy peered at the screen of her computer in her refrigerated, windowless office. She seemed wired and shaken from the meeting. The principal had returned to her own office, saying quietly — but not quietly enough — to Wendy that she should come by once the visitors were 'off the premises'. No doubt the prospect of a dressing down preyed on her mind.

'Here we are,' she said now. 'Ingrid Valk, Estonian national, date of birth the first of May 2005. And here's the new emergency contact she entered, though as I say, I must have tried the number more than ten times over a couple of days and it just rang out. I'll write it down for you.'

'Can you just print everything that's on the screen?' Lola asked.

'Yes. Yes, okay.'

A printer behind her whirred into life. A page slid from it. Wendy reached for it and passed it to Lola.

Lola scanned down it and read: *Emergency contact: Ewan Cathrie.* A mobile number was beside it but no address.

'Ingrid's photograph was linked to her study visa,' Wendy said. 'That's in a different folder. Give me a moment.' She tapped at her keyboard. 'Here we are — oh! That's strange.'

'What is?'

Wendy frowned at her screen in confusion. 'Ingrid's photograph has been deleted.' She put a hand to her mouth.

'Deleted by who?' Lola asked.

But Wendy didn't answer, just continued to stare at her screen.

'Wendy?' Lola exchanged glances with Anna.

'It must be a mistake,' she said, but didn't sound convinced.

'Could she have done it herself? The way she changed her emergency contact?'

'Not in this part of the system. It relates to her visa, you see.'

She was clearly worried now.

'Excuse me a moment.' She lifted her phone receiver and dialled a four-digit number. 'Oh, Danny, could you pop into my office for a second?'

She put the phone down. 'Danny McDougall is our data officer,' she said. 'He'll know what's happened.'

A second later there was a small knock at the door.

'Come in,' Wendy called, and a skinny young man stepped in, dressed all in black and with long dyed-black hair. He eyed the visitors shyly. 'These ladies are from the police,' she told him. 'Just checking on one of our international students. Only her photo's been deleted.'

'Deleted from the visa file?' he asked her, seeming unfazed that the police were asking. 'Don't really see how that could happen.'

'Well, indeed. Here, have a look.'

She got up and he took her chair, then wiggled the mouse and tapped a couple of keys.

'You're right, it's not there,' he said. He clicked into another window and frowned. 'It's not in the uploads folder, either. Strange.' He peered up at her, waiting for another instruction.

'Wouldn't we have kept a paper scan of it?' she asked him.

'Yes. This student left the course at the end of the last academic year,' he murmured, reading the screen. 'Could she have asked for her photo to be deleted?'

'No,' Wendy said. 'There'd be a note on the file. Marisa might know . . .'

'Who's Marisa?' Lola asked.

'My deputy,' Wendy said.

'These paper records . . .' Lola said, 'could you check them easily?'

Wendy looked to Danny for an answer.

'Should be straightforward,' he said. 'They'll be in the archive. Just need to find out how they were coded.'

'How long would that take?'

He pushed out his bottom lip. 'Within the hour, I reckon.'

'We'll find it and send it over,' Wendy said.

'That's fine,' Lola said. 'DS Vaughan will give you her email address. Please do treat it as urgent.'

'Of course.'

Wendy led Lola and Anna back to the lift in thoughtful silence. She seemed even more tense and nervous than before, saying nothing, her eyes averted and her hands working away at each other.

When they were in the lift, Lola said, 'Prue Carstairs didn't want you to contact us, did she?'

Wendy's look of wide-eyed alarm told her she'd hit home.

'You did the right thing,' Lola went on. 'The lawful thing.'

Wendy nodded then looked down, blushing.

'Remember that, if she tries to break you down. Don't let her bully you and don't apologise.'

A tiny nod. 'It's just that she cares so much about this place and its reputation.'

'But not her staff?' Lola asked kindly. 'Or her students?'

Something changed in Wendy's expression. She bit her lip and took a breath as though she had something to say—

At that moment the lift doors opened and they were disgorged into the reception, now abuzz with students and staff.

Wendy led them to the reception desk to sign out. There was a short queue, and while they waited Lola noticed a board with posters pinned to it advertising a host of activities, including lectures by guest speakers. Something caught her eye — a speaker's photograph that Lola recognised. It was

Lawrie Dixon, grinning over his shoulder with those dead eyes. She stepped closer to read it. *Considering a career in cyber?* it asked. *Come and meet cyber forensics expert and business entrepreneur Lawrence Dixon.* The lecture was to take place on a Wednesday evening three weeks from now.

Anna appeared at her shoulder. 'I signed you out as well,' she said.

'Look at that,' Lola said quietly, and nodded to the poster.

'Thank you for coming in,' the registrar said, and they peeled their attention away from the poster. 'We'll get that photograph to you as quickly as we can.'

She wanted to say more. Lola could tell.

'Walk outside with us, would you, Wendy?' She led the way through the automatic doors. At the bottom of the steps, away from the stream of people coming and going, Lola said, 'There's something else, isn't there?'

'No! Honestly, it's nothing.'

'Wendy,' Anna came in, her tone several degrees cooler than Lola's, 'you need to tell us anything that might help with our inquiry.'

'What's "nothing"?' Lola asked. 'Look, why don't we go somewhere away from here and have a chat, just us three? We're parked just along the road. We could even sit in the car and talk.'

Wendy stole another look at the building behind her, then jumped in fright.

Prue Carstairs stood at the top of the steps glaring down at them, her chest heaving with angry exertion.

Knowing her subordinate had seen her, the principal lifted a wrist and tapped it meaningfully.

'I have to go,' Wendy said in a small, breathless voice. 'I'm sorry. You've been very kind.'

And she hurried up the steps and followed Prue Carstairs back into her gleaming lair.

CHAPTER NINE

11.27 a.m.

Lola's team met back at Helen Street to talk through their various leads. She told them about Tiina Valk.

'Kirstie's been on to Interpol again,' Anna said, nodding to the constable to pick up the thread.

'They're going to find us a senior contact in the Estonian police,' Kirstie said. 'Hopefully they'll be able to find the Valk family for us.'

'That's good,' Lola said. She looked at Aidan Pierce. 'Have you seen Desmond Anderson yet?'

He looked at her balefully, clearly still fuming about the questions she'd asked him yesterday. 'Yes,' he said shortly. 'He confirms Dixon's story. Dixon called him after the fact. He stayed with Mrs Dixon while her husband went out driving about.' He shrugged, his way of saying he had no more to add.

Lola thanked him curtly.

She looked to Anna. 'What next?'

'The van, boss. Jonno and Marcus have been contacting drivers who passed under the motorway bridge.' She looked towards Jonno.

'We got lucky, boss,' Jonno said. 'One guy's dashcam caught a small dark van turning into Waukglen Road at 2.34 a.m. The van's reg plate is obscured, possibly with mud, which is suspicious in itself.'

'The van didn't pass under the motorway bridge,' Anna said, picking up the narrative. 'That's not to say it didn't pick up Tiina Valk and make its way to Darnley via another route. We're now going back into all the CCTV and dashcam footage we've already obtained to see if we can see where it came from and where it went afterwards.'

'Quite possibly with a tiny baby as a passenger,' Lola said quietly.

The room fell silent.

'Have we had nothing back from any of the ports?' she asked tetchily.

'Not according to Cath from Organised Crime,' Anna said.

'And what about calls from the public about the baby?'

'Nothing indicative,' Anna said. 'A couple of improbable sightings.'

'Any more from the industrial estate where Tiina was last caught on camera?'

'Still waiting,' Jonno said.

'And what about the lad on the bike who talked to the officer at Darnley?'

'Again, nothing yet,' Anna said gloomily. 'Do you think we should make an appeal for him to come forward? We could stress the need to eliminate him from our inquiry.'

'Do it,' Lola said. 'Keep it low-key so the papers don't read too much into it. Tag it onto our daily update.'

Lola looked at her pad. 'Nothing more from Wendy Baker at the university?'

Anna clicked at her laptop. 'An email's just come in,' she said. 'She's attached Ingrid Valk's photograph.'

'Let me see.' Lola stepped round the table to look over Anna's shoulder. She said nothing, just stared at the image of Ingrid Valk.

'My God,' Lola murmured, eyes transfixed by the young woman staring back at her.

Ingrid Valk was blonde and strikingly beautiful . . . and the spitting image of the petrified Marta Dixon.

* * *

1.05 p.m.

'So, come on,' Lawrence Dixon said tersely. 'What's this about?'

They were in the kitchen of the flat in Garnethill: Lola, Kirstie, Dixon and the austere solicitor Jeremy Wilder. Marta was in another room. She'd come into the hallway when Lola and Kirstie had arrived, but Dixon had taken her elbow and pushed her back through the doorway — quite roughly, Lola had noticed. Her face was blotchy, her eyes red.

'Do you know anyone called Tiina Valk, Mr Dixon?'

He stared then frowned and pushed out his bottom lip. 'No,' he said, then seemed to understand the reason for the question. 'Why, is that her — the woman who took our boy?'

'We need an official confirmation but, yes, we think it could be.'

She watched him very carefully, observing his reaction, trying to read his thoughts.

'*Tiina Valk*,' she said again, emphatically.

'No,' he said. 'I've never heard of her.'

'She's Estonian,' Lola said now.

'Is she?'

'Like your wife.'

Dixon shrugged. 'A coincidence.'

'What exactly are you implying?' Jeremy Wilder said crisply.

'You've spent a lot of time in Estonia, Mr Dixon,' Lola went calmly on. 'I saw on your LinkedIn that you worked there for two years.'

He nodded and swallowed. 'I worked at the NATO Cyber Centre of Excellence. Marta and I met while I was out there.'

'You must have met a lot of people.'

'Yes, but . . .'

'Are you sure you don't know that name?'

'Absolutely.' He was getting annoyed now.

'My client has answered your question, DCI Harris,' the solicitor said.

She acknowledged the fact with a nod.

'Tell us about Marta's family.'

'About—? You'd be better asking her, surely?'

'We will, but we want to hear it from you.'

His breathing started to become laboured.

'She's from Tallinn. Grew up there. She has an older brother. Her father is still alive. Her mother died when she was a child.'

'Have you or Marta had contact with her family since Adam was taken?'

He shook his head. 'Her father is elderly. He's very frail. She didn't want to worry him.'

Lola gave nothing away but made a mental note to ask Marta if that decision had indeed been hers.

'So Marta has no sisters?'

'No.'

'What about female cousins?'

'Cousins? I'm sorry, this line of questioning—'

'I'd like to show you a photograph,' she said and turned to Kirstie.

Kirstie produced a folded sheet of paper. She opened it and passed it to Dixon. He snatched it from her, turned it and looked at the black-and-white image of Ingrid Valk. His face gave nothing away.

'This isn't the woman who took Adam,' he said at last.

'I didn't say it was.'

'Who is it, then?' He continued to stare at the image.

'Does she seem familiar to you, Mr Dixon?'

He blinked but said nothing. Then he put the page down and pushed it back across the kitchen table to Lola.

'I don't know who she is,' he said with some dignity.

He squared his shoulders and looked Lola hard in the eye. Lola could tell he was employing every gram of self-control to appear unrattled.

'Her name,' Lola said, 'is Ingrid Valk. She's the sister of Tiina Valk. She was a student here in Glasgow, but she left her course and her accommodation sometime in the summer . . . and hasn't been seen or heard from since.'

'Like I say,' he said gruffly, 'I don't know her.'

Lola took the page, folded it and gave it back to Kirstie. Dixon seemed to relax a little.

'You're giving a lecture at Clyde University in a few weeks' time, I understand,' she said now.

He frowned and seemed to need a minute to recall. 'Yes, I am,' he said. 'A talk about careers. Why?'

'Who invited you?'

He blinked. 'I don't remember. I'm sure I'll have an email somewhere. I expect it was a computing lecturer.' He narrowed his eyes. 'Why?'

'Clyde University is where Ingrid Valk studied.'

'Is it?'

Lola said nothing for several seconds, only watched Dixon as he tried to hide his discomfort. Then she asked quietly, 'Mr Dixon, do you know where your son is?'

'What?' Dixon's eyes widened. It felt as if all the air had been sucked out of the small, shiny kitchen. 'Of course not. Why are you even asking me that?' He turned to his solicitor. 'Jerry?'

'What exactly are you suggesting, DCI Harris?' Jeremy Wilder asked.

Lola ignored him again, and kept her gaze fixed on Dixon. She let the silence last for several seconds, then stood quickly up, making her chair scrape loudly on the floor so the two jumped.

'Mr Dixon, we're done for now,' Lola said. 'We'll talk to your wife next. DC Campbell, would you fetch Mrs Dixon? Mr Wilder, I expect you'll want to stay.'

* * *

1.27 p.m.

Dixon was furious, hissing at Jeremy Wilder in the hallway, making the solicitor flinch and remonstrate. At one point Dixon returned to the open kitchen doorway and informed Lola that he wouldn't permit his wife to be interviewed unless he was present. That if he wasn't there, he'd instruct her not to speak.

'Your attitude is frankly alarming, Mr Dixon,' she said.

Kirstie came out of the living room, leading Marta Dixon. Her husband said something to her, making her flinch away from him. The solicitor put a calming hand on Dixon's shoulder.

'Hello, Marta,' Lola said as the young woman came into the kitchen. 'We just want to have a wee chat through things, that's all.'

Wilder was back, pulling irritably at his double cuffs. The door into the hallway was now firmly closed but no doubt Dixon was behind it, listening.

Marta's face was still puffy with crying. 'Is there any news?' she asked.

'I'm afraid not,' Lola said, noting she'd asked the question, where her husband had not.

Marta closed her eyes. Lola took a moment to study her. She was clearly still very upset and frightened. But distressed? Not exactly. Why wasn't Marta Dixon climbing the walls? Why wasn't she out in the streets, screaming for help to find her son? Lola would be for sure. Was it because Dixon had sedated her, as her friend Sarah had done the day before?

'Marta,' Lola began, 'is it true you haven't spoken to your father or brother since Adam was taken?'

She nodded, her eyes averted.

'Why not?'

She shrugged, still avoiding eye contact.

'Adam's your father's grandson,' Lola pointed out gently. 'Don't you think he'd want to know?'

Marta's face crumpled at that.

'Did you decide not to tell him?'

She hung her head.

'Or was it Lawrie who decided that?'

'He's old,' Marta said in a whisper. 'It would be a shock. We thought it best.'

'And your brother?'

Her face darkened. 'We don't speak.'

'Do you have a sister, Marta?'

The solicitor broke in: 'Mr Dixon has already told you the answer to that question.'

Lola gave him a look, then turned back to the young woman. 'Well, Marta?'

She frowned in confusion and shook her head.

'What about female cousins?'

The frown deepened. 'No!'

'Do you know anyone by the name of Tiina Valk?' Lola asked.

Marta shook her head and lowered her eyes.

'She's Estonian.'

Marta peered up at her from under her brows. 'I don't know every Estonian,' she said, a touch moodily.

'Do you know anyone with that surname? Valk, V-A-L-K.'

'Probably, if I think about it. It's not uncommon.'

Lola waited, then asked mildly, 'Don't you want to know why I'm asking?'

The question jolted Marta and she looked immediately terrified. She gave a quick, anxious nod.

'We think Tiina Valk is the woman who took your son. The woman who is now dead.' She waited a second then asked, 'Marta, are you sure you don't know her?'

'I don't.' It was a miserable whimper.

The reaction wasn't right. Where was the horror, the rage? Where was the furious impulse for revenge?

'Tiina has a sister,' Lola went on calmly. 'Her name is Ingrid. None of her family and friends have seen her. Not for months.'

Marta pushed out her bottom lip and gave a small shrug.

'I'd like to show you a photo of her, to see if you recognise her.'

Lola nodded to Kirstie and Kirstie handed her the folded page. Lola opened it.

'This is her,' she said, handing it to Marta and watching carefully. 'This is Ingrid Valk.'

Marta looked physically pained, as if she had to strain every sinew to peer at the page.

'Well, Marta?' She must see what Lola saw, what her husband had surely seen but denied.

'I don't know her.'

'Does she look familiar to you?'

An evasive, almost insolent shrug, followed by a shake of the head.

Lola said, 'My colleagues and I see a striking resemblance between her . . . and *you*.'

Her eyes opened wide, though she tried to hide it. She coughed out an attempt at a laugh, then her face changed. Her eyes became hard and her lip sneered. 'Because all foreigners look the same to you? Yes, I have blonde hair, I'm slim. I'm pretty.' She thrust the page back at Lola and glared.

Lola said nothing, just took it and contemplated that image again, glancing up at the woman who sat opposite her, then back down, taking time to compare the faces.

'Marta,' Lola asked, 'what's going on here?'

Marta's mouth pursed but she didn't speak.

'Do you know where your son is?'

It was as if Lola had slapped her. She lifted her chin a little, then looked sharply away, her pale cheeks reddening.

'Marta,' Lola began conversationally, '*are you Ingrid Valk?*'

Marta's eyes became like saucers, full of fear.

'This is outrageous!' the solicitor yelled.

'Was Tiina Valk your sister?' Lola asked. 'If she was, we will find out. It'll be relatively easy, whether you choose to cooperate or not.'

'How dare you?' Marta Dixon whispered, then got suddenly to her feet. Her chair toppled with a crash. 'How *dare* you?'

Lola went calmly on: 'Marta, does Adam wear an ankle tag?'

Another petrified look, then she turned to Jeremy Wilder.

Wilder rose and said something very quietly to his client whose shoulders rose a little.

'Marta?' Lola prompted.

Marta Dixon returned her frightened gaze to Lola. She was breathing hard, barely containing panic, Lola suspected.

Lola waited.

'No,' Marta said in a whisper. 'No tag.'

'Did you tell Jeanie Quigley Adam wore one?'

She looked quickly down at her hands. 'No.'

The door opened, and Lawrie Dixon stood there, nostrils flaring, teeth bared.

'That's enough,' he snarled. 'Come on, Marta. You don't need to talk to them.'

His wife nodded and got up. Dixon reached out and took her by the arm to pull her from the room.

'Mr Dixon,' Lola said, still sitting calmly, 'we aren't finished.'

'Oh yes you are.'

Lola met Jeremy Wilder's eye. The solicitor looked more than a little embarrassed.

'Lawrie,' Marta whined, while he still gripped her arm, 'please . . .'

'Shut up,' Dixon hissed. 'Just don't say another bloody word.'

Lola got to her feet.

Dixon spat something else, this unheard, in his wife's ear, then thrust her out into the hallway. Then he turned back to Lola.

'I *knew* we shouldn't have told you. You can't help us. You don't even want to. You just want to accuse *us*, Adam's parents.'

'You and your wife are hiding something, Mr Dixon,' Lola said. 'I know it. You know it.' She turned to the solicitor and said unpleasantly, 'I expect you know it too, or at least suspect it.'

Wilder looked outraged while Dixon looked as if he was about to explode.

'You won't tell me, but I will find out,' she told him. 'One way or another.'

'I won't have this!' Dixon yelled. 'I'll stop you. I can, you know. I can ruin you.'

'Good luck with that,' Lola said.

She led Kirstie from the flat. Marta's loud, almost animal sobs followed them into the stairwell, seeming to ring in Lola's ears all the way back to the car.

* * *

2.04 p.m.

In the car, still shaken from the confrontation, Lola checked her phone and saw a missed call from a mobile number she didn't recognise. Whoever it was had left a message.

'Oh. Hello, DCI Harris. It's — it's Wendy Baker here.' She talked quietly, as if she was keen not to be overheard.

Lola paused the message and put the speaker on so Kirstie could listen too.

'Sorry to call like this,' Wendy said, 'but I've been thinking, and . . . well, I'm now fairly certain something's *not right*. It was the fact that photograph had been deleted. There's only one way that could have happened. I've raised it but I'm wondering if I should have talked to you first. And there's more. Oh gosh . . . this is going to sound melodramatic, I know it is, but I couldn't explain in front of Ms Carstairs. Could we meet? Away from the university, I mean. Maybe you could come to my flat. I might ask a colleague to join me too. It wasn't me who noticed the pattern and she can explain it better than I can. You see, this thing with Ingrid Valk — it's the fact she's the *third*! And . . . well, I think I know who's behind it.'

CHAPTER TEN

2.23 p.m.

Lola had tried calling Wendy Baker before she drove back to Helen Street but it had just rung out and gone to voicemail. She'd left a short message saying she was free now if Wendy wanted to call, but that she'd try her again in a short while. She called again after she'd parked at Helen Street. Once more, no reply.

Anna spotted Lola and Kirstie as they came into the office. She jumped up and hurried over, looking excited.

'We've managed to get CCTV footage from the office park where Dixon has his business,' she said. 'It seems Dixon was telling us the truth. Want to see?'

They followed Anna to her desk. Anna sat and turned her laptop screen towards them.

'It's in two parts and just a few seconds long.'

The image was black and white and the frozen image showed the corners of two buildings separated by grass. It was nighttime and the glow from a streetlight cast angular shadows across the lawn.

'That's Dixon's unit on the left,' Anna said. 'The guy appears at the bottom of the screen. Ready?'

'Aye, go on.'

Anna pressed play.

Nothing happened for a couple of seconds, then a tall, slim, hooded figure appeared at the bottom of the screen and made its way between the buildings to the corner of the one on the left — Dixon's unit. The figure paused at the corner and looked about before slipping out of sight down the side of the building. The clip finished.

'And this second clip is from four minutes later,' Anna said and pressed play.

The scene was the same. This time, the hooded figure appeared round the corner then retraced its steps, hurrying now.

'We only have Dixon's word for what was said,' Lola pointed out, feeling oddly deflated. Part of her had wanted Dixon's story to be disproven.

Anna peered at her.

'Dixon's still lying,' Lola said. She told Anna about their confrontation at the flat. 'I'm going to talk to the super about it. Meantime, would you try and call Wendy Baker for me? She left me a message saying she has new information, but now I can't get hold of her. She wanted me to ring her personal mobile, which seems suggestive.'

She read out the number.

'And try to find some more images of Ingrid Valk, would you? There must be something on social media somewhere. I put it to Marta Dixon that she was Ingrid Valk and she denied it, but she looked petrified. Something very strange is going on here and I mean to find out what.'

* * *

2.47 p.m.

'They're both lying,' Lola told Elaine Walsh, 'but only about part of it. No question they're frightened of something or

91

someone. Tiina Valk took their child — there's no denying the video evidence from the house, unless it's some kind of elaborate "deep fake". We've got CCTV footage that seems to confirm Dixon was indeed visited at work. I just don't buy the far-fetched story about the Russians. And now there's Ingrid Valk, Marta's apparent doppelganger.'

Elaine sat back, deep in thought.

'When I saw Ingrid's photograph,' Lola went on, 'I was convinced she and Marta Dixon were the same person. But you know, sitting in that kitchen with her just now . . . I started to doubt myself. I held the photo up to compare it with the flesh-and-blood woman sitting opposite me — and I wasn't so sure anymore. Her eyes look different, her chin, the angle of her jaw — there are subtle differences.'

'Another relation, then — a cousin?'

'Possibly, though Marta denies it. We could check but it'll be complicated and take time.'

'You could ask Marta for a DNA sample,' Elaine said. 'Compare it to the DNA of the dead woman. Then you'd know if they were sisters or otherwise related. Of course, she'd have to consent. We don't have any evidence at the moment to compel her. It could be interesting to see how she reacts. A refusal could be telling.'

Elaine became thoughtful once more.

'Do we know how Tiina Valk got into the Dixons' house yet?'

Lola turned a page in her notes; Anna had sent her an update from IB earlier. 'There's no sign of forced entry,' she said, reading. 'All the doors have smart locks on them, which are activated by a palm reader. There's a keypad as well, with a ten-digit code you can use.'

'So Tiina had the code?'

'It seems like it. Unless one of the Dixons left the door on a latch for her.'

'Surely not . . .'

'As I say, something isn't right, boss. What would we expect in a case of kidnapping? Distress, panic, fury, desperation — all of that. You'd expect the parents to be out of their minds. But Dixon seems frightened and defensive — even obstructive — as though he's about to be found out. Then there's Marta. Yes, she's terrified, panicking too, but she also seems weirdly in denial. Fatalistic as well, as though she already knows her son is gone.'

'What are you saying?' Elaine probed.

'I . . . I think there's a chance they know who has their child and where he is.'

They watched one another for several seconds. 'You think they're in on it?'

'I don't think so,' Lola said. 'As I say, their fear is very real. I just think there's a lot they're not telling us, and I don't understand why.'

'Has Dixon been doing something illegal, do you think?'

'Maybe. He said he's going to try to stop me asking questions. I wonder if he'll try to get ACC Thompson to intervene on his behalf.'

'He might,' Elaine said. 'Tread carefully. Be professional and courteous and keep meticulous notes. I'll deal with the ACC.'

'Thanks, boss.'

She got up to leave.

'Lola, before you go . . .' Elaine said, changing her tone.

Lola slid back into her seat.

'I wondered how things were with Sandy, after . . . you know — the announcement.'

'Oh, that.' Lola took a deep breath and let out a groaning sigh. Elaine waited. 'We met up last night,' Lola said.

'Oh?'

'On neutral territory. Some Chinese place neither of us had been to before. He apologised — for not telling me all that time. I told him I get it. But then . . . he asked me to go with him to meet the kid this Saturday — with her mother, obviously.'

Elaine's eyebrows went up. 'And what did you say to that?'

'I lost it, I'm afraid. I accused him of treating me like a support animal, then he did that whole "hurt" thing, which was all the more annoying, if I'm honest.'

Elaine said nothing.

'I love him, Elaine,' she went on. 'He knows I do and I think it's mutual. But this . . . it changes everything. And yet — why should it?'

'Good question.' Elaine sat up, eyes narrowed and off into a corner of her office.

'What are you thinking?' Lola asked drily, recognising the expression.

'I'm wondering if it's about children,' Elaine said very gently. 'Tell me to mind my own, if you like, but . . . something like this has to throw up feelings.'

Lola didn't reply. She looked at her hands, as if the topic was one she could hold and turn over to examine. At last she looked up and met Elaine's gaze. 'I don't know,' she said, and swallowed. 'I'd like . . . I'd like to think it wasn't about that. But then I think about all those years I wasted on Joe. Three decades, Elaine. And now I'm forty-seven.'

Elaine let the words settle for a moment.

'Have you said any of this to Sandy?'

'In the past. I've said to him that it was something I'd come to terms with. That I didn't mind.'

'And is that still the case?'

'I don't know.'

'Could you say any of this to him?'

'Maybe. But I think it's for me to deal with. Thanks, boss,' she added. 'Thanks for asking.'

'You know where I am, Lola.'

'I do.' She smiled and got up to go.

* * *

94

'I can't get hold of Wendy Baker,' Anna said when Lola returned to her desk. 'Do you think we should try to reach her through her colleagues?'

Lola thought for a moment. 'I'll try her one more time.'

But the call rang out once more, then went to voice-mail. Lola googled the university's main phone number and dialled.

'Can I speak to Wendy Baker in the registrar's office, please?'

'Calling now.'

Grating music played.

'Her extension is going to voicemail. Would you like to leave her a message?'

'Is there anyone else in the registrar's office I could talk to?'

'I'll check for you. Hold please.'

More tinny music played.

'Putting you through now.'

'Thank you.'

'Hello,' a quiet woman's voice said. 'It's Marisa Singleton in registry speaking. How can I help?'

'Oh, hello,' Lola said. 'I was wondering — do you know happen to know where Wendy Baker is?'

A pause. 'Erm . . . in a meeting, I think. Let me look at her calendar . . . She's in with the principal and the curriculum heads right now. Can I take a message?'

'When is she due out?'

'Five, it says, but these things can run on. Can I ask who's calling?'

'It's DCI Harris from Police Scotland,' she said. 'It's very urgent.'

'Oh! I see. Erm . . . I could ask the principal's PA to interrupt the meeting.'

'If you wouldn't mind.'

'I'll go down the corridor and talk to her myself. Give me a number and I'll ask Wendy to call you back — or I'll call you if there's a problem.'

'Thank you,' Lola said. 'What did you say your name was?'

'Marisa. Marisa Singleton.'

'Thank you, Marisa.'

While she waited she checked her personal phone. Sandy had sent a message.

I thought I should take Maisie a present. I'm no good at this kind of thing. Any ideas?

She reread the message then typed: *Nice idea. Sorry, no clue what kids are into these days.*

He began to type a reply straight away. Lola watched the three dots and felt her blood pressure rise.

Then his message appeared: *Any thoughts about Saturday? I'd love you to be there.*

She stared into space for a second or two, then decided there was no point delaying things.

You go on your own, she typed. *You can tell me about it afterwards.*

'Are you okay, boss?' Anna asked, arriving at her desk and making her jump.

'Yes.' She put her phone down. 'What is it?'

'News. The Tallinn police have found Tiina Valk's father and aunt. They're going to pay a visit to the flat to break the news. They'll ask if they feel up to talking to us, and if so then my contact will organise a translator. I said we'd make ourselves available to suit them, but the sooner the better. Oh, and we've had a call from a woman who thinks she saw Tiina Valk in a coffee shop off King Street, talking intently with a—' she consulted her notepad — 'skinny young man with freckles and sandy hair. Sounds like the cyclist chap the officer saw at Darnley yesterday morning. DS Pierce is trying to get a glimpse of him on security footage from businesses around King Street. He'll show anything he finds to the officer, but it's a promising lead.'

'Thanks, Anna.'

Lola's work mobile began to ring. She recognised the number of Clyde University's switchboard and pressed answer.

'Oh, hello. DCI Harris? It's Marisa Singleton here. I'm really sorry, but Wendy didn't turn up at the principal's meeting. I've asked around. Someone saw her heading down to reception about two forty-five, but no one's seen her since.'

CHAPTER ELEVEN

3.19 p.m.

The university's director of human resources was in the meeting Wendy should have attended. She came out to take Lola's call.

'Obviously I'm concerned too,' the woman said, 'but she may be dealing with something important — a student with a visa problem, or maybe a personal appointment.'

'Is it like her to miss meetings without telling anyone?' Lola asked.

'Frankly, no, it isn't. In my experience, Wendy is very reliable. And this is urgent, did you say?'

'It's connected to a murder inquiry.'

'Oh! Oh dear. Is Wendy involved in some way?'

'The university is,' Lola said. 'Were you not aware we'd met with Wendy and the principal earlier today?'

'No,' she said darkly. 'No, I wasn't.'

'Then I suggest you talk to Ms Carstairs. Meantime, I need to find Wendy Baker. I need her home address. Could you get that for me now?'

'Okay,' the woman said. 'Give me five minutes and I'll ring you back.'

* * *

Wendy Baker had a tenement flat at the top of Great George Street in the Hillhead area of the city's West End. Lola took Kirstie with her and found a space to park outside.

She rang the buzzer then, after waiting and buzzing again, pressed the service button, used by delivery people. The occupant of another flat unlocked the door.

Lola led the way up the echoing tiled stairwell to the second floor.

But no one answered when they rapped the knocker on the storm door.

Lola knocked on the door opposite. A lad in his teens appeared, looking as if he'd only just got out of bed.

'Police,' Lola said, holding out her ID. 'We're trying to contact Wendy Baker next door. Have you seen her today?'

He frowned and pulled at his blond locks. 'No. Sorry.'

'When did you see her last?'

'A week ago? Sorry. Not sure.'

'You don't have a spare key do you?'

His eyes widened. 'Shit, is it serious or something?'

'Do you?'

'No. Soz.'

'Do you know who might have one?'

His eyes narrowed. 'Angela might. She's lived here the longest.'

'Which flat is she?'

'Ground floor, underneath this one.'

'Thanks.'

Lola sent Kirstie down to knock. The constable was back in two minutes, an older woman climbing slowly after her. She had loose grey hair and was wearing a ratty green cardigan.

'I'm Wendy's neighbour Angela,' she told Lola. 'I hope nothing's wrong. I told your colleague I'd be coming in with

99

you. I'd prefer that. Going into your neighbour's is one thing, handing over a key is something else.'

She unlocked the storm door then the inner door, taking her time, then led the way into the flat.

Lola and Kirstie divided the rooms between them, Lola checking the bathroom, dining room and kitchenette. Everywhere was clean and neat — exactly what Lola would expect having met the flat's owner. On the hallway wall, beside a coat rack hung with jackets, scarves and a bright-green tote bag with writing on it, was an old-looking photograph of Wendy smiling away in a graduation gown, flanked by an older couple who beamed with pride. Her parents, no doubt.

'Nothing, boss,' Kirstie told her when they met again in the hallway.

'Thank you, Angela,' Lola said. 'You can lock up then we'll leave you. If you see Wendy return, would you ask her to ring me on this number at once?' She handed her a card.

They were back in the car and about to head off when Anna called.

'Boss, did you find Wendy Baker?' she asked.

'Not yet. Why?'

'A 999 call came in thirty minutes ago. A woman answering Wendy Baker's description has been found dead just off Garscube Road.'

Anna's words winded her. 'Really?' she managed.

'Colleagues from central are there now. DI Charlie Noble is in charge. I'm heading out there now.'

'Give me the address,' Lola said, 'and we'll meet you there.'

Lola asked Kirstie to drive. That way she could replay Wendy Baker's voice message and pay close attention to her words. The hand she held her phone in trembled. She'd known Wendy was holding something back when they'd stood by the campus steps. She should have made Wendy speak to them, taken her away from the place and away from the influence of the domineering Prue Carstairs.

The message played. Lola heard again the anxiety in the Wendy's words as she referred to the deleted photograph:

There's only one way that could have happened. I've raised it but I'm wondering if I should have talked to you first.

Then, in relation to Ingrid herself: *it's the fact she's the third!* The third what?

There was a sliver of hope: the colleague Wendy mentioned, the one who'd 'noticed the pattern' and who could 'explain it better' than Wendy.

Did she mean Marisa, the deputy Lola had spoken to briefly?

'I won't stay long at the crime scene,' she told Kirstie as they arrived and were looking for a space to park. 'Just long enough to check it's her. If it is I'll head straight to the university campus.'

* * *

5.11 p.m.

Central Subdivision's officers had been efficient, cordoning off a whole section of the street, focused on the entrance to an alleyway where the body apparently lay.

Just beyond the cordon, Anna was talking to a stocky woman with short curly grey hair. Anna spotted Lola and Kirstie and beckoned them over.

'This is DI Noble,' Anna said.

'DCI Harris?' Noble reached for Lola's hand and shook it heartily. 'I've heard a lot about you. Seen you on occasion but we've never spoken. DI Vaughan was explaining a possible link with your case down in Darnley.'

'I'd like to see the body,' Lola said. 'Time's against us, I'm afraid. If I know it's Wendy Baker, then I can make a move.'

'What sort of move?' Noble eyed her curiously.

'I mean to find out what she knew. Wendy Baker left me a message this afternoon, saying she had further information about a student who disappeared from the university. She hinted one of her colleagues had information about it. That person could be in danger now. If we can get to them first then they might be able to tell us who's doing this.'

'Sounds sensible. Can we keep in touch, though? I don't want to drop any threads.'

'Of course.'

Noble called an IB officer over to equip Lola and Anna with forensic suits. Kitted out, they filed into the alleyway towards a tent, using stepping plates to protect any evidence.

'Ashra, can we get inside for a minute?' the officer called to an unseen colleague.

'Sure.' A figure emerged from the tent. 'All yours,' Ashra said, tugging down the face mask.

'Take your time,' the first officer said to Lola, who went first, steeling herself.

Wendy Baker lay on her side, her back arched and her head at an unnatural angle, eyes starkly open and her mouth open in a silent scream. Blood was matted in her hair. Lola stepped further into the tent and inclined her head to get a proper look into the face.

Lola looked with pity and regret at the woman on the ground. *I'm so sorry*, she told her silently. Then she backed wordlessly out of the tent and let Anna go in.

'Have you any idea how long she's been dead?' Lola asked the IB officer who lingered a few feet away.

'We're still waiting for the police surgeon to arrive, but an hour, we reckon. Maybe a little longer than that.'

'So, around four o'clock?'

The IB officer shrugged. 'Quite possibly.'

Anna had reemerged from the tent.

'I'll go see that principal,' Lola told her, hearing anger cracking in her own voice. 'This is an indirect result of her culture of secrecy and control, and I'm going to make sure she realises that.'

CHAPTER TWELVE

5.45 p.m.

There was no one at the campus reception desk, just a button you could press after five thirty.

'It's DCI Harris from Police Scotland,' she said when a tinny voice answered. 'Is the principal still in the building?'

The voice said something indistinct, then cut out.

A minute later a security guard appeared, a small wiry man in his thirties.

'You want to see our Prue, eh? Without an appointment?' He whistled.

'It's urgent,' she said.

'I'll call her,' he said, smirking. 'Wish me luck.' He went behind the reception desk and picked up a phone.

Lola looked about the atrium. The café was still open and there were a few students sitting on the other side of the glass security barrier, hunkered down in seats.

'Evening, Ms Carstairs,' the security man said, clearly rolling out his best telephone voice. 'It's James from security here. Police lady for you. In reception, aye, that's right.' He made a face at Lola, an exaggerated wince as if he was getting an earful. 'Aye, okay. Well, I can't really leave my post, unless . . . aye. Okay. Sorry, Ms Carstairs. Of course, that's quite all right. I'll bring her right up.'

He put the phone down.

'Her PA's finished for the day,' he said. 'I've to escort you. This way.'

'Do you like working here?' Lola enquired when they were in the lift. James's eyes widened.

He made a silent gesture to a camera in the corner of the lift's ceiling, and whispered, 'Walls have ears as well as eyes.'

'I get you,' she replied drily.

They arrived at the same floor she and Anna had come to earlier. James led the way past the open-plan area and the closed door of Wendy's office. Lola spotted the young man who'd tried to help Wendy find Ingrid Valk's photograph on the system.

'One minute,' she said to the security guard, and walked quickly to the lad's desk. He had earphones in, so she waved a hand in front of his face and made him jump.

'Danny, isn't it?'

'Oh, hi,' he said, then eyed the security guard behind Lola. 'You were here earlier, weren't you? Were you looking for Wendy again? Only, she's not around, so—'

'I'm seeing Prue Carstairs.'

'Oh.' Judging by the look in his eyes, the principal struck fear into everyone who worked here.

'Do you work with Marisa?'

'Yeah, but she's away home too. Marisa's my boss. Can I help you?'

He had an open, eager face, despite a 'gothy' appearance.

'What is it you do here?'

'I look after student data.'

'You're not leaving any time soon, are you, Danny? Only, I might want a wee chat.'

He glanced back at his screen then gave her a glum, ironic look. 'I'll be another hour at least.'

'Good. I'll catch you on my way out.'

'Good luck with the principal,' Danny said, a twinkle in his eye.

Lola turned to the security guard. 'Lead on,' she said.

Prue Carstairs' office was at the end of a long corridor. The door stood ajar. Her desk was set at right angles to the door and she was jabbing irritably at a keyboard, stopping now and then to look at the keys. She must have known they were in the doorway, but ignored them, even when the security guard gingerly knocked on the doorframe.

'Your visitor, Ms Carstairs,' he said loudly.

The principal didn't so much as turn but reared round in her seat. 'Yes?' she demanded, gripping the arm of her chair with both hands.

'Thank you,' Lola said to the guard, and smiled.

'Right you are,' he muttered and stepped away.

'Good afternoon, Ms Carstairs,' Lola said. She went into the office and kicked away a door stop so the door fell quietly shut.

'What is the meaning of this?' Carstairs demanded.

'I'm here with upsetting news,' she said and went to the desk to stand over Prue Carstairs.

'Oh?' Carstairs sat up and squared her shoulders. 'I hope it isn't a student you're here about.'

Lola sat in one of two chairs on the other side of Carstairs' big desk. There was a box of tissues in easy reach, no doubt in high demand in this office.

'Well, come on out with it,' Carstairs said.

'I'm afraid your registrar Wendy Baker has been found dead this afternoon, in an alleyway about a quarter of a mile from here.'

She stopped and waited for a reaction.

The principal didn't speak or move. Her pale blue eyes stared through Lola rather than at her. She remained like that for several seconds, then her eyes closed. She took deep breaths that made her nostrils flare.

Then she opened her eyes, lifted her chin and peered down her nose at Lola. 'Are you sure it's her?' she asked stiffly.

'I saw the body before I came here. It's the same woman I met with you earlier today.'

Carstairs nodded then seemed to sag a little. 'I see. What happened to her?'

'We don't know yet.'

She seemed to be struggling to take it in. 'This is . . . most unfortunate.'

'Wendy called me this afternoon, Ms Carstairs. She said she had more to tell me about Ingrid Valk. She wanted me to call her and possibly see her at home. She implied she didn't feel able to talk at work.'

Carstairs' face coloured at that, but from anger rather than embarrassment, Lola felt sure.

'I mean to find out what she wanted to tell me,' Lola said coolly. 'I mean to talk to your staff and I'll expect them to tell me the truth.'

'The truth about *what*?' she asked.

Lola hadn't intended to quote Wendy's words but the moment seemed right. 'About Ingrid Valk being "the third".'

A glimmer of alarm. 'The third what? I don't know what you mean.'

But the pink had deepened and her jaw now trembled. 'Ms Carstairs?'

The principal sat up, squared her shoulders and asked, 'Has Wendy's mother been told?'

'Not yet. Is she her next of kin?'

'Yes.'

'If you could give me her details, then we'll break the news.'

Carstairs nodded, then tapped at her keyboard. 'She's local. She lives in the West End, I believe. Yes,' she said, peering at the screen, 'here we are. Queensborough Gardens.' She tore a page from a pad and wrote on it, then handed it to Lola without eye contact.

'Now,' Lola said, 'about Ingrid being "the third" . . . If you know something and you're holding it back, then you would be obstructing a police inquiry. What do you know, Ms Carstairs?'

'Nothing!' she half shrieked. Her fist came down hard on her desk, making a Sellotape dispenser fall on its side. She jumped and stared as if shocked at her own action. More quietly, she muttered, 'I know nothing. *Nothing.*'

She flapped about, rearranging her desk, righting the Sellotape dispenser and moving a stapler alongside a hole punch then squaring her keyboard. Then she turned her gaze back to Lola and asked acidly, 'Was there something else?'

'We'll need access to any email or phone accounts Wendy had here, and access to all digital files she might have had access to through her computer.'

Carstairs' expression was one of sheer, gripped horror. Her mouth worked but no words came out.

'I expect your IT colleagues can help with that. This is an emergency, so perhaps you could contact them to arrange that in the next hour if possible. I'd also like to contact Marisa Singleton. I believe she worked with Wendy.'

'She's her deputy, yes.'

'I'd like a contact number for her, please.'

The woman huffed. 'Very well.'

'Oh, and I'd like one for you as well, Ms Carstairs.' She got up. 'That's everything I can think of just now.'

* * *

6.24 p.m.

Danny the data clerk was still at his desk. Lola got the distinct impression he'd been watching for her return from the principal's office. She went over.

'Can we have a chat?'

'Erm . . . if you like.' His eyes flittered along the corridor in the direction of Carstairs' office.

'Don't worry about her,' Lola assured him.

'Did you . . . want to talk here or . . . ?' He glanced over at a glass cube of a meeting room, the door of which stood open.

'Somewhere private would be good.'

He rose and led the way to the cube. A light came on automatically as he walked in. Lola followed, closed the door after her and sat.

'How can I help?' he asked, nervous now.

'How closely do you work with Wendy Baker?' she asked.

He stared for a moment. 'Oh . . . fairly closely. I mean, she's the big boss in this department. She's my boss's boss.' He frowned. 'Is everything all right? She's not in any trouble, is she? She's really nice. Kind — unlike some others in this place.'

'Oh, like who?'

'I shouldn't have said that.' He eyed her, biting his lip. 'Something is wrong, isn't it?'

Lola ignored the question, asking, 'Have you ever heard Wendy talk about a student called Ingrid Valk?'

'She's the one you were asking about earlier, isn't she? The one whose photo was missing from the system? Wendy didn't explain what it was about, just that it was urgent — because you needed it.'

'So you hadn't come across Ingrid Valk before?'

He looked uncomfortable. 'I'm not certain,' he said after a moment. 'Her name did seem familiar. Her surname, anyway.'

He peered out through the meeting room's glass wall, nervous now.

'She won't like me talking to you like this,' he said.

'Who won't?'

'Old Prue. She was very angry with Wendy earlier. Marisa heard her after you'd left, yelling at Wendy in her office. Marisa said Wendy was in tears about it. Prue's a big bully.' He pulled a face. 'We're all looking for new jobs.'

'Is this your first job?'

'Yeah. Started here two weeks after I graduated.'

'Did you study here at the university?'

He nodded. 'Data management and information systems. Sounds boring, doesn't it? Guess it was in parts, but data is everything these days. I mean, everything we do involves data in some way.'

'I suppose it does. And data security is therefore critical.'

'Just a bit!'

'And where are you from?'

'Clydebank. My mum's still there. I've got a wee place in Dennistoun.'

'Back to Ingrid Valk,' Lola said gently.

'Yeah, sorry. Look, I'm pretty sure she's one of the students who left her course and didn't inform us. We had to do a bit of running to try and find her — well, I say "we", I mean Wendy and Marisa and some of the Student Services people. We have to report them, you know, because of their visas.'

Something seemed to occur to him, making him frown and withdraw a little. He looked at his hands.

'What is it?' she asked.

'Nothing. I mean . . . sorry. It's just — well, it's not for me to tell you any of this. I'd rather you spoke to Marisa and asked her. It's just . . .' His eyes strayed back to the office beyond the glass wall. He started to get up. 'Look, I should be getting back to my work.'

'Sit down please, Danny,' she said firmly.

He did as he was told, eyes wide with apprehension.

'Now, I'm going to tell you something in the strictest confidence, because time is important and I need you to understand why you must help me.' He looked now. 'I'm afraid Wendy Baker is dead.'

He stared for what seemed to be an age, then frowned and gave a nervous laugh. 'What?' he asked. 'I — I don't understand.'

'We don't know what happened exactly,' she said, softening her tone. 'But we're investigating.'

His face was a picture of disbelief, as if he knew this must be a prank. He was so young he might never have encountered death before, let alone the brutal kind.

'You're serious, aren't you?' he said. 'Oh God . . .' He sank down in his chair, looking sick. For a moment she thought he might be about to burst into tears.

'I'm afraid so,' Lola said. 'And there's a chance her death is connected to Ingrid Valk. Now you understand why I need you to tell me what you know.'

But he was distracted. 'I can't believe it. Wendy was so nice to me.'

She waited a few more moments and Danny began to pull himself together. His face moved as if he was battling with himself.

'Please, Danny.'

He nodded, resigned. 'It was the way she'd gone missing that worried Wendy. The way she just vanished like that, and no one knew where she was.'

'What about it?'

'As I say, you're better talking to Marisa, but . . . well, it wasn't the first time, was it? It had happened twice before.'

Lola frowned, peering hard into the young man's face. 'I'm sorry, Danny. Are you saying Ingrid had gone missing *twice* in the past?'

'No!' He shook his head vehemently. 'No, not her — two other students. Two other students had gone missing before Ingrid, and the way they disappeared, it was *so* similar. You see, *Ingrid was the third.*'

* * *

6.47 p.m.

Lola let Danny return to his desk while she remained in the glass cube and phoned Marisa Singleton.

She broke the news about Wendy's death, though without giving any details, and asked her to come to the university

110

immediately. She'd be there in ten minutes, Marisa told her in a small, frightened voice. She only lived three streets away.

'Good,' Lola said. 'And please don't say anything to anyone. I'll see you when you get here.'

Next Lola called Anna Vaughan and asked her to release one of the constables.

'I'll send Kirstie,' Anna said.

'Ask her to buzz me when she arrives and I'll come down and get her. Any updates about Wendy Baker's death?'

'Yes. The owner of a café saw her walking up Garscube Road towards Maryhill around three o'clock. He knew her because she used to buy coffee and cakes from him. He was bringing in his pavement sign and says Wendy went hurrying past, heading in the direction of Maryhill. He said "hi" and she acknowledged him but seemed distracted and upset. But listen to this, boss: the café is further *up* Garscube Road than the place where she was found dead and presumably killed.'

'Meaning what?'

'If she came from the university campus then she was heading for somewhere *beyond* this chap's café. She must have been killed on her way back, sometime later. So the question is, where was she going?'

'IB put her time of death at around four, didn't they?' Lola said. 'So where was she for the hour between when the café owner saw her and the time she was killed? I assume DI Noble is requesting CCTV?'

'Yes. Doorbell cameras, the lot.'

'I'm trying to picture what's at the top of Garscube Road.'

'A whole lot of places,' Anna said. 'Industrial estates, a few wholesalers, small businesses, quite a lot of tenement flats too. Hopefully cameras will show us where she went. Did you get information about her next of kin?'

'I've got her mother's details. Could you pass them to Charlie Noble? Let her take that particular job.'

Lola read out the information.

'Before I go,' Anna said, 'I heard from the Estonian police ten minutes ago. They've seen Tiina and Ingrid's father and aunt. They've confirmed the photograph taken at the mortuary shows their daughter Tiina. They're obviously very shocked but they're willing to talk to us this evening. The aunt has some English but the father none. It'll take an hour or so to get a translator in place. I've suggested eight p.m. our time, which is ten p.m. theirs.'

'Could they possibly do an hour later? I'm reluctant to rush things here.'

'I'm sure that'll be fine. Will we aim to talk to them from Helen Street?'

'Yes. Failing that, we can do it from a car. Ah—' She peered through the glass wall of the cube and saw a woman hurrying into the open-plan part of the office. 'I think that's Marisa Singleton here now. Talk to you later, Anna.'

She opened the door of the glass cube and called, 'Marisa?'

'That's me,' the woman answered and hurried over.

'I'm DCI Lola Harris. We spoke on the phone.'

'Yes.' She was in her forties, a thin woman with curly black hair. Her face was a picture of misery. She'd clearly been crying. 'What on earth happened? Does her mum know yet?'

'She'll know very soon. And we don't know what happened,' she added pointedly, 'but we're investigating.'

'Oh God. You mean . . . ?'

'I mean, we're *investigating*. One of my constables is on her way here. When she arrives, we can talk.'

She nodded. 'Does the principal know?'

'I've spoken to her, yes.'

Marisa reached for the back of a chair and sat down, then gave Lola a wary look. 'Does she know you're talking to me?'

'Don't worry about that,' Lola said darkly. 'You leave Prue Carstairs to me.'

Her phone buzzed in her hand.

'That's my constable,' she said. 'I'll go down and get her.'

* * *

They used the glass cube for the interview, Lola and Kirstie sitting on one side of the table, Marisa facing them, her back to the door and the glass wall. Lola didn't want her distracted by the possibility that Prue Carstairs might materialise at any moment.

Lola explained what Danny had told her, about Ingrid being the third student to go missing.

'It's imperative you tell me everything you know,' she said. 'You won't get into any trouble. I'll make sure of that.'

Marisa nodded but looked unconvinced.

'Now, tell me about the three students.'

'We track early leavers,' Marisa said. 'Partly to understand why they've left the course, but also because if someone was in the UK on a study visa then we have to inform the Home Office. Last autumn I spotted something. A South Korean student had left her course without warning and a Chinese student had gone missing about the same time — and the circumstances were quite similar.'

'Oh?'

'Yes. I'll tell you about the South Korean student first. Her name, if I remember rightly, was Yunhee Kim. She was studying communications. A good student, according to her lecturers — until she stopped attending classes in the April of last year. She missed a couple of lectures and then a meeting with her tutor, saying she was ill. She provided a doctor's note, but visa regulations mean we have to require attendance except in the direst of circumstances. We wrote to her, inviting her to a meeting but she didn't reply. I asked Student Services to contact her and they tried to, even paying her a visit at her accommodation — but they learned she wasn't living there anymore. Her flatmates didn't know where she was but there was talk of a boyfriend. Now, the fact she'd moved

113

to another address without telling us was hugely concerning, because of the visa rules.

'But just as we were about to sound the alarm — by which I mean, contact the Home Office — she emailed me, saying she'd been ill and that she was going to start classes again that week. I replied, asking her in for a meeting and she came. Wendy and I explained the importance of attendance and of staying in touch. She got quite upset at that. She didn't look well at all, the poor thing. She said she was living with her boyfriend and was sorry she hadn't given us her new address. I asked her to write it down for us there and then, but she claimed she couldn't remember it, which was very odd. She promised to provide a new address or to move back to her shared flat within the week, and we gave her the benefit of the doubt.'

'Did she send her new address?'

'She emailed to say she'd moved back into her shared flat. I made a note on the system and wrote a reminder to myself to check she had in fact gone back there. She took her assessments in May but I'm afraid she failed two of them. We notified her of the need to resit two assessments in August, but she didn't show up, and then she failed to register for her third year. We tried to contact her again but we couldn't get hold of her.' She looked sheepish now. 'She hadn't moved back in with her former flatmates. I have to say I was very annoyed when I found out she'd lied.'

'Did you contact her family?'

'We were going to,' she said, a little stiffly, 'only . . . it seemed we didn't have their details anymore. The student had changed her emergency contact on her own electronic records. It was for someone here in Scotland. A man. There was a number but it just rang out. It wouldn't even let me leave a message. I sent a text message but didn't get a reply.'

'Did you contact the police?'

Marisa gave her a long look then shook her head. 'No,' she said. 'No, we didn't. Wendy and I discussed it, then she spoke to Prue — to Ms Carstairs, I mean — and Ms

Carstairs told us not to. She said it would be bad publicity and became quite cross with Wendy, reminding her about the importance of international fees and how important the university's reputation was for attracting students from abroad. She also pointed out that students do leave courses and for all sorts of reasons. Sometimes they don't tell us why. Plus, the student was an adult . . . Then the next day, I spotted that another student hadn't registered for her third year. So, we got back on to Student Services and asked them to try to locate her.'

'This was the Chinese student?' Lola checked.

'Yes. Another very bright girl who'd been studying accounting. She'd never missed a class and always turned up for her assessments. She just didn't show up to re-register in the autumn.'

'When had the university last been in contact with her?'

'A few months before. We don't monitor students' whereabouts over the summer break, so she could have been missing since the end of May. We tried to contact her, but her UK number was dead. There was an emergency contact, for her grandmother in China. A colleague who speaks Mandarin talked to her but the lady seemed very confused. She kept repeating that her granddaughter was in London — she seemed to think that's where she'd gone to study. Student Services talked to the student's former flatmates . . . and that's when they learned she'd moved out of her shared flat in April — about the same time as Yunhee Kim, the Korean student. Chan Wen, the Chinese student, had sworn her flatmates to secrecy, saying she was in love with a man she'd met and was going to live with him. She continued going to classes from this man's place.

'Wendy was really very worried so she talked to the principal again, but Ms Carstairs said it was the students' decision and that we should inform the Home Office and then move on. Wendy was just on the verge of informing the Home Office when Yunhee, the South Korean student, reappeared — she just arrived at the Student Services desk and said she was here to register for her third year, two weeks into the new term!'

'Did you let her re-register?'

'Wendy and I interviewed her and asked where she'd been. She said she'd been ill, that she'd had a sort of breakdown, but that she was much better now and keen to resume her studies. She seemed quite full of herself, actually. Well, Wendy wasn't sure we should readmit her. Then she took Ms Carstairs' advice and Ms Carstairs insisted she should be allowed to continue: because of the fees, Wendy suspected. We asked about her emergency contact and she said it was incorrect and changed it so that it was for her mother in Seoul. Now this was all very well, but then she chose to leave anyway, just before Christmas, saying the course was dull. She even asked for her money back. Ms Carstairs spoke to her herself but then conceded she had every right to leave, but we kept a third of her fees. Yunhee didn't seem overly bothered. A lot of attitude, that girl.'

'And where is she now, this Yunhee?' Lola asked.

'She talked of starting another course somewhere in Scotland,' Marisa said. 'I'm sure the Home Office people could confirm if she applied for a new study visa — and if she was granted one.'

Lola made a note to check.

'I don't think we ever mentioned it after that. There's so much work to do and so many students to monitor — I think we just forgot about them. But then, when Ingrid Valk didn't register for her third year last month, we made our usual enquiries — and found the same pattern again! Missed classes, moving out of the flat she'd shared, rumours of a mysterious boyfriend — and her emergency contact had been changed too — the same way Yunhee's emergency contact had been.'

She took a deep breath and said, quietly, almost guiltily, 'This time Wendy didn't go to Ms Carstairs. She went to the police herself — just to ask for advice. She spoke to a sergeant at the police station in Charing Cross. Told him everything and showed him records. He made notes, but he didn't think there was enough evidence to warrant any kind of investigation. He seemed to think that if the Home Office had been informed then that should be an end to our role. Wendy said he tried to reassure her, suggesting the young women must have gone home, and that Wendy had done everything she possibly could.'

She paused and took a peek over her shoulder out into the office, as if Prue Carstairs might be prowling there.

'Two days later,' she said, in a low voice, 'Wendy and I were called in to see Ms Carstairs. She said she'd "had word" that Wendy had gone to the police, though she didn't say how she knew. She was *furious* and accused us of risking the university's reputation as a safe place to study and cast doubt on our ability — and willingness — to look after our students' interests.' Her voice became choked and she put a hand to her mouth. 'I'm sorry. It's just . . . Ms Carstairs was *vile* to Wendy. She even said she'd considered suspending her. She made Wendy apologise and promise not to speak of it anymore — and said the same went for me. So, we obeyed her. I tried to talk to Wendy about it but she said it was best that we just did our jobs. And then, two weeks ago, Tiina Valk appeared, wanting answers about her sister, and we couldn't give her any. When Wendy saw Tiina's photo on the news this morning, she told me she was going to ring you and if it meant losing her job, then so be it — those were her very words. I told her I was right behind her.' She was choked again. 'But this is so much worse and now . . . now Wendy's dead.'

Lola gave her a minute to collect herself.

'Can you give us all the information you have about the South Korean and Chinese students?'

'Of course,' Marisa said. 'I'll ask Danny to find that for you. I'll ask him right now.'

'Please.'

Marisa rose from her seat — then froze, staring out into the office. Lola peered round her and saw an ominous pink-clad figure approaching between the desks.

'Oh God,' Marisa whispered.

Lola got up and went quickly to the door. 'Stay here,' she said to Marisa, then opened the door and left the cube, just as Prue Carstairs arrived, eyes ablaze.

Lola pulled the door closed after her then stood blocking it.

'What is going on?' Carstairs demanded, peering over Lola's shoulder. 'Is that Marisa Singleton?'

Lola saw Danny McDougall cringing at his desk across the office.

She said calmly, 'My colleague and I are interviewing Marisa Singleton in relation to her colleague's death.'

'What exactly has she said to you? I have a right to know.'

'No you don't, Ms Carstairs. This is a police interview.'

Carstairs made to push her out of the way but Lola stood her ground.

'Would you kindly move?' the principal said. 'That staff member answers to me in the absence of her line manager and she talks to no one without my being there, even you!'

Lola said icily, 'I know you tried to prevent Wendy Baker from reporting those girls' disappearances. Then you bullied her and threatened to suspend her when she took the initiative.'

Carstairs reared up, her lips drawn back to reveal long teeth.

'I'm not having this,' she snarled then narrowed her eyes. 'Wait till the chair of my board hears about this.'

'You don't intimidate me,' Lola said calmly.

Carstairs' eyes blazed with renewed fury.

'Now, please stop trying to block a police investigation — or you risk being charged with obstructing an investigation.'

Carstairs opened her mouth, ready to speak, then changed her mind, snapped it shut, and turned and marched furiously away.

Lola re-entered the glass cube to find Marisa looking frightened to death.

'You see what it's like here?' she asked in a whisper.

'I do. I'm sorry.' She smiled sympathetically. 'I'd get out if I were you, and fast.'

Marisa smiled sadly back. 'I'm trying, believe me. We all are. Now, give Danny and me five minutes and we'll dig out all the information we hold on those two students.'

CHAPTER THIRTEEN

8.51 p.m.

Assistant Chief Constable Alec Thompson phoned Lola as she was parking at Helen Street. She was a few minutes early for the call to Estonia with Anna, so said she could talk.

'I've just spoken to Lawrie Dixon,' the ACC said smoothly. 'He's horribly worried, understandably. I expressed my support and assured him my best people are on the case. I suggested he step down from his advisory role for the duration of — well, until we know what's what. He agreed it was the right thing to do. I did what you wanted and asked him to surrender his devices and give us access to his accounts, but I'm afraid he's unwilling.'

'I see, sir. Did he give a reason?'

'Yes. He expects to be contacted by whoever has taken his son. He insists on keeping his devices with him. As you know, DCI Harris, we have no grounds to seize them. As for the other question,' he went on, clearly short of time himself, 'Lawrie and his wife are not willing to go public. I'm sorry.'

'I see.'

'Let's treat the Dixons with the care and support they need, DCI Harris.'

'Of course, sir.'

He hung up and Lola sat for almost a minute, staring at the blank screen of her phone, wondering what exactly Thompson had meant, what exactly Dixon had said to him, and how much he'd believed.

* * *

9.02 p.m.

The screen of Anna's laptop showed Henno Valk and his sister Irma Nugis sitting at a table in a brightly lit meeting room a thousand miles away, flanked by a senior detective and an interpreter. Mr Valk, a big man, was hunched and grim-faced. Irma, thinner and older-looking, inclined her head and looked mournful.

The detective spoke in English, allowing pauses so the translator could communicate with the siblings.

It took time, but Lola was able to express condolences and check to her satisfaction that the dead woman at Darnley Glen was indeed Tiina Valk.

The pair confirmed they'd seen Tiina three weeks before, giving dates for when she'd arrived back in Tallinn from Australia. She'd asked them about Ingrid, whom she hadn't spoken to for some time. Tiina had fallen out with her sister a year ago, apparently offended by Ingrid's attitude to their father. Henno himself had heard from Ingrid only once, in March — or so he thought. She'd needed money. He'd sent some. Ingrid had broken his heart, he told Lola and Anna tearfully, with her self-serving ways and her lack of care for her father; now his heart was breaking again, this time for his other daughter.

Lola asked about Tiina's work and her education before that. 'Something in computers,' he said.

She liked sport, including running and climbing, Irma told them. 'Always outside. Always moving, never still.'

'Did Tiina tell you she was coming to the UK?' Lola asked, then waited for the answer in English.

'She said she planned to visit friends in London,' came Henno's answer. 'I asked if she would try to see Ingrid. She said perhaps.'

'Did she contact you again after you saw her in Tallinn?'

'No.'

She'd thought long and hard about her next questions — how to probe into Tiina's possible criminal behaviour without adding to her father and aunt's trauma.

'Was Tiina ever in any kind of trouble with the police or other authorities?' she asked, then watched the pair's faces as the translator passed the question on.

Henno looked shocked. Irma began talking angrily.

'No, it's unthinkable,' the translator said for both of them. 'Never anything like that.'

'Did Tiina have any Russian friends?'

That went down even worse.

The translator relayed Henno's furious words: 'Tiina wouldn't spit on any Russian.'

'I see.'

Lola asked the father to provide photos of both his daughters. He wanted to know why they needed a picture of Ingrid.

'We'd like to try to find her,' she explained, not adding she feared it was unlikely they'd find Ingrid alive.

The Estonian detective said he'd organise for any photographs to be scanned and sent to them.

Finally, Lola thanked the pair and expressed her condolences once more.

They came off the call exhausted.

Anna checked her phone.

'What is it?' Lola asked.

'Tiina's best friend in Estonia wants to talk to us,' Anna said wearily. 'Tonight, she says. Doesn't matter how late it is.'

'That's sounds a bit more promising,' Lola said. 'Can you send her a Teams link for ten minutes' time? Time for us to nip to the loo and get coffee from the machine.'

* * *

9.55 p.m.

'Tiina was very worried about her sister,' Kaia Tamm said. She was teary-eyed but calm and, luckily, her English was excellent. 'We were in touch often, texting a few times a week all the time she was in Australia.'

'Why was she worried?' Lola asked.

A deep breath. 'They'd had a falling out, but they reconnected earlier in the year. Then Tiina found out Ingrid was involved in something she didn't approve of. She didn't say what, but she hinted it was illegal and could get her into trouble. About a month ago I heard from her that she'd asked a friend to go to Glasgow to look for Ingrid. That he couldn't find her. So she said she was going to come to Europe. She would fly to Tallinn to see her father and her aunt, and me too, she hoped. Then she was going to go to Scotland. And she wasn't going to leave until she'd found Ingrid "and rescued her from herself". She said she wanted to bring her back to Estonia.'

'Did the two of you meet?'

'No.' She hung her head, perhaps overcome at the realisation that no meeting could ever happen now. 'No, I was away. My work sent me to Helsinki for a few days. I arrived back the day Tiina left.'

'Do you know Ingrid well?'

'Not really. I've met her. She's a few years younger than Tiina.' She made a face. 'She's different from Tiina.'

'What do you mean?'

'She's silly. Entitled. Selfish. And she'd do anything for money — which is why I think Tiina fell out with her in the first place.'

Lola sat thinking for a minute, battling tiredness now.

'Tiina's male friend in the UK,' she said. 'Did she mention a name?'

The woman on the screen blinked as she thought about it. 'I don't remember,' she said at last. 'Oh — just a minute.'

She reached for a phone and began tapping. 'Our text conversations,' she said, eyes on the screen. 'Wait, please.'

She scrolled, pausing now and then to read. Lola realised how tense she was and forced herself to relax.

'Here,' Kaia said suddenly. 'Yes. This was our conversation. Let me read through it.'

Her lips moved as she read over the words. Occasionally she smiled but then looked pained with emotion again.

'It's in Estonian, so I'll translate,' she said. '*My friend Anthony will go to Glasgow from this weekend. He owes me, but it's nice of him to do this. He says he has friends there and he's sure he can find Ingrid, if anyone can.*' She looked up.

'Had she mentioned this Anthony before, or did she mention him again?'

Kaia refocused on her screen then shook her head slowly. 'I'm sorry, I don't think so. I'll check, but . . .'

'Could you email me screenshots of that conversation, Kaia? To the address you used before. Don't worry about translating it.'

'Of course. I'll do that right away.'

'Thanks. And do you happen to have any recent photos of Tiina or of Ingrid?'

'Of Tiina, definitely. I'll look and see if I have any of Ingrid. If I do, Tiina will be in them too. I don't like Ingrid. I don't mind saying that. I don't understand why Tiina was so bothered. But she always wanted to do the right thing.'

She bit her lip as if a worry had occurred to her. Something she maybe shouldn't say . . .

'What is it, Kaia?' Lola asked sharply.

'An idea, that's all. And probably mean of me.'

'Tell us anyway,' Lola said.

'Tiina's death,' Kaia said. 'I wouldn't be too surprised if, well . . .'

'What?'

'If it turned out it was all because of Ingrid. That it was her fault.'

* * *

10.34 p.m.

Coming off the call, Lola stretched to revive herself then told Anna about ACC Thompson's call.

'It worries me,' she said, and suppressed a yawn. 'The fact the ACC is even talking to Dixon — or rather that Dixon is talking to the ACC.'

'I saw Dixon earlier,' Anna said. 'I called by after I'd been at Garscube Road.'

'And?'

Anna took a moment before speaking. 'I think he's keeping his wife sedated,' she said at last. 'Marta was so sleepy. There was a friend with her, a Sarah Finnie, glaring daggers at me the whole time. I wasn't trying to interrogate Marta, just asking how she was doing. Then I asked if she'd taken anything and Finnie jumped in saying, "What sort of question is that?" Then Dixon interrupted and said his wife was tired because she wasn't sleeping. How could she when their child was out there somewhere? I don't like him, boss. I don't trust him. I know we've got all that CCTV footage confirming his story, but . . .' She sighed, seeming to struggle to put her thoughts into words. 'I wonder if it's half true. That Adam was taken because of something Dixon refused to do — or perhaps because of something he had done that they didn't like. Something corrupt or criminal. Something he can't admit to, and that's why he's so shifty and defensive — frightened too. Because he *is* afraid of something.'

'You might just be on to something . . .' Lola murmured.

125

'I think he knows or strongly suspects where his son is. What if he's trying to get him back and he's terrified we'll either scupper his own plan to get the boy back — or that we'll find out what he's been up to?'

'Ingrid Valk was doing something illegal,' Lola murmured, 'according to what Tiina told Kaia.'

Anna eyed Lola closely. 'Boss,' she said drily, 'Marta Dixon isn't Ingrid Valk.'

Lola said nothing.

'She *isn't*,' Anna pressed. 'I know they look similar, but it's not her.'

'But the similarity is significant,' Lola said, unwilling to surrender the hunch. 'It *cannot* be a coincidence, and yet I can't imagine what it means. Why did Ingrid's sister take Marta's child? Kaia called Tiina "a good person" and yet she stole a baby.'

They sat in weary silence.

'How are we supposed to find Adam with so few leads?' Lola asked now. 'I don't suppose we've had any more calls?'

'Kirstie's monitoring everything closely. Nothing, boss.'

'We have to find that van . . . It's our only hope, unless we can get to the bottom of what the Dixons know. Anything else before we say goodnight?' She stretched again, groaning this time. Her brain swam with tiredness.

'I've got a list from the National Crime Agency of all unidentified people found dead in the UK covering the last six months, updated at the start of last week. I glanced through it but nothing jumped out. I'll look properly in the morning. Did you know about 150 unidentified dead people are found each year in the UK? Shocking, isn't it? Imagine being one of those people, condemned to anonymity for all eternity.'

'I think we need to go back further than six months,' Lola said, 'and check for any unidentified young women of East Asian origin too.'

She went into her bag and pulled out a cardboard wallet.

'Courtesy of Clyde University,' she said, pulling out papers. 'One is a Chinese student named Chan Wen, who is still unaccounted for; the other is a South Korean student named Yunhee Kim who went missing but then turned up, claiming she'd had a sort of breakdown. She could be studying at another institution. The Home Office should be able to tell us.'

Anna accepted the papers and had begun to leaf through them when her phone buzzed.

She peered at the screen.

'Photos from Kaia Tamm,' she said. 'Looks like she's found one of Tiina and Ingrid together. Here.'

Lola took the phone and examined the photograph of the two sisters, sitting at a table in a bar or restaurant. Tiina, on the left, was dark, sitting back, smiling a little; Ingrid sat forward, a confident blonde, beaming for the camera, looking entirely conscious of her good looks. One of them was dead, they knew for sure. Was the other too?

'I need to sleep,' Lola said. 'You know, Anna, I'm convinced it's all to do with the university. I've felt so ever since I saw that poster of Dixon, grinning away in the reception.'

She shook her head and reached for the door.

'Night, boss.'

'Night, Anna.'

CHAPTER FOURTEEN

Friday 31 October
9.15 a.m.

Lola had emailed Prue Carstairs first thing, asking her to provide a list of Ingrid Valk's lecturers so they could be contacted. Carstairs had replied curtly to say she would see to it.

A short video had appeared on the university's social media channels and website, in which Prue Carstairs, garbed in black rather than pink, expressed her personal condolences to Wendy Baker's family and friends. Lola watched it sitting in her parked car while she waited for Kirstie to arrive. In it, the principal oozed dismay at the sad news, describing Wendy as 'a respected colleague and dearer friend', making Lola dislike Carstairs all the more.

There were TV cameras and reporters outside the campus and a harassed-looking DI Charlie Noble was busy answering questions. Lola lingered nearby.

Her interview over, Charlie approached Lola.

'A lot of interest,' Lola commented, eyes on the huddle of reporters. 'Hopefully it'll help.'

'Already had a good response to the appeal for information,' Charlie told her. 'Only released the news at seven this morning and we'd had over fifty calls last time I checked. Two callers reckon they saw Wendy on Garscube Road, tying in with the café owner's story. What I'm hoping for is dashcam footage. Something that shows her going in somewhere. We're carrying on with door knocking. Keep everything crossed for us, eh?'

'Will do.'

'So, what d'you reckon?' Charlie said, voice confidential now. 'Do we make it public there could be a link between your case and mine?'

'Not yet,' Lola said, eyes on the reporters, a couple of whom were watching them beadily. 'Not until we know for sure.'

'You're probably right. But there must be a link, don't you think?'

'I do,' Lola said. 'We'll be holding a press conference at four today. Feel free to come along. I'm going to name our victim and give an update on what actions we've taken to find the baby. I won't go any further than that, so I'll be interested to see if anyone asks about a connection.'

'I'll be there,' Charlie said, 'but I'll keep a low profile. Creep in at the back once you're underway.'

Lola caught Kirstie's eye and signalled it was time to go in.

Marisa Singleton collected them and took them up to a meeting room on the third floor. Danny McDougall was there with a small pile of printed paper, which he pushed across to Lola once she was sitting.

'These are the names and phone numbers of the three students' personal tutors,' he said. 'Ms Carstairs said you wanted them. I haven't warned them you'll be ringing. I've also got the names and phone numbers — where we've got them — for Ingrid Valk's former housemates and also a woman who shared a flat with Chan Wen. I don't have anything for Yunhee Kim on the system. Sorry.'

Lola looked at the details for Ingrid's housemates. There was a note of the address where they'd lived during the last academic year. The two young women had since moved to another place, in Partick. Something occurred to her. She looked up sharply at Marisa.

'Yesterday you said each of the three women had moved out of their regular accommodation, taking most but not all of their things?'

'Yes,' Marisa said. 'That's right, isn't it, Danny?'

'Think so,' he said.

'What happened to their things that were left behind?'

Marisa stared, wrong-footed. Danny frowned.

'It was our Student Services people who went round to the flats,' Marisa said. 'They reported back to us, but . . . Erm, give me two minutes.'

She stepped out of the little room.

'I just spoke to a colleague in Student Services,' she said when she came back. 'Apparently there's a locker where they keep items students have left in their accommodation. They only keep things for a year, for obvious reasons. She says anything Ingrid left behind should still be there.'

'Where is it?' Lola asked.

'In the Student Services department. I'll take you round.'

Lola and Kirstie filed after her, Danny coming too. The Student Services department was on the same floor, but round a corner. Marisa spoke to her colleague, who handed over a key then led the way to a floor-to-ceiling locker with a sliding tambour door. Marisa bent to unlock it and rolled the door up.

There were shelves inside, and cardboard archive boxes lined up, each labelled neatly.

'And here it is,' Marisa said, and made to reach for it.

'Let us get that,' Lola said, and nodded to Kirstie, who was already snapping on forensic gloves.

Marisa stepped aside, a little flustered.

Kirstie reached for the box and Lola indicated a desk she could put it on.

'Would you give us some space?' Lola asked Marisa and Danny.

'Of course,' Marisa said, pulling her colleague away gently by the elbow.

At Lola's nod, Kirstie lifted the lid of the box.

Inside was a labelled plastic bag, tied at the top. Kirstie lifted it out, unknotted it, then peeled down the sides. Inside were some clothes, a few books, a stuffed toy that resembled a pixie, and a handful of papers, including fliers.

Lola pulled on some gloves too and between them they picked through the items. The books were textbooks relating to Ingrid's course, one on understanding economic theory, another on banking law. Lola flicked through them, looking for anything that might have been noted inside them, or for items that might have been secreted between the pages. Then she turned her attention to the papers.

There was a European driving licence, a print-out of credits Ingrid had achieved in her first year at the university, a leaflet for a medical centre and a booklet about vitamins and minerals and how to get enough from your diet. There was also a bright-green leaflet for an organisation called Dear Green Place. Lola had a sudden memory of seeing the same shade of green somewhere very recently. For a moment she couldn't place it, but then remembered: there'd been a tote bag in that shade of green in the hallway of Wendy Baker's flat. She recalled the font of the writing on it and looked at the logo on the leaflet in her hand. Yes, surely the same organisation.

Welcome to Glasgow, one of the world's great cultural cities! the cover read. There was a cartoonish image on the front of smiling people of different skin colours and wearing different cultural garbs. Lola opened it and read the text on the first page. *Dear Green Place is your one-stop shop for making the most of your time here.* An image of a very friendly lady in a green suit beamed out: one of those people with shining eyes and perfect smiles who were always on this kind of material.

131

And then she spotted handwriting on the leaflet. A phone number had been circled and a date and time noted:

Jen, 18.30, 10 Dec.

'Is the university connected to this organisation?' Lola asked, holding it up.

'They're one of our key partners,' Marisa said. 'They coordinate induction week activities for our international students, taking them to their accommodation and settling them in, helping them register with medical centres, that kind of thing. The international students all come a week earlier than the other students to give them time to adjust. Employees from Dear Green Place take them on the bus tour of the city and out to Loch Lomond for an afternoon. They even take them on a bit of a pub crawl, though nobody has to drink. It's just a bit of fun.'

'Does someone called Jen work there?' Lola asked.

'Yes,' Marisa said. 'Paolo is the manager and Jen works with him, but I think she's part-time.'

'Where are they?' Lola asked.

'Queen's Crescent,' she said. 'Not far from here.'

'I'd like to talk to them,' Lola said.

'Danny can give you Paolo's mobile number, can't you, Danny?'

Danny nodded. 'Give me a minute,' he said and hurried away.

'Paolo and Jen are wonderful,' Marisa said. 'So student-centred.'

Lola returned the leaflet to the pile.

Kirstie was finishing going through the pockets of the clothes.

'Nothing, boss,' she murmured.

'Put it all back in the bag,' Lola said. She stripped off the gloves.

'We'll take it away,' she said to Marisa. 'We'll make sure it finds its way back to Ingrid's family in Estonia.'

'Oh, have you located them?'

'Yes, we spoke to her father and aunt last night. We told them about Tiina.'

Marisa put a hand to her mouth. 'Oh, how sad. I do hope Ingrid is safe and well somewhere. Oh—'

Prue Carstairs had appeared at the edge in the open-plan area. She was draped in the same black garb she'd worn in her mournful video and appeared all the more formidable for it.

'A word, please,' she called to Lola, who went over. 'The chair of my board wishes to speak to you face to face.' She bunched her lips and narrowed her eyes. 'He'll be here at eleven, in my office.'

'That might be possible,' Lola said, hackles up. 'Obviously the demands of a live case come first.'

'I expect they do.'

Lola's phone started to ring. She saw it was Anna.

'Excuse me,' she said, and moved away so she could answer.

'Lawrie Dixon says he's heard from the people holding his son,' Anna said. 'I'm going to the flat in Garnethill right now. Meet me there?'

'Yes, fine,' Lola said, grimly pleased to have a reason to snub Prue Carstairs and her chair. 'I'll be ten minutes.'

She went back to Carstairs. 'Sorry, but I've been called away,' she said. 'Ask your chair to wait for me, would you? Or get me a phone number and I'll call him when I have a minute. Needs must, I'm afraid.'

Prue Carstairs scowled, breathed hard so that her nostrils flared, then turned and stumped away.

Danny reappeared. 'Paolo DeSalvo's number,' he said, and handed her a Post-it note.

'Thank you.'

On their way out of the building, Lola asked Kirstie to call the personal tutors of each of the three students.

'Ask each of them how they found the student, what behavioural changes they noticed before they went missing, what classmates might have said, whether any had particular friends — and if so, what their names were. I'll hang on to the housemates' details and give them to Anna. She can organise to talk to them. Right—' she reached for her car keys — 'next stop for me: Garnethill.'

* * *

10.17 a.m.

'It came by email,' Lawrie Dixon told Lola and Anna.

They were in the kitchen of the flat, Dixon and his solicitor sitting across the table from them. Marta was in the living room with her friend Sarah Finnie.

'I can show you the text,' Dixon went on. 'I copied and pasted it into my notes app. I don't want to show you the original email so please don't ask me to.'

She held her tongue — for now — and took his phone from him. She held it so Anna could see too.

> *Mr Dixon,*
>
> *Your boy is currently safe and well. Our priorities have changed. We no longer require the program code but our work to date has incurred costs. Transfer £250,000 in bitcoin to the following account by midnight tonight and you will have your boy back by lunchtime tomorrow.*
>
> *Do not show this to the authorities. Just do as we ask.*

It wasn't signed.

'I didn't copy and paste the bitcoin address or the address of the email it came from, for obvious reasons,' Dixon said.

'Because you don't trust us?' Lola asked.

'Yes.'

Lola looked at the solicitor. Jeremy Wilder quickly averted his gaze, perhaps embarrassed by his client's behaviour.

She took out her phone and snapped a photo of Dixon's screen.

'If you don't trust us, why bring us here?' she asked, dropping her phone back in her jacket pocket. 'Why even bother to show us this? You provide evidence but block our ability to do anything about it? I don't understand.'

Dixon sat up and took a huffing breath. 'Because I want you to back off,' he said, his words clipped, as if he was only just containing his anger. 'You've done nothing to help us, only endangered our boy, but I'm going to get him back. I'm going to give them what they want, and I'm asking you to keep away.'

'Sir, your son was kidnapped,' Lola said, just about keeping a lid on her frustration. 'You were threatened by foreign agents. Your wife and son's lives were threatened too — or so you've told us.'

He glared. 'You still don't believe me, do you?'

She searched for a way to answer but struggled. Just then she caught sight of something in the shadows of her brain. A glint of something she couldn't quite make out . . .

'We can't step away, Mr Dixon,' she said simply. 'We just can't.'

'*Why?*'

'Because a woman is dead.'

'A child kidnapper! Who cares?'

'*I* care. I want to understand why she did it, and who killed her. Your son's disappearance is intimately linked to her death.' She thought about mentioning Wendy Baker, but decided to keep quiet about that for now. 'The people who did this are out there and they're dangerous.'

They watched each other over the table. In the silence Lola could hear Marta sobbing in the living room. Occasionally the sobs formed words Lola couldn't make out.

'What exactly are you saying?' the solicitor enquired.

'That if Mr Dixon tries to hinder our inquiry then he will be breaking the law,' Lola told him quietly. 'We could arrest him and seize his devices and gain access to all his accounts.'

The solicitor drew an alarmed breath and looked at his client. Lola looked too. Dixon's expression was stony but his eyes gave away his fear.

'Get out,' Dixon spat. 'Get out of here before I throw you out.'

'Lawrie—' the solicitor began.

Dixon stood up, and his chair screeched backwards. Lola turned to Anna, nodded and rose.

In the hallway, she paused, eyes on the closed door to the front room. She reached for the handle and went in.

Marta Dixon sat hunched on the edge of a leather sofa. She turned her face away. Sarah Finnie had been standing by the window and strode across to Lola.

'She's in no fit state to talk to anyone,' she warned.

'Is that right?' Lola asked. 'How are you doing, Marta?'

Marta lifted her face but didn't meet Lola's eye. Her face was blotchy and wet with crying and she looked ill.

Lola crouched so their faces were level.

'Have you seen a doctor yet?' she asked.

She shook her head and glanced up at Sarah.

'She doesn't want to,' Sarah said. 'It's her choice.'

'I'd feel happier if a doctor examined you,' Lola said gently.

'I'm okay,' Marta said. 'Gen— Genuinely, I'm fine.' She glanced at Sarah.

'If you say so.'

Marta's face was flushed now. She hunched her shoulders and looked horribly uncomfortable.

'I think you should go,' Sarah said, the chill in her tone intensified.

There was a commotion out in the hallway and Dixon appeared in the doorway. 'I told you to leave!'

'Can't you see how frightened she is?' Sarah Finnie demanded.

'I can,' Lola said quietly, eyes on the trembling woman on the sofa.

Frightened of what, she wondered.

10.50 a.m.

'He wrote the note,' she said to Anna. They sat in Anna's parked car to share thoughts before going their separate ways. 'I'm sure of it. That he won't show us the supposed email is one thing, but the language is what gives him away.'

'Why would he do that?' Anna asked.

'I don't know, but it's part of a bigger scheme to stop us finding out what's really going on.'

She seethed as she thought about Lawrie Dixon's manner, the way evasiveness alternated with aggression, fear alternated with cunning. She thought of the frightened sobbing woman in the front room of the flat and felt her blood pressure rise. Why would any father risk his son's life like this? Why would the child's mother let him?

'I'm going to smoke him out,' she said coolly. 'I need to think how to do it — and I'll need the super onside, of course. Anything for me before I head back to the university?'

'An update on the list of unidentified dead people,' Anna said.

'Oh?'

'I got more information from the NCA, going back over the past eighteen months. There are three unidentified females on the list who are thought to be of East Asian origin, including what appears to be one accidental death and two likely suicides. The timing could fit for Chan Wen being one of the two suicides. Marcus has gone back to the NCA to look a bit deeper.'

'Good. Another job for you, I'm afraid.' She opened her bag. 'I got names and contacts for each of the three students' housemates. Can you get someone to root them out and arrange interviews? Start with Ingrid, then Chan Wen. Leave the South Korean student for now — we know she's probably okay, though we will need to find her and talk to her. We need to know the circumstances in which the students disappeared, any suspicious behaviour they exhibited, and what the house-mates themselves suspect happened.'

'Leave it with me,' Anna said. 'By the way, I've put the information you gave me last night about the three students into a table. It helps me remember who's who along with timings. Want me to email a copy?'

'Please,' Lola said.

They said their goodbyes.

Back in her own car, Lola listened to a voice message from Paolo DeSalvo, director of Dear Green Place, saying he'd be more than happy to talk to Lola, though he couldn't promise he'd be much use.

'You could come to the hub,' he said. 'Tell me a time and I'll be there.'

She looked at the clock and texted a reply. *Can we say 12.30?*

He came back immediately. *Perfect. The hub is in Queen's Crescent at St George's Cross.* He gave the address and added: *Ring this number if you don't get a reply from the buzzer.*

Next she called Deborah Truebig from Corporate Comms to check plans for the press conference at four. Deborah expected a full house and suggested Lola be there by three thirty so they could talk through her script.

'That's fine,' she said.

She looked at the time. The chair of the university's board had wanted to see her at eleven, according to Prue Carstairs. Well, she'd be late and that was tough.

She called Superintendent Elaine Walsh's mobile, but it rang out, no doubt on silent while she was in a meeting. She emailed her instead:

Can we have fifteen minutes ahead of the press conference? I need your view on tactics.

Then she put the car in gear and drove back to Garscube Road and the campus of Clyde University.

11.20 a.m.

Lola parked and took a minute or two to look over the table Anna had prepared based on the information they'd received.

Name & Nationality: Yunhee Kim, South Korean

Studying: Communications (2nd year)

Disappeared: August 2024 (uncertain)

Notes: Had moved out of shared flat in April but moved back in May. Late registering for 3rd year, then dropped out, believed to be studying elsewhere. Checking with Home Office. Emergency contact changed to a Scottish man's name (no answer); later changed back by student to give her mother's details.

Name & Nationality: Chan Wen, Chinese

Studying: Accounting (2nd year)

Disappeared: Completed 2nd year inc. all assessments in May 2024 but failed to register for third year in September

Notes: N/A

Name & Nationality: Ingrid Valk, Estonian

Studying: Business finance (2nd year)

Disappeared: May 2025, after completing 1/3 assessments. Failed to register for 3rd year in September. Housemates said she moved in with a boyfriend (name unknown). Reported to Home Office.

Notes: Emergency contact changed to 'Ewan Cathrie' by student, number not answered.

The table provided a helpful reminder of the key facts, and Lola noted the critical period around the three students' assessments in the late spring, and their failure to re-register for their courses in September — or in the case of the Korean student, a two-week delay in registration.

Still ruminating on the data, she got out of the car and walked the short distance to the campus building.

* * *

11.27 a.m.

Prue Carstairs was a different woman. She simpered and fussed over Lola as she introduced her to 'our wonderful chair, Gerald Linklater, MBE'.

Linklater was a striking, almost theatrical figure. In his seventies, he was immensely tall and thin, with a hawk's beak nose and lots of flowing white hair that seemed purposefully coiffured to double the size of his head. He had on a beautifully tailored grey suit, complete with pink pocket handkerchief. He rose lithely from Carstairs' desk and took Lola's hand in his own papery dry one. He gripped it a little too tightly and his steely blue eyes bore so piercingly into hers that she felt as if he was trying to see inside her mind. Then he smiled. Rather, his lips stretched back to bear crooked little teeth.

'Do have a seat,' he purred.

'Shall I pour?' Prue Carstairs said, and began dithering over a tray bearing a teapot and cups.

'Black for me, please,' Lola said.

Carstairs lifted the teapot. 'Gerald has been our chair for three years now,' she twittered. 'Such leadership. Such rich business experience too. We're very blessed.'

The rictus smile stretched Linklater's thin lips once more.

'What kind of business?' Lola asked.

'IT,' he said.

'Gerald's microchips control many of the satellites currently in orbit,' Prue Carstairs said, more like a proud wife or mother than university principal.

'Really?'

'He chairs and sits on numerous boards and committees too.'

Linklater nodded. Carstairs passed Lola her cup, then sat in a chair at the side of the desk, fanning herself as though she was in the throes of some erotic flush.

'Such as?' Lola asked, recognising she was being prompted, but curious enough not to resist the temptation.

'I advise the leadership of your *own* organisation,' he said, and his smile tightened some more.

'How interesting,' she said breezily. 'In what area?'

'Technology and its applications.'

'Including cyber security?'

There was the tiniest hesitation. 'Not specifically.'

Prue Carstairs gave him an odd, curious look.

'Have you worked in cyber security, though?' Lola asked him.

He looked briefly annoyed before regaining his composure. 'Security is an integral part of all digital technological development,' he said tightly. 'At least it should be. Now, you must be very busy, so shall we turn to business?'

'As you wish,' Lola said.

'What I "wish" is to make an appeal to your discretion,' he said.

'Oh?'

He inclined his head again. 'We deeply regret the loss of our colleague, Miss, err . . .' He looked to Carstairs.

'Ms Baker,' the principal said quickly.

'Yes,' he went on smoothly. 'It seems to me her death must be the result of an accident or mistaken identity — or perhaps the work of a deranged person, a derelict. It cannot be connected in any way to this institution.' He paused and those steely blue eyes peered closely at her before the grin reappeared. 'Is that understood?'

Lola took a breath. She'd dealt with so many men like this in her career, who tried to intimidate her from under a thin veneer of politeness.

'Unfortunately, I believe Wendy Baker's death is connected to her work here,' she said. 'My colleagues and I are accruing evidence to that effect. I believe the death of a young woman called Tiina Valk is connected to this place too.'

His face gave nothing away. He appraised her through narrow slits.

'Nonsense,' Prue Carstairs came in. She gave a high, nervous laugh. 'Sheer nonsense.'

'Indeed,' Linklater muttered. '*Dangerous* too.'

There was a subtle, sinister emphasis on the word.

'Dangerous to whom, Mr Linklater?' Lola asked.

He blinked, a slow lizard blink.

'To the reputation of the university,' he said. 'To the well-being of our students. To the reputation of our great city as a destination for learning.'

'I'm not interested in reputations,' Lola said. 'I'm interested in people's safety and their right not to be murdered in the street.'

'We know you are asking questions of a number of people,' he went on. 'Seeking access to data that really does not concern you. I know Prue here has been helpful to date, but

I am asking you to respect the integrity of our systems and processes.'

'I'm sorry. What does that mean?'

'We take care of our students, especially our international ones. We make them *most* welcome here, we nourish them through education and the very best pastoral support, we celebrate their achievements and—'

'Allow some of them to go missing and not report it?' Lola enquired airily. 'Prevent concerned staff members from calling the police? Even admonish and threaten those who seek advice from the authorities because they're so concerned for the students' welfare?'

He sat back, eyes narrowed and lips pursed, and considered her with unmistakeable disgust.

'I am going to continue investigating,' she said, 'whether you like it or not. It's my duty to find out what happened to the three students who disappeared from here under strikingly similar circumstances. If there is evidence to connect their disappearances to the deaths of Tiina Valk and Wendy Baker, and to the disappearance of a two-month-old baby, then I will make that connection known. If I find that this institution, including its board and management, have connived at criminality, then I will make that known too — *as publicly as I can.*'

She got up. Linklater looked like thunder. Beside him, Carstairs looked quite stricken. Frightened, in fact.

'You'll excuse me,' Lola said. 'I have a job to do.'

She was at the door when she made a decision. She wheeled round, making the pair of them start.

'You'll know Lawrence Dixon,' she said to Linklater, and smiled as she waited for him to react.

He blinked. Beside him, Carstairs frowned.

'Who?' he asked, but in a voice high with strain.

'*Lawrence Dixon,*' she said, slowly and clearly. 'He's giving a lecture about careers in cyber security for students here. There's a poster in reception.'

'Is there?' He shrugged then said lightly, 'I don't know him from Adam.'

'Really? Funny you should say that. Adam is the name of Mr Dixon's son.'

She watched as he bridled, then turned and left the room.

In reception a few minutes later she tried to find the poster for Dixon's lecture again, but it was gone. In its place was a bright-green poster for Dear Green Place, advertising a get-together event for international students. *Come and make new friends!* it exhorted in a cheerful font.

***

12.09 p.m.

Queen's Crescent housed a mix of residential properties and third-sector organisations. Lola found number twenty-one sandwiched between a private health clinic and a women's charity. Paolo DeSalvo met her at the main door, all smiles; a skinny, dark, thirty-something Italian with a neat little beard.

He led the way into the bright front room of the house, which was filled with colourful armchairs, low tables and shelves of books and fliers. There was a bookshelf marked *Scottish literature* and stands holding leaflets and fold-out maps. Posters on the walls advertised social evenings and English lessons. The room still had its original elaborate cornicing and perhaps its original huge, wood-framed sash windows, judging by the draught.

'Please, have a seat,' he said. 'Danny didn't tell me very much, but I'm happy to tell you what I can. Now, can I get you a coffee, perhaps? We have an espresso maker — none of your instant rubbish here.' He beamed.

'No, and I don't have a lot of time,' she said, 'but thanks.'

'Okay!' He wasn't in the least put out and cheerfully picked one of the armchairs opposite her. 'It's about a student, someone's sister — that's right, isn't it?'

144

'Yes,' Lola said. 'But first, tell me what you do here.'

'Of course! We're a charity, endowed by a trust and in receipt of donations where people wish to give them. We are here to provide specialist services to international students arriving in Glasgow. These services include practical help with accommodation, registering with a doctor and travelling about. We offer some welfare and funding advice and help them to make friends. Oh, and we offer some help with study skills — essay-writing, that sort of thing. We work with a number of universities and colleges in the city, though not all.'

'How many students do you work with?'

He thought for a moment, eyes on the ceiling. 'More than two thousand last year, and that number is only growing.'

'Including students at Clyde University?'

'Yes. They're only a small institution, but they still bring — I don't know, maybe 170 to 180 international students a year. We welcome them, take them to their accommodation, talk to each one individually and invite them to join us in a number of activities.'

'We?'

'We have part-time staff, often former students themselves, so they have a range of languages between them. My colleague Jen organises all the social side, including bus tours of the city.'

'And you've been providing this service for a number of years?'

'Seven,' he said. 'Myself, I've been here four years.'

'And Jen — what's her surname, by the way?'

'Crossley. I'm the only full-time employee,' he said now. 'Jen's post is funded differently. Now — if you'd perhaps tell me how I can help you . . .'

'Of course. The student we want to ask about is Ingrid Valk, studying business finance. She should be in her third year now, but she apparently left the course in the summer.'

'Valk . . .' He frowned and leaned forward.

'Ingrid Valk,' Lola said slowly.

He shook his head. 'I'm usually good with names. Bear with me, please.' He rose from his seat, went to a shelf in a corner of the room and came back with a tablet. Installed in his chair he tapped away for a few seconds. 'Ingrid Valk, Estonian,' he said, reading his screen. He turned it and held it out for Lola to see. 'Is this her?'

'That's her,' Lola said. It was a colour version of the grainy image the university had provided.

DeSalvo was scrolling now. 'Yes, studying business finance,' he said. 'Lived at Firhill Mount in her first year.'

'Firhill Mount — what's that?'

'A student accommodation complex by the canal,' he said. 'Exclusive to Clyde University's international students. Some even stay into their second year. This says Ingrid moved into private rented accommodation in the West End in her second year.' He peered over the screen at her now. 'You said she left the course. Are you worried about her?'

'Yes, Mr DeSalvo—'

'Paolo, please.'

'We are worried, Paolo. Nobody knows where she is, including her family. We're looking for all the help we can get. Now, I have reason to believe she may have had an appointment with your colleague Jen on the tenth of December — presumably last year.'

'Oh?' He frowned.

'Might you have records of appointments?'

'Possibly,' he said and scrolled at his screen again, then tapped a couple of times.

'Hmm. There's nothing recorded on the system about any appointment, I'm afraid. It shows that she attended a welcome event at the city chambers — that's where city councillors welcome the students. She also went on a bus tour and a trip out to Loch Lomond in her first week. All of that was organised by Jen, though. I look after the hub, finances and welfare services.'

'Has Ingrid used any of those services?' Lola asked.

He scrolled on his tablet. 'Not according to this. I'm so sorry.'

'It's okay. You mentioned the charity is funded through a trust.'

'That's right. The Lara Shulman Trust. Set up by Mary Shulman and her late husband in memory of their daughter, an American from New England, who came to study in Glasgow and who . . . tragically died.'

'That's very sad,' Lola said.

'Isn't it? It happened twenty years ago. Lara Shulman was homesick and very lonely and . . . well, she ended her own life. Her parents didn't want that to happen to any other young person coming to the city.'

'I see. Could you give me Jen Crossley's number, please?'

'Of course. I told Jen I was speaking to you, so it won't be a surprise to her.' He smiled sadly. 'I'm just sorry I couldn't be of more help.'

* * *

12.43 p.m.

'It's Jen speaking,' a voice answered. There was a lot of background noise — tannoys and people talking indistinctly.

Lola was back in her car, parked on Garscube Road. She introduced herself. 'I was wondering if I could come and see you.'

'What's it about?'

'An international student who has gone missing from Clyde University, Ms Crossley.'

'A student?' Her voice was hard to make out against the noise. Lola shut her eyes to concentrate. 'When did this happen?'

'At the end of the last academic year, so it seems,' Lola said. 'You might have come across her. Where are you now?'

'Ah . . . Edinburgh, I'm afraid. Obviously I'm happy to talk, but I'm about to get a train to Fife for a meeting. Can we talk now?'

There was something familiar about the way Jen spoke: a confident, unflustered, middle-classness that could easily tip from assertive to off-hand. The tone might, though, be the result of having to talk loudly over background noise.

'I have five minutes — if it'd help?' she prompted now.

'Thank you, Ms Crossley. The student's name is Ingrid Valk.'

'Ingrid Valk . . . I don't recognise the name. Couldn't Paolo help?'

'No, I'm afraid not. We've found a leaflet for Dear Green Place among Ingrid Valk's possessions,' she said. 'She — or someone else — had made a note on it. It appears to be for an appointment with Jen, at 6.30 p.m. on the tenth of December.'

'Oh, but that's almost a year ago.'

'Might there be something in your diary?'

'Could be. I'll check when I'm on the train. I'll text you if I find anything.'

'Text me either way, would you?'

'Of course.'

148

CHAPTER FIFTEEN

1.33 p.m.

But Jen Crossley couldn't help. She apologised by text, saying she had no record of a meeting with Ingrid Valk or anyone else for that time or date. She said she'd be in touch if anything else occurred to her.

Back at Helen Street, Superintendent Elaine Walsh was tied up in a meeting somewhere in the building. Anna was at her desk, as were Marcus and Jonno, so Lola suggested a catch-up then led the hunt for a meeting room. Kirstie appeared in the corridor and Lola called for her to join them too.

'I'm convinced Lawrie Dixon is lying,' she told the team when they were seated. 'This ransom note he says he's received. It talks about Dixon "getting his boy back". That's what Dixon calls Adam. "My boy." He's written the thing himself, I know he has. It's the reason he won't show us the original message or let us go anywhere near his devices. I've had enough of it.'

'What are you proposing?' Anna asked.

'I want to drag him out into the light,' she said. 'I want to inform Dixon we consider him and his wife suspects in their

149

son's disappearance — and that we plan to say as much at this afternoon's press conference.' Anna's eyes were wide. 'Don't worry, I don't actually plan to do anything of the kind. But I think Dixon might panic and tell us what's really going on. I'm going to clear it with the super when she's free.'

Anna nodded and smiled.

'Right. Where are we up to, Anna?'

Anna flicked back a few pages in her notebook.

'DS Pierce has found brief CCTV footage showing a woman who could well be Tiina Valk — though her face isn't clear — turning a corner a few metres away from the coffee shop where a witness reported seeing her. She's in the company of a young man and his face is much clearer. The officer who spoke to the lad at Darnley says he's ninety-nine per cent sure it's the same person.'

'Can I see?' Lola asked.

Anna turned to Marcus.

'I've got it here,' Marcus said and turned his laptop so Lola could see.

'That is a good image,' Lola said, studying the sandy-haired figure, who'd looked up and almost directly at the camera as he rounded a corner in the company of a dark-haired woman who walked with her head down.

'Yes, get it out there,' she said. 'Ask him to come forward or for anyone who recognises him to call. What else?'

Anna turned a page. 'We've got the name of a friend Tiina was living with in Sydney, plus a phone number. She might know what Tiina was up to or be able to put us on to other friends of Tiina's, or her employer. I've left a message and I'll try again later if I don't hear back. As for Ingrid, the body of a female of her height and build was found at a recycling centre in Lancaster on the tenth of August. Face badly disfigured and the body partially burnt. Authorities in the north of England have tried to identify her but there's been no match on any database of missing persons. They're still holding the remains.'

'The tenth of August?' Lola asked, thinking fast. 'Ingrid was last seen in May. Ask for a DNA test and have it checked against Tiina's Valk's.'

'Already requested, boss.'

'Good. What about the South-East Asian woman who committed suicide in London — the one who could be Chan Wen?'

Anna looked to Marcus to answer.

'The timing does seem to fit,' he said. 'The police are still holding her remains and we've asked for the PM report.'

Lola turned a few pages in her pad and found her notes about the Chinese student. 'Chan Wen had a grandmother,' she said. 'One of the university staff spoke to her when they couldn't locate Wen, but she was confused and couldn't help. We could ask Interpol to contact the police in her home city and request a DNA test from a family member.'

'It might take some time,' Anna said.

'There might be a quicker way to make an initial identification,' Kirstie said. 'I've been speaking to the students' personal tutors. Chan Wen's said she was very shy and self-conscious. She had a birthmark on her neck that seemed to bother her. She wore scarves to cover it up.'

Lola looked to Marcus. 'See if there's a note about the suicide having a birthmark, would you?'

Marcus went into his laptop. 'It's here,' he said. 'This is from the brief description they've circulated. *Deceased had a palm-sized port-wine birthmark on the left side of her neck.*'

Lola felt a prickle of excitement.

'As soon as we get the PM report, let's show photos of her face to the tutor — to her flatmate too. Good work, everyone. Okay, Anna, what else?'

'I've heard back from the Home Office about the South Korean student who vanished and reappeared,' Anna said. She checked her pad again. 'Yunhee Kim is indeed studying again, at one of the other universities here in Glasgow. I've contacted their Student Services department to get an address as a matter of urgency.'

'Excellent, Anna,' Lola said. 'And any news about the van?'

'We've made some headway with CCTV, boss,' Marcus said. 'It heads into Paisley and turns off for Crookston. Goes past the castle, but then there's a dead zone without any cameras. We know it didn't pass the shopping centre at Silverburn, so it likely took a left into Cardonald. We're seeking footage from out that way.'

'I think we need to go public about the van,' Lola said, thinking aloud. 'I'm not sure it'll do any good but that baby is still missing. We need to be able to say we did everything we could — despite Dixon hindering us every step of the way. Marcus, can you pull some good stills of the van from the film?'

'Sure can,' Marcus said.

Lola turned back to her list of ongoing leads.

'Back to our missing students,' she said. 'Ingrid's housemates.'

'I've contacted one of them and she's getting hold of the other,' Anna said. 'I'm hoping to see the two of them later today.'

'I want to be there,' Lola said. 'What about Chan Wen's housemate?'

'Still trying to get hold of her.'

'Keep trying. Kirstie, did you speak to Ingrid's and Yunhee's personal tutors too?'

'Yes, boss.' Kirstie consulted her notes. 'Ingrid's tutor wasn't very flattering about her. She said Ingrid was "wilful" and "not very mindful of rules and processes". She often handed work in late, sometimes not at all. "A strong personality." She told me which modules Ingrid took. I got the impression she wasn't particularly bothered when Ingrid dropped out. Yunhee Kim's personal tutor described her as a good student, "very clever, very ambitious." But she was from a poor background, he said. She'd managed to get to Scotland to study through sheer determination and grit. She had a couple of jobs on the go all the time she was studying at the university.'

'Are international students allowed to work on a study visa?' Lola asked.

'Up to twenty hours a week,' Kirstie said. 'Though I did get the impression her hours might have gone over that. The tutor said they'd had to have words about the impact of working on her ability to study. He said she was just desperate for cash. She even sent some of it back to her mum in Korea.'

Lola turned to Anna. 'Any updates from Charlie Noble on Wendy Baker's murder?'

'She says she's got another witness who claims she saw Wendy Baker in the hour before she was killed,' Anna said, 'at the top of Garscube Road. She was outside a betting shop, on the corner of a junction, and looked as if she was waiting for someone — a lift perhaps. Charlie's got her officers checking cameras for that spot.'

'Good.' She recalled Wendy's voice message on her phone, when she'd said that Ingrid had been '*the third*'. She'd added, '*I think I know who's behind it.*'

Was it that person she'd gone to meet at Garscube Road? The one she'd been waiting for on that corner?

She suddenly recalled Paolo DaSilva talking about the dedicated student accommodation by the canal. You'd reach that via Garscube Road. Was that significant?

'I'll catch up with Charlie Noble myself later,' Lola said. 'Now, are we any closer to identifying and finding Ewan Cathrie?' Lola asked the room. Both Ingrid Valk and Yunhee Kim had named Cathrie as their next of kin on their university records.

'No trace of anyone of that name in Scotland,' Marcus said. 'And the number's registered to a burner phone. No name associated.'

Lola's phone rang. It was Elaine.

'Lola, are you free to come my office just now?'

'I'll be with you in two minutes, boss.'

* * *

Lola went over her script again on the way to see Elaine. She was confident of the case she needed to make: a clear, point-by-point argument as to why she believed Lawrie Dixon was lying, and how she proposed they might smoke him out. She suspected Elaine would be less than enthusiastic and was ready to spell out the risks to the safety of the Dixons' baby if they didn't act.

She knocked.

'Come in,' Elaine's voice replied.

She went in to find Elaine wasn't alone. A man was getting to his feet. She recognised him at once.

'ACC Thompson,' she said, putting on a smile to mask her surprise.

'DCI Harris,' he said. 'We haven't met in person.' He put out a hand. Lola took it. 'Sit down, please,' he said. There was something chilly in his smile.

Lola sat, glancing at Elaine, whose eyes were stony, her lips pursed.

Lola steeled herself. She was in trouble, she knew it. Her thoughts raced as fast as her heart.

Elaine said, 'ACC Thompson has something to tell us.'

Lola nodded and squared her shoulders and gave the ACC her full attention. He was fifty-ish, broad-shouldered and solid-looking, with freckles and faded, close-cut red hair in a pronounced widow's peak.

'I spoke to Lawrie Dixon again earlier today,' he said. 'As you're aware, we know one another and he trusts me.'

'Sir?' She longed to glance at Elaine, to see how she'd reacted to that.

'He told me about your visit to the safe house this morning — and about the exchange you had.'

She said nothing and could feel her face setting.

'DCI Harris, Lawrie told me the truth.' He paused. 'And now I'm going to tell it to you.' He took a deep breath. 'The

154

story he told us, about being approached by Russian gangsters in Germany was — in his words — a pack of lies. He wasn't threatened to force him to hand over software for illicit use, and he wasn't visited by one of the gangsters' associates on Thursday evening at his office.'

'He was visited by someone,' Lola said. 'We have it on film — a man with a hood up arrived and left a few minutes later.'

'Lawrie has explained that too — *if* you would allow me to speak.'

She glanced at Elaine, who shot a warning look in return. Lola folded her hands in her lap.

'The ransom note he showed you the text of — that was false too.'

'I knew it, sir.'

He raised an eyebrow. 'Oh?'

'I've suspected he was lying since I first met him. But I had no other way to explain everything that's happened.'

'Lawrie explained everything and it makes perfect sense to me. A couple of months ago he gave what could be called "insider information" — though I have to say I'm not convinced it meets the criteria — to a business acquaintance, to do with a takeover of a cyber security firm by a multinational corporation. The associate invested heavily in the firm that was due to be taken over, only for the deal not to go ahead and for the firm to fold. The acquaintance lost a quarter of a million pounds — and he wants his money back, from Lawrie. Lawrie refused, so this individual went to extremes. He hired thugs to kidnap Lawrie's son and hold him until Lawrie paid up, which he means to do. Lawrie is sorry he lied to you, to us. He is mortified that his actions have led to this, and terrified he might be charged with insider trading — though I assured him that was unlikely, based on what he told me. He is extremely embarrassed, DCI Harris.'

Lola processed the information. It explained why Dixon was so frightened but why he'd been so unwilling to involve the police, and why he'd forbidden Marta from alerting them when she feared she was being followed. It explained the holes in his story and his half-baked attempts to explain them away.

'Who is this former business associate?' Lola asked.

'Lawrie won't name him. He's terrified for his son's safety. He thinks he can get him back — and he's asking us to take a step back . . . which I told him we would do.'

'But it's a crime, sir,' Lola said, unable to conceal her amazement. 'The child could be in serious danger.'

'Exactly, DCI Harris. Put yourself in his shoes.'

She looked at Elaine, whose eyes were firmly fixed on her desk.

She put a hand to her forehead as she thought hard. Yes, it answered a number of questions, but there were others it did not. Tiina Valk had been no hired thug. She'd come to Glasgow with one intention: to find her missing sister. She'd then, unaccountably, taken a child from its parents — from its mother, who very closely resembled her own sister.

'A woman is dead,' Lola said. 'Someone killed her. That person probably took Adam Dixon away with them. If they'd kill her, they could harm him. Sir, we have to get the child back. There's more to this, I'm sure of it.'

He was looking at her very warily now, almost suspiciously.

'It is my view, DCI Harris — and Superintendent Walsh here agrees with me — that Adam Dixon's safety would be compromised by our further involvement in efforts to retrieve him, or to link his disappearance publicly to that woman's death.'

Lola looked at Elaine again and waited for her to meet her gaze — to deny, even wordlessly, that she'd agreed to any of this. But Elaine didn't look up.

'We're holding a press conference at four, sir,' she said, hearing her voice tremble. 'The media and the public are waiting for answers.'

He narrowed his eyes. 'A bit of a circus, by the sounds of it.'

'Sir—'

156

'We are ceasing all investigation into Adam Dixon's kidnap,' Thompson told her. 'Organised Crime will take over the investigation into the woman's death. You, DCI Harris, are free to work on other cases.'

'Boss—' Lola began, eyes on Elaine.

He cut across her, almost shouting: 'You will draft a statement with Corporate Communications that I will approve. It will explain that we were mistaken to conclude the woman had a baby with her. That the CCTV footage was . . . *inconclusive.*'

'The registrar at Clyde University was murdered yesterday!' Lola half yelled. '*She* identified the dead woman at Darnley Glen. There's a connection, sir. Other students have gone missing over the past couple of years. This isn't the whole story. It can't be—'

'Central Subdivision CID are investigating that unfortunate woman's demise,' he said.

She reeled, tears of frustration welling.

'Thank you for your work on the case thus far, DCI Harris,' Thompson said in a voice that cracked with ice, 'but your efforts here are no longer required.'

'Sir—'

'Don't say any more, DCI Harris,' he snapped, then frowned and asked nastily, 'You're a temporary DCI, isn't that right?' He looked to Elaine to verify. 'A substantive inspector but hoping for a permanent promotion?'

She stared, her lower lip trembling. 'But that has nothing to do with this. Frankly—'

'Go,' he told her. 'Effect my instructions. Keep your head down and your nose clean.'

She staggered to her feet, swayed and had to hold the back of the chair for a moment.

Then, without another look at him — or at Elaine, who she hoped was in silent agony — she left the room and stalked past her desk, down the stairs and out of the building.

CHAPTER SIXTEEN

2.23 p.m.

Lola drove to Asda, a stone's throw from Helen Street, parked at an extremity of the car park, then called Anna and asked her to come and find her. 'I'm in the far corner,' she said shakily. 'I'll explain everything when you get here.'

Elaine tried to call her on her work phone, but Lola rejected it and turned the phone off.

She reached for her personal phone, ready to turn that off too, and saw messages from Sandy:

I'm at Braehead looking for a present. What do you think of this?

He'd attached a photo of a silver necklace with a heart pendant.

'For God's sake, Sand,' she said and rolled her eyes, then felt bad and replied, *Yes, very nice.*

He started to type a reply.

Going into a meeting, she typed, then pressed send and turned that phone off too.

Anna's Volvo appeared in the space to Lola's right. She came round and climbed in beside Lola.

'Is this something to do with the ACC, by any chance?' she asked.

'What makes you say that?'

'Kirstie saw him with the super. She said they both looked pretty grim.'

'I'm sure they did,' Lola said, eyes fixed on the grey railings that separated the car park from the motorway, endeavouring to steady herself, to stop her voice from shaking.

'He told me to shut down the inquiry into the missing boy,' she managed.

'He *what*?'

'ACC Thompson's talked to Dixon and Dixon's convinced him. I don't know how — maybe they're friends, freemasons or something. Anyway, he says Dixon's done something he regrets and he just needs to pay off the folk who've taken Adam and we've to leave him to get on with it.' Anna's face was incredulous. 'Oh, and Organised Crime are going to take the lead on Tiina Valk's death from now on. We've not to worry our heads.' She took a deep, deep breath, but it was as if she couldn't fill her lungs. She gasped some more.

'My God,' Anna breathed. Her eyes found the dashboard clock. 'There's a press conference in an hour and a half. What are we supposed to do? Do we—'

'Cancel it,' Lola said. 'On Thompson's instruction. I'll tell Deborah Truebig. She won't be very happy, but it's tough.'

'And Wendy Baker? The connection between Tiina and Ingrid and the university?'

'Central can deal with it, according to Thompson. Great, isn't it? A real vote of confidence.'

Anna looked as horrified as Lola felt, which was blackly satisfying.

'I know, Anna,' she said. 'I know.'

Anna reached into a pocket for her phone. She looked at it buzzing in her hand. 'Superintendent Walsh,' she said quietly. 'Should I answer?'

She nearly said no, then changed her mind.

'Yes, do,' she said, 'but you're not with me and you don't know where I am. 'Kay?'

Anna put the phone to her ear.

'It's DI Vaughan here,' she said, bright and breezy. Lola could make out Elaine's calm, assertive voice but not the words. 'No, ma'am. No, I haven't . . . Right now? I'm just in the car, about to head to Darnley . . . Yes, a potential witness who saw the van, and— Oh . . . Oh, I see. Yes, understood, ma'am . . . Yes, yes, of course, I'll tell her if I see her. Bye for now.'

She closed the call. 'I expect you could work out what that was about.'

'Where's DCI Harris? Don't go talking to any witnesses? The situation has changed?'

'She's asked me to see her the minute I'm back from Darnley.'

She looked sick. As sick as Lola felt.

'Is there a potential witness at Darnley?' Lola checked.

'Not that I know.' She looked at Lola, biting her lip. 'What going on, boss?'

'I don't know.' She stared at the railings again. At the ratty brown vegetation that grew through them, withered by poor soil and motorway fumes. 'I'm very hungry,' she said. 'You don't fancy fetching us something to eat, do you? I can plot better on a full stomach.'

Anna smiled. 'Me too, boss. Give me five minutes. Any special requests?'

'Mini Scotch eggs,' Lola said, feeling slightly better already. 'And Irn Bru. Full fat.'

'Coming right up,' Anna said.

* * *

2.54 p.m.

While Anna was in the supermarket, Lola put her work phone back on and winced as the notifications for missed calls poured in. She rang Deborah Truebig.

'We have to cancel the press conference at four,' she told her. 'There've been developments. I'm sorry.'

'It's late, but if you insist . . . Do you want to reschedule?'

'Not yet. It's complicated and I can't go into detail. Sorry, Deb. Someone will be in touch.'

She turned the phone off again and resumed seething at the railings.

Were Dixon and ACC Thompson friends, or associates in some fashion, as she'd suggested to Anna? It was possible, and could explain why Thompson had made him his so-called 'cyber tsar'. Or was the ACC just being politically savvy — safeguarding his own reputation by protecting the man he'd appointed to a prominent role?

Or was it something else — something more serious? Dixon was a cyber expert and would know how to hack. Could he have something on Thompson?

You're being ridiculous now.

Then what else? *Who* else?

There was Gerald Linklater, MBE, the tall grey man with the voluminous white hair. He'd said he advised Lola's employer on — what was it, 'technology and its applications'? She'd asked him if that included cyber security and he'd answered defensively. He might know the ACC. They'd have met, for sure. Had he used some sinister 'application of technology' to dig up dirt on the man? But why would he? To protect the precious university? No one could be that enamoured of an institution, surely . . .

She'd asked Linklater if he knew Lawrie Dixon and he'd denied it. Did she believe him? Would a senior business leader, a specialist in IT, not know the man appointed as Police Scotland's 'cyber tsar'?

She realised she knew very little about ACC Thompson.

She turned her personal phone back on and googled his name, finding a news article about his appointment to Police Scotland. She read:

Alec Thompson will take up the newly created post of Assistant Chief Constable for Policing in a Digital World in February 2025. Previously he served as Chief Superintendent (Special Projects) with West Pennine Police, a post that quickly became a focal point for innovative policing practice using new technology.

Thompson led a 'root-and-branch' review of policing methods in the wake of a number of cases of drug and people trafficking, where criminals had made use of encrypted messaging services to conduct their activities.

Thompson, who is 48 and grew up in Dundee, is married to Janet Lee Thompson, a social sciences professor at the University of Preston. They have one son.

Next she googled 'Lawrence Dixon + Alec Thompson', but there were dozens of results. There would be: Dixon was Thompson's appointee, so there were countless photos of them, grinning at events. She closed the tab and googled 'Gerald Linklater + Alec Thompson' instead. A couple of results bore fruit, but nothing juicy. They were named as attending an event, a big economic forum in Edinburgh where digital technology was discussed.

She peered out across the car park and saw Anna in the distance, coming her way clutching paper bags and a couple of bottles.

She used the remaining seconds to google 'Lawrence Dixon + Gerald Linklater' — for the sake of completeness.

And there it was: the top result a photograph of the two of them, with another couple of men, beaming away in suits.

She enlarged and studied it. They were at the unveiling of a plaque. She clicked the link and a press release appeared. *Directors of Highwire Cyber Ltd Celebrate Most Successful Year Yet*, read the headline.

Anna climbed in and passed Lola a plastic container with six mini Scotch eggs inside. 'It didn't look like much, so I got you these to go with them,' she said, and handed her a bag of

162

carrots. She held up a six-pack of cheese and onion crisps. 'I got these too, in case you wanted something more substantial.' She saw Lola's face. 'What is it?'

'Lawrie Dixon and Gerald Linklater know each other,' Lola said. 'They're directors on the board of a company — or were. Though what it means . . . who knows?'

* * *

3.22 p.m.

They ate their picnic fast, passing up carrots for crisps and swigging Irn Bru. 'Right,' Lola said, wiping her hands on a Kleenex. 'What do we do now?'

Anna looked at the dashboard clock. 'Whatever it is, we have to act fast,' she said. 'The super is expecting me, then that'll be me off the case too.'

'You said you'd already requested DNA test results for the woman found at Lancaster, didn't you?' Lola checked.

'I asked for the PM report too. Got a reply sharpish to say they've got it on file and it wouldn't be long.'

'Did you give them your name?'

Anna nodded.

'Go back to your contact and ask them to email it to me rather than you.' She saw Anna's expression change and said, 'I don't want you getting into any hot water over any of this. Same with any info about the dead woman in London. Ask our contact at the NCA to send the PM report direct to me.'

'Of course.'

'Can you give me the name and contact details for Tiina Valk's friend in Sydney? I'll speak to them. As for Ingrid Valk and Chan Wen's housemates, I've already got their details, so I'll go see them myself this afternoon. Oh, and did you get a new address for Yunhee Kim?'

Anna checked her email inbox on her phone. 'Not yet,' she said. 'I'll ring and chase it. Boss, I'm worried about you going off on your own. Is there a way I can help?'

'No. I'd rather you do as the super tells you. I'll be fine.'

Anna nodded. 'You can call me,' she said, 'but get me on my personal number. I'll do what I can.'

'Thanks, Anna,' Lola said. 'Right, you go. We haven't seen one another since the team meeting, all right?'

Anna returned to her own car and drove away.

Lola went into her phone and found a phone number. She rang it.

'Tatjana?' she said when a nervous voice answered. 'It's DCI Lola Harris here from Police Scotland. I'd like to talk to you and your flatmate Kristel this afternoon if possible . . . Yes, it's about Ingrid Valk.'

CHAPTER SEVENTEEN

3.41 p.m.

Lola was on the approach road to the Clyde Tunnel when Sandy rang. She answered on hands-free.

'I'm very busy!'

'I know,' he said. 'I'm still at Braehead. I bought the necklace but there's a bracelet too, only it's got dark blue gemstones in it. I thought—'

'Sounds fine,' she snapped. 'Good idea. Get it.'

'Okay, but—'

'Got to go. Sorry.'

She was emerging from the other end of the tunnel when her phone rang again. This time it was Elaine. She'd rarely called Lola's personal phone before — not unless there was an emergency or Lola had called her first.

Elaine would tell her to come in, she knew it. She'd warn her, in no uncertain terms, and Lola would have no choice but to obey. Lola took a deep breath and jabbed the reject icon on the dashboard screen. Her body reacted with a shiver of dread.

What was she doing?

Her job, that's what — while powerful people tried to stop her.

But it was a job she might lose. And what then?

She pulled off the expressway and parked to call Sandy back.

'It's me,' she said when he answered.

'Too late,' he began, 'I already bought it. I thought about maybe a gift set from Boots as well. Or is that too much?'

'Sandy, I need to tell you something — and ask you something.'

A pause. 'Oh?'

'If I left my job could I still come and work with you?' she said in a rush. 'I know you said I could in the past. Does the offer still stand?'

Another pause, longer this time. Then he laughed. 'Aye, of course . . . Lola, has something happened?'

'Aye,' she said. 'Aye, it has. And it's still happening. Only, I can't talk right now.'

'Lola—'

'I love you, Sandy.'

'Wha—'

'Sorry. Got to go.'

And she hung up. She didn't drive for almost a minute.

* * *

4.03 p.m.

Tatjana Kallas and Kristel Sepp lived in a rented ground-floor tenement flat in Fortrose Street in Partick, off busy Dumbarton Road. They appeared to have quickly tidied the living room ahead of her. A pile of books, papers, clothes and bags teetered beside an armchair.

'Thank you for seeing me,' Lola said, and sat in an arm-chair with a tartan throw over it. It was dark in the living room and the window gave straight onto the pavement. People passed by, their elbows almost brushing the glass.

Tatjana was blonde like Marta Dixon but of a squarer build, Kristel was dark and suspicious-eyed. The pair sat on a small IKEA-style settee and eyed her with half-nervous, half-mutinous expressions.

'You lived with Ingrid Valk for a year, I understand. In Dowanhill, wasn't it?'

'Yes, in a flat off Highburgh Road,' Kristel said.

The two women exchanged quick glances, as if to check they were still on script.

'Did you like her?' Lola asked.

Both nodded readily enough, though one of Kristel's eyebrows was raised. 'Until she disappeared and stopped paying her share of the rent,' she said. 'We had the lease until August, so she missed three whole months.'

'Are you both from Estonia?' Lola asked, already knowing the answer from the information Danny McDougall had provided.

They nodded in unison.

'I'm from Tallinn, like Ingrid,' Tatjana said.

'Tartu, in the south,' Kristel said.

'Did you know each other before you came to Glasgow?'

They shook their heads.

'Or Ingrid?'

'No. We met when we arrived, in our first week,' Tatjana said, 'just over two years ago. We were all in the same student accommodation near the canal and we became friends. We decided to live together in our second year. Maybe after that too, if we got on.'

Lola thought for a few moments. 'So you were here for the induction week?'

'That's right.'

'With Dear Green Place?'

'Yes,' Tatjana said. 'Paolo and Jen. As I say, that was more than two years ago. Seems like a lifetime.'

167

'Tell me about when Ingrid disappeared,' Lola said.

Another of their surreptitious glances, and a small nod from Kristel to Tatjana.

'We knew she had a boyfriend,' Tatjana said. 'Neither of us realised it was so serious . . . maybe we should have done.'

'Tell me about the boyfriend.'

'Ewan,' Tatjana said, then spelled it, as if the name might be new to Lola. 'Another student, but not at our university. At the other one here in the West End.'

'Did you know his surname?'

They shook their heads.

'Was it Cathrie?'

'Don't know,' they said at the same time.

'Did she ever show you a photograph of him?'

More shaking of heads.

'And what was he studying?'

'Medicine, I think,' Tatjana said after a moment's thought. 'Or biomedical something-or-other. He was busy or shy or whatever, and anyway he had his own place — no housemates — so Ingrid liked to go there. She was in love, you could tell.' She laughed to herself.

'How could you tell?'

'Oh, you know — the usual way people act when they're in love, and . . .'

'And?'

'Nothing. Ignore me.'

'When did you last see her?' she asked now.

'The end of May,' Tatjana said. 'The twentieth, actually. It's my sister's birthday so I remember it. She was out in the daytime and there was no sign of her in the evening. But I heard her about midnight after I'd gone to bed. I heard her in the room next to mine and then moving about in the hall. I put my head out and asked if she was okay. She seemed nervous. She had a bag with her — a big one, as if she was going away. I said, "Is everything all right?" and she said she was going to Ewan's. "Forever?" I said, though of course I was joking. "I'll be back," she said. And that's the last time I saw her.

'A couple of weeks later, someone from the university came round. They said they'd tried to contact Ingrid because she'd missed two assessments. We said she was at her boyfriend's. They made a big fuss about her moving out and we told them she hadn't, not permanently. They asked us which was her bedroom and we went in. Some of her things were there but not many. And then she didn't pay the rent at the start of June, or July . . . We were pissed off.'

'*Really* pissed off,' Kristel came in.

'And you haven't seen or heard from her since?'

They shook their heads in unison.

Kristel said, 'Tatjana heard the university had told the visa people, didn't you?'

Tatjana nodded.

'Do you remember any people Ingrid seemed particularly friendly with?'

Tatjana looked strained. 'Not really . . . I'm sorry.' She gave a shrug.

'You've both been very helpful,' Lola said.

* * *

4.35 p.m.

Lola checked her personal phone as she was leaving. Anna had texted a contact card for Yunhee Kim, the South Korean student who'd moved to study at another of the city's universities. Yunhee was potentially the key to understanding what had been going on, having apparently vanished then reappeared. There was a phone number and a street address. Lola briefly weighed the likelihood of Yunhee taking flight if she merely phoned, and decided to go straight round in person.

Back in the car she punched the postcode into her GPS, fastened her seat belt and drove.

The flat was no student residence, but in an expensive-looking development near the canal above Maryhill. Lola found the buzzer in the smart entry lobby. *Kim*, said the label beside the button — no other surnames, suggesting Yunhee lived here alone. Hadn't her personal tutor told Kirstie she was very poor?

Lola rang the buzzer and waited, then rang it again. Nothing.

She cursed and reached for her phone, then rang the mobile number.

It was answered after two rings. 'Yes?' a voice answered.

'Delivery for Ms Kim,' Lola said breezily.

'What delivery?' the voice asked suspiciously. From the background noise, it sounded as if she was out and by a busy road.

'Don't know. I just deliver. It's in a box. Looks like a gift.'

'A gift?' She sounded suddenly interested. 'I'm out right now. Just take it up to the fifth floor and leave it. Press the service buzzer. Someone will let you in.'

'Oh, right,' Lola said, acting hard. 'Only, I need a signature. Sorry. When will you be back?'

The woman gave an exasperated sigh. 'Five minutes,' she said. 'Just wait, all right?'

'Fine by me.'

Lola pressed the service button and someone let her into an inner lobby where a lift stood open. She went in and selected 5.

She found Yunhee's flat at the far end of the fifth-floor hallway, indicated by a nameplate on the door. The hallway was nice. It was carpeted, clean and there were real plants in pots.

There was a fire door to the side of Yunhee's door. Lola opened it and went through into a stairwell. No point giving Yunhee more warning than she needed to.

She waited tensely, thinking and rethinking her approach. In time, she heard the lift *bing* and then footsteps approach along the hallway. When they were near, she opened the fire door and stepped out into the corridor. The woman saw her and jumped, then stared at her, key up like a weapon.

'Who are you?' she asked in a high, frightened voice.

'My name's Lola Harris,' she said. 'I'm a detective with Police Scotland. Are you Yunhee Kim?'

The terror on her face confirmed it.

'Can we have a chat?'

'No,' the young woman said, eyes darting to the door of her flat, then behind her, back along the corridor. 'No! I can't talk to you.'

'Who says?'

'I just can't!'

'Please, Yunhee. You see, women are dying and I don't want you to be next. I need to talk to you. I need to understand what happened to you last summer.'

'Fuck you!' the woman suddenly spat. She made to push past Lola, key up, ready for the lock, except Lola wasn't about to move.

'How do you afford to live here?' she asked her. 'Very fancy for a student.'

'None of your fucking business!'

'Yunhee—'

She put a hand out to hold the woman's arm, but Yunhee threw it off. Suddenly she pushed Lola — hard, so Lola half fell into the wall. Then Yunhee was through the fire door and into the stairwell.

'Stop!' Lola bellowed, scrambling after her, ignoring the pain in her arm and shoulder. She flew down the stairs, hearing the young woman going before her.

Lola was only down as far as the second floor when she heard a door crash open below. She coursed down the remaining flights and burst from the doorway into daylight.

A car — a very new, very expensive-looking blue Mini — screeched from the car park in front of the flats. Lola glimpsed Yunhee at the wheel.

4.42 p.m.

Back in the car, Lola very gingerly opened her work phone and looked at her emails. There were several, including one from Elaine entitled 'RING ME IMMEDIATELY'. She ignored it and went into an email headed 'PM REPORT'. It was from Anna's contact in London and attached the post-mortem report on the young woman who'd committed suicide there — the one who was possibly Chinese and had a birthmark like the one Chan Wen's tutor had described. There were photographs attached to the report, including a clear one of the young woman's face, where she looked merely asleep. The birthmark showed clearly on the photograph.

Lola found the contact name and number for Chan Wen's old flatmate and called her. A young woman answered after seven or eight rings in a very quiet voice.

'Hello, is that Tan Min?' Lola asked.

'Yes,' the voice whispered. 'Who is it, please? I'm in the library. Can't speak very loudly.'

'My name is Detective Chief Inspector Lola Harris from Police Scotland,' she said.

'Oh, your colleague called me too. Just a while ago. She left a message. I'm sorry, I haven't called her back yet.'

'You don't need to, but I'd like to talk to you, and urgently — in the next hour, if possible. It's about your former flatmate, Chan Wen. Could we meet? I can come to you.'

A brief silence, then, 'Yes, okay. Near St George's Cross?'

'Perfect.'

'Okay. We can go to Café Cavino on Great Western Road. Give me fifteen minutes, okay?'

Lola found a parking spot near the café and paid with her phone. She was jangled. Elaine had tried her again on her personal phone while she was driving. She'd let it go to voicemail. A notification told her Elaine had left a message.

'Sorry, Elaine,' she muttered, and climbed out of her car.

There were booths in the café and she saw a woman of East Asian appearance peering out from one at the back. She waved shyly and Lola went over.

'Tan Min?' she asked.

'You can call me Min.'

Lola squeezed into the booth opposite her.

A waiter arrived with a menu. 'Just coffee for me, please,' Lola said. 'Black.' She looked at Min. 'What would you like?'

'Matcha,' Min said, putting on a smile for him. 'With soy.'

He went away.

'The matcha is why I come here,' she confided. 'Not everywhere does it.'

'Thank you for meeting me,' Lola said.

She nodded and smiled again, but now it looked strained. 'You want to talk about Wen . . .'

'Yes. She was your friend?'

A nod. 'We were very good friends — so I thought. We lived together until summer last year, when she left one night.' She gave a helpless little shrug. 'Didn't even say goodbye, just took her things and moved out.'

'Where to, do you know?'

She shook her head.

'Did you hear from her after that?'

'No. Do you — do you know where she is?'

The waiter came with Lola's coffee and saved her from answering. 'The matcha's just coming,' he said.

Lola looked her straight in the eye and said gently, 'Min, I'm afraid there's a chance Wen is dead.'

Min said nothing for a moment, then nodded sadly, eyes down. 'I thought she might be. I don't know why.' She swallowed. 'What — what happened to her?'

'We don't know. And we don't know if it is her. A young woman was found in London a year ago. She'd taken her own life.' She paused to let the information sink in. 'Police believed she was of East Asian, possibly Chinese origin. They tried to

173

identify her but failed. I have a photograph of her, taken after she died. She looks peaceful in it, as though she's sleeping. I'd like you to take a look at it.'

Min put a fretful hand to her mouth. 'I don't know . . .'

'Just a quick glance.'

The matcha arrived, milky green with a beautiful leaf pattern drawn in the foam. Tan Min put her hands round it as if suddenly needing its warmth. 'Okay,' she whispered miserably.

Lola took out her phone and found the email from Anna. She opened the photograph of the young woman, eyes closed, lips slightly parted. She turned the screen to Min.

Min peeked at the screen then drew in a sharp breath.

'Take a few seconds,' Lola said gently.

'It's her,' Min said. 'Yes, it's her.' She shut her eyes tight and put a hand to her mouth. She sniffed and tears squeezed from the corners of her eyes.

Lola found her a tissue.

'How sure are you?' she asked after a minute.

'It's her. I know it is. When did it happen? When did she . . . ?'

'Last autumn,' Lola said. 'Drink your tea. Take your time. Then I'd like to ask you a few questions about Wen.'

She nodded and took a sip of her matcha latte. Green foam stuck to her upper lip. She used another of Lola's tissues to wipe it away.

'Did you know one another before you came to Glasgow?'

Min shook her head. 'We're from very different parts of China. I'm from a city near Shanghai in the north-east. Wen is — was — from Shenzhen, in the south, near Hong Kong. We met in the first week, on a bus tour. We realised our rooms were on the same corridor at Firhill Mount — you know, near the canal?'

Lola nodded.

'We became friends. We decided to live together in our second year. But then . . .'

'Then what?'

She was silent for what seemed a long time, and Lola sensed something important was coming.

Min leaned in and said clearly but quietly, 'I didn't approve of what she did. I know why she did it, but it was wrong. I told her so.'

Lola braced herself. 'And what was that, Min?'

'She was struggling. She worked so hard but still she couldn't understand what they needed her to understand! And the essays and assessments were getting harder and harder . . .'

'She was struggling with her course, you mean?'

A small nod. 'And so she asked for help.' She bit her lip.

'What kind of help?'

Min's eyes darted about the café, as though people might overhear.

'You can say anything to me,' Lola said softly.

Min leaned in. 'She paid for an essay,' she said. 'She told me she'd done it, but afterwards when it was too late. I cried! I did. I told her it was wrong — and a big risk!'

'You mean — Wen paid someone to write an essay for her?'

Min nodded, looking utterly miserable.

'Who did she pay?'

'I don't know. I don't think she knew either. It was all arranged. And then she did it again,' Min said now. 'We began to fall out. She said she was desperate. She begged me not to tell anyone. If her family in China found out, they'd be so ashamed. And then . . .'

She stopped and looked long and hard at Lola.

'Then what, Min?'

'Then they asked her to pay some more — the people who'd got the essay for her. But not in money. She was asked to do something.' Min squirmed. 'With a man. She had to . . . to go to bed with him. I said to her, "No! You can't do this!" I told her to go to the police. I said, "It's blackmail!" But she was so frightened by then. She didn't want anyone to know about the essay, you see?'

175

'Who made Wen do this, Min? Who are you talking about?'

Min swallowed and eyed Lola miserably. 'The people at Dear Green Place,' she whispered. 'They organised the essay too.'

'I see.' It took Lola a moment to collect herself. 'Paolo, or—'

'Not Paolo,' Min said. '*Jen.* I know it sounds incredible. Jen's so nice — so normal — but she isn't really.'

'Let me get this straight, Min. Jen Crossley from Dear Green Place sold Chan Wen an essay and then blackmailed her to have sex with a man?'

A second nod. Lola's skin crawled.

'One man, or *men*?'

'One.' She put both her hands to her mouth as if in a last bid to keep the words in there. 'I haven't told a soul, but now I know she's . . . dead . . .'

Lola took a moment to line up her questions.

'Did she tell you who this man was?'

'No.'

'Who else knew?' Lola asked.

'No one,' Min whispered. 'No one else.'

One man. Blackmailed to have sex with one man. Was this 'the boyfriend'? The one Ingrid had had too?

'Min, does the name Ewan Cathrie mean anything to you?'

'Ewan . . . ?'

'Ewan Cathrie.'

She shook her head.

Lola thought of Yunhee. Yunhee who was from a poor family but had managed to get herself to Glasgow to study and who'd worked all hours to fund herself — and to send money home to her family . . . but who now lived in an expensive apartment block and drove a shiny new car. And she thought of Tatjana's off-hand remark about Ingrid and the conversation that had followed:

She was in love, you could tell.

How could you tell?

Oh, you know — the usual way people act when they're in love . . .

Lola remembered when she and Sandy first got together, and how she'd seen her sister Frankie a few weeks later and Frankie's comment: 'Someone's happy!' And how Lola had replied: 'What do you mean?' And Frankie's reply: 'You've put on a few pounds, Lola. Don't worry — it always happens. People eat when they're in love.'

And with a shiver of realisation Lola began to understand.

'Min,' she said, her breathing shaky, 'I'm going to leave you now. I'll need you to make a statement in due course, so I'll be in touch.'

'Okay,' Min said, her face sad but willing.

'I'll pay for your matcha,' Lola said. 'You take care.'

* * *

5.20 p.m.

She almost threw herself into the car and went into her work phone to find yet another missed call from Elaine, but no further voicemails. She still hadn't listened to the first. Elaine would know she was angry and would be expecting a maverick behaviour in response. It had happened before. She'd always been able to talk Elaine round in the past, but didn't see how that could happen this time; now she wasn't just defying Elaine, but the ACC — and that was beyond serious.

She found the post-mortem report on the woman she now believed to be Chan Wen and scanned it for the information she wanted — the information she hadn't thought to look for beforehand. And there it was, the words hiding in plain sight:

Uterus size and perineal tearing suggest deceased had recently given birth, possibly within last three months.

'My God,' she murmured aloud.

Chan Wen had bought an essay and been blackmailed into having sex with a man in order to carry his child. Some weeks later she had chosen to end her own life.

Lola felt physically sick.

There was another email waiting for her — this from the Lancashire police attaching the post-mortem report into the unidentified woman whose body had been found at a recycling centre in Lancaster — the woman Lola felt in her bones was Ingrid Valk. She opened the pdf and scanned through it, peering hard to read the writing on the small screen of her phone. The dead woman had died of asphyxiation, she read, probably as the result of strangling with some kind of thin cord.

Lola scrolled on, then found the text she was looking for.

Her skin prickled. Just like Chan Wen, the dead woman at Lancaster had given birth in the weeks preceding her death too.

Babies no one knew about . . . babies for whom?

A snatch of conversation occurred to her: Jeanie Quigley's words when Lola had gone to see her on Wednesday evening.

She went into her phone and found Jeanie's number. She dialled.

Jeanie answered by reciting the number.

'Jeanie, it's Lola Harris here.'

'Oh! Oh, Lola. Is there any news?'

'I'm afraid not. Jeanie, I want to ask you something.'

'Yes. What is it?'

'The other night, you were talking about when Marta's father came to visit her after Adam was born. You said her father described Adam as a "little miracle".'

'That's right.' There was fondness in her voice. 'Well, it's true.'

'Why is it true, Jeanie? Why is Adam a "little miracle"?'

'Well . . . because Marta wasn't ever supposed to have children, was she?'

'Wasn't she?'

'She'd been ill as a girl. She'd had something — oh, what is it called? Lupus something. It affects the kidneys. She told me all about it. It causes all sorts of complications, including when it comes to pregnancy. But then, a miracle happened.' Lola could hear her smiling into her phone. 'Off she went for a few months on that extended trip of hers, and when she came back, Adam was born!'

'Thank you, Jeanie,' Lola said.

She came off the call and sat quietly for a full minute, then, driven by a steely anger, she googled 'Jen Crossley + Dear Green Place Glasgow'. A number of results appeared and Jen was named twice, but there were no photos.

She remembered Jen's cheerful, businesslike and assertive voice when they'd talked on the phone. She'd sounded so competent, so pleasant. Not at all the type of person to exploit vulnerable students so far from home . . . Let alone through an organisation set up to combat loneliness and provide support.

A text from Anna's personal number flashed up. She opened it.

That's me off the case too, boss. The super is on a war footing, just to warn you.

* * *

6.01 p.m.

Anna's personal phone rang five or six times before she answered with a quiet, 'Hi.'

'Can you talk?'

'Give me two secs,' Anna said. Lola heard a door open then close. 'I can now. Go on.'

'I think I've worked it out,' she said. 'Jen Crossley of Dear Green Place has been exploiting female students and forcing them to have babies for other people. Chan Wen

179

was blackmailed into it; I suspect Yunhee Kim was possibly paid for it; and I don't know about Ingrid Valk, but the dead woman at Lancaster had given birth just before her death. If that was Ingrid, then *that makes three* — just like Wendy said.'

'My God, boss. My God . . .'

They were both silent for several seconds.

'Marta Dixon believed she couldn't have children,' Lola went on, 'then one day she had apparently given birth to a baby boy — after several months away from home. Anna, I think Adam Dixon could be Ingrid's son.'

'We could check his DNA against Tiina's,' Anna said, then caught herself. 'Or we could if he wasn't missing . . .'

'*Exactly,*' Lola said.

'So Dixon knows where Adam is and that's why he's hiding him?' Anna said. 'It explains also why he's so scared — he's scared we'll find out about Ingrid. Do you think he killed Ingrid? Tiina too?'

'I don't know.'

They were silent again.

'Should you try to talk to the super?' Anna asked. 'Persuade her we need to keep investigating?'

'Not yet,' Lola said. 'I need to know more. I need to try to get some concrete evidence. I need to understand more about the link between Dear Green Place and the university. I think I'll go to the university and face down Prue Carstairs. I want to put all of this to her and see what she says.'

Anna was quiet for a moment.

'What is it?'

'I've just seen an email come in,' Anna said. 'It's from the lab in Lancashire. Boss, the body in Lancaster — there's a perfect match with the DNA from Tiina. It's her, boss. The dead woman found at Lancaster is Ingrid Valk.'

* * *

180

'I'm still at the university,' Prue Carstairs barked when Lola called her mobile. 'Where else would I be? *Some* people may slack off on a Friday; others are a good deal more committed!'

'I'm coming in to see you,' Lola said.

'Suit yourself. One of the security people will escort you.' She hung up.

Lola drove fast, both phones safely off again.

James, the security guard who'd taken her in the other day, was in reception. 'Here for another face-off with the big yin, are you?' he asked, eyebrow raised.

''Fraid so,' she said.

He led the way to the lifts.

'Do you know Mr Linklater?' she asked him when they were in the lift.

'Wouldn't say I know him,' the man said quietly. 'He comes and goes. Here most weeks — some weeks more than others. Swanning around like he owns the place.'

'Does he own it?' she asked mildly.

He frowned and pushed out his bottom lip. 'Wouldn't put it like that. Close to his heart, though he's invested a fair penny of his own money in it, so they say.'

'Who says?'

'Ah.' He lifted a hand. 'I'm saying nothing.' The lift pinged. 'Here we are. After you.'

Halfway along the corridor, in sight of Prue Carstairs' slightly open office door, he stopped. 'You know where you're headed?'

'I do.'

'Best of luck, hen,' he said and made a face.

Lola proceeded on her own.

Through the gap, Lola could see Carstairs was on the phone, hunched over her desk. 'Indeed,' she heard her say. 'Indeed, indeed, indeed. I could *not* agree more.' There was some huffing and puffing.

Lola rapped loudly on the door, making her jump.

'Who is it?' the principal asked, hand over the phone receiver.

'Me, Ms Carstairs,' Lola said and went in.

Carstairs glowered. 'I'll call you back,' she said into the phone. 'Yes, all right. Goodbye.'

Lola closed the door and went to take a seat.

'What is this about?' Carstairs asked, sitting up straight and facing her visitor.

'I want to know more about Dear Green Place,' Lola said.

'What about them?' She managed to sound both uninterested and offended by Lola's interest.

'How are they funded?'

That earned a scowl. 'What business is that of yours?'

'Your registrar was murdered, Ms Carstairs.'

'I know that, but . . . Honestly, I . . .' She ground to a halt.

'It's funded through a trust, I believe.'

Carstairs narrowed her eyes and breathed. 'For the large part, yes. The Lara Shulman Trust, in honour of a young woman who struggled with loneliness on her arrival in Glasgow some time ago. Our international alumni are encouraged to give donations to the trust to enable more of its work. Some have even named the trust in their wills, I believe.'

'Who are the trustees?'

Carstairs' eyes became very small. Lola readied herself to be pulled up for impertinence.

'Mary Shulman, of course,' she said. 'Then there's myself. Gerald Linklater became a trustee last year. A couple of others: an accountant who kindly volunteers his time, and a woman who acts as secretary. Now, is that everything?'

'Not quite. How is Paolo DeSalvo paid?'

'How is he *paid*? I do not see—'

'Ms Carstairs!'

'He has a salary paid through the trust, overseen by a sub-committee, chaired by me.'

'And Jen Crossley. Who pays her?'

'I—' She caught herself and her expression darkened. 'That's a different arrangement.'

'Different how?'

Carstairs glared at her with intense dislike, then peered at a clock on the wall.

'Ms Carstairs,' Lola began. 'Prue—'

'We shall have tea,' the principal said, suddenly, surprisingly, and eased herself up out of her seat.

'Actually, I'd rather have information.'

'You don't want a cup? Fine. I myself happen to be thirsty all of a sudden.'

She bustled to a corner of the office where there was a mini-kitchen with a sink and kettle.

Lola sat on her impatience and waited.

Two minutes later, Carstairs was back at her desk, a steaming mug in hand.

'You haven't asked me why I'm asking about Dear Green Place,' Lola said.

'I'm sure you have your reasons,' Carstairs said sniffily. She wiggled her mouse and feigned interest in her computer screen.

'Criminal exploitation,' Lola said softly. 'That's the reason.'

That got the principal's attention. Her eyes darted to the door, which Lola had closed behind her.

'Exploitation? Of whom and by whom?'

'Female international students, by employees of Dear Green Place.'

'But—'

'It is my belief, Ms Carstairs, that Jen Crossley, working on her own or with someone else, has been grooming young women to carry babies for payment — or through blackmail.'

Carstairs' face became puce and her lower lip trembled. 'This is . . . this is an *outrageous* suggestion — and quite possibly slanderous. I hope you have proof of what you're saying.'

Her eyes were on the door again. Lola turned to look. There was a narrow vertical window in the door itself. Out in the open-plan office area of the floor she could see lights had come on, as though someone was approaching. Carstairs had been on the phone when she arrived. To whom, Lola wondered.

'As a result of their activities,' Lola went coldly on, 'two of your former students are now dead, along with your registrar, who'd worked out what was going on. Meanwhile a young child — who I believe was born to one of the dead women — is still missing. So you see why I need to find Jen Crossley — and fast.'

The door behind her opened and a figure slipped nimbly into the room. Gerald Linklater closed the door softly behind him, but just before it closed, Lola was sure she'd glimpsed another figure just outside.

'We meet again,' Linklater said, an unpleasant smile curling his thin lips.

'Oh, Gerald, thank goodness!' Carstairs cried, immediately on her feet and going to him.

Lola rose calmly and faced the pair, who stood so close they were almost embracing.

'Mr Linklater,' she said nicely. 'I'm having difficulty making Ms Carstairs here understand the importance — and urgency — of my request. Perhaps you can help.'

He wrinkled his nose. 'Help you? How?'

'How is Jen Crossley paid for her work with Dear Green Place?'

'Jen . . . ? How would I know that?'

'Because you're a trustee, sir.'

He shot Carstairs a shifty look.

'I'm so sorry, Gerald,' she heard Carstairs whisper to him, a little teary now, like a lover who'd betrayed the man she loved.

'Oh, yes,' Linklater said and mugged a smile. 'Yes, of course. I remember. She is paid with an honorarium, I believe.'

'What's that, sir?'

184

'A payment for professional services. It's—' he cleared his throat — 'paid from the scholarships and hardship fund, I believe. Isn't that correct, Prue?'

He peered at Carstairs, who nodded, eyes down.

'I need to talk to her. I have her phone number but I need her address.'

'Why?'

'She's been saying terrible things,' Carstairs cut in. 'That Jen has been *exploiting* our students!'

'She's been *what*? What nonsense!'

'I only wish it were,' Lola said.

He looked at her long and hard, doubtless hating her. Then he stepped apart from Carstairs and reached for the door and opened it. He made a signal to someone Lola couldn't see, then came back in.

'Who's out there?' Lola asked.

'Someone to see you, Ms Harris,' Linklater said.

'Oh?'

The snake smile was back on his lips.

'We know you're here unofficially,' he said. 'We know, too, that you have been instructed to step away from the case.'

'Do you?'

The smile widened, the thin lips stretching.

Lola heard footsteps outside the room. It took every fibre to keep calm. She stood, arms at her side, and waited.

Whoever it was had arrived outside the door.

'Come in!' Linklater barked out.

The door opened. Lola froze.

'DCI Harris,' Elaine said, gazing at her in such intense dismay Lola felt weak. 'Come with me, please.' To Linklater she said, 'Thank you. I'll take things from here.'

CHAPTER EIGHTEEN

6.56 p.m.

Neither Lola nor Elaine spoke during the long walk through the building and down in the lift.

Lola felt oddly calm, as if a splinter of ice had lodged in her brain and numbed her anxiety.

Don't plan a speech, she told herself. *Answer questions simply and make it clear you now have evidence. Real evidence. Then you can ask a question or two of your own . . .*

'I'm parked on the street,' Elaine murmured coolly when they reached the reception. 'We can talk in the car.'

Lola nodded to show she'd heard.

She followed Elaine out through the glass doors and down the steps. Elaine headed right, in the direction of Garscube Road.

Traffic was heavy and they had to wait for a gap, then Elaine went first. Lola was almost at the pavement on the opposite side when she felt eyes on her — and looked sharply left. A black car pulled quickly out from the pavement where it had been parked. A hand snapped a sun visor down to hide the driver's face and then the car took off, screeching and causing a couple of pedestrians to jump hurriedly out of its way.

'Lola?' Elaine called sharply.

But Lola couldn't tear her eyes away. She memorised the registration plate.

'Is there a problem?'

Lola kept her eyes on the car as it disappeared up Garscube Road.

'I think we should drive somewhere away from here,' she said. 'I think it would be safer.'

* * *

7.16 p.m.

'I tried to call you four times, left two voice messages and sent a text,' Elaine said.

They were parked on Queen Margaret Drive by the Botanic Gardens, both staring resolutely ahead.

'I know,' Lola said.

She was still so calm.

'You chose to ignore me.'

'Yes. I'm sorry, but I had my reasons.'

'Oh, I'm sure of it.'

Silence descended. Elaine's breathing told Lola how angry she was. Still, Lola remained calm.

'How did you know I was at the university?' she asked.

'A tip-off,' Elaine said.

'From Carstairs or Linklater?'

'Linklater. Though I didn't speak to him myself.'

'He's mixed up in it,' Lola said. 'I'm not sure if Carstairs is, but I wouldn't be surprised.'

'Lola—' Elaine turned to look at her — 'you have to leave this.'

Lola kept her eyes determinedly straight ahead.

'You were given an instruction — *I* was given an instruction by the assistant chief constable.'

'I know,' Lola said.

'The ACC took a measured view,' Elaine went on, 'based on his own conversation with a man he knows very well. Given the unique circumstances of this crime, he *instructed* us to step away, with a view to saving that child's life. But you chose to defy him. To defy me.'

'I did.'

'*Why?*'

'Because it was the right thing to do. I thought the ACC had been lied to and manipulated. I thought he was being a fool. I still do.'

Elaine gave a frustrated sigh. 'Do you think I'm a fool?'

She didn't answer.

'I'll take that as a yes.'

'I don't think you're a fool, boss.'

More silence.

'I have to take action against you,' Elaine said now. 'You do understand that?'

'I did it because they're killing women,' she said.

'And both women's deaths will be investigated.'

'But investigated separately,' Lola pointed out, 'though their deaths are inextricably linked.'

Elaine groaned with irritation.

'There are more deaths. Ingrid Valk, Tiina's sister, is dead. Chan Wen, another student, is dead, too, though she committed suicide.'

Elaine was looking at her curiously now.

'Ingrid Valk gave birth in the weeks before she died,' she said, knowing she had the super's attention. 'I think her baby was handed to the Dixons. I think Tiina went to get the child back — and was killed for her trouble. I suspect Lawrie Dixon knows exactly where his son is and is keeping him away from us in case it occurs to us to take his son's DNA . . . and test it against Tiina's.'

'Are you being serious?' Elaine asked.

'Deadly,' Lola said. 'From what I can piece together, Lawrie Dixon married Marta in hopes she'd inherit her father's business. The father's too much of a misogynist to entrust it to his daughter, and Marta's brother is a bit of a waster, by all accounts. The old man came to Scotland to meet Adam shortly after he was born and dotes on the boy, apparently. If you look at photos of Adam, he does look like Marta, boss — it's the reason they chose Ingrid. Anyway, Marta's father is talking about changing his will in Adam's favour . . . so I hear.'

'This is incredible,' Elaine said.

'I think a charity associated with the university, and which is supposed to help international students, is in fact being used to groom young women to have babies for wealthy couples who want a baby with the "correct" ethnic profile. Some might be paid, which we know is illegal, but I also know that a young Chinese woman was blackmailed over the fact she'd used an essay mill for one of her assignments. She killed herself — possibly from shame.'

She stopped, suddenly choked with emotion and anger, then forced herself to go on:

'Her former housemate can identify the body from one of the PM photos,' she said. 'The PM report says the dead woman gave birth weeks before she died.'

'Lola—'

'Then there's Yunhee Kim, who disappeared from the university for a number of months and returned with enough money to buy a flat in a trendy complex. I tried to talk to her but she refused. She said she "wasn't allowed".'

She paused to study her boss's face and was pleased to see how sick she looked.

'Lawrie Dixon was director of an IT company in Edinburgh at the same time as Gerald Linklater,' she went on. 'He's the creep who had you come and collect me just now. Linklater has a very intense relationship with the university. He's also a trustee of Dear Green Place and did *not* like me asking questions about Jen and how she's paid.'

Elaine peered up at her, a strange look in her eyes.

'What is it?' she asked.

'A thought, that's all.'

'What?'

'I'll keep it to myself for now.'

Lola shrugged.

'What evidence have you got?' Elaine asked.

'It's all circumstantial, if that's what you're really asking me. For now. Yunhee Kim is the key to this. I need to get her to talk. But I can't do that if I'm off the case. Boss, ACC Thompson is wrong. He's wrong to protect Dixon just because he's his "tsar" or whatever he calls him. Dixon's spun him a line and he's believed it. It's wrong and the ACC is wrong and someone should tell him.'

That strange look was back on Elaine's face . . .

'What is it?' Lola asked her, then she realised. 'Was it ACC Thompson who told you where I was? Linklater contacted him and he "instructed" you to come and take me away?'

'Yes,' Elaine said simply. 'Yes, it was.'

Her boss looked suddenly very pained. She put a hand to her forehead. Lola saw it was shaking.

'Oh God, Lola . . .'

'What?'

She opened her eyes. 'I need to check something.' She scrolled, clicked, then enlarged something on her screen. 'The Chinese student you spoke about a minute ago — when did she die?'

'If it is her — and we only have her old housemate's say-so — then last September.'

'And she gave birth how long before she died?'

'The post-mortem report estimated three to four weeks.'

Elaine had her phone out now and tapped, her mouth set in a grim line.

Lola waited, wondering what on earth she was checking.

She'd found whatever she was looking for and sat staring at the screen, holding her breath. Finally she passed the phone to Lola.

190

Lola looked at the photograph of a man in a dinner jacket, a woman in a kingfisher-green dress beside him, grinning away. It was on a pdf from a glossy magazine that reported on political events.

'ACC Thompson and his wife, Janet.'

'Lee,' Lola said. 'I didn't realise she was . . .'

'Chinese?' Elaine asked. 'She's from Hong Kong. That photo was taken last Christmas at an event at Holyrood Palace, hosted by the first minister. I was there. Look at the caption under the photo.'

'ACC Alec Thompson and his wife Professor Janet Lee Thompson will be spending their first Christmas with their new son, Noah, born in August.'

Lola passed the phone back and the two of them stared at one another.

'We can't leave this, boss,' Lola said. 'We need to find Yunhee Kim and get her to make a statement. And we need to find Jen Crossley.'

Elaine nodded. 'What do we know about her?'

'Very little. But she's being protected — by Linklater, I think. She runs the social and pastoral side of things for Dear Green Place — which gives her direct access to the students — but she's not salaried. She's paid on some kind of "honorarium" through a fund. I asked Prue Carstairs and Gerald Linklater for information just before you came and pulled me out of there.'

Elaine frowned. 'Gerald Linklater is a successful business-man with a number of public appointments,' she said. 'Why on earth would he cover up for this Jen?'

'He might if he had a stake in what she's doing,' Lola said. 'If there was money in it — and power.'

'Power over the young women?'

'Power over the people he and Jen provide children for. Someone's pulling ACC Thompson's strings, boss. No doubt about that.'

Elaine jumped and reached into her jacket. Her phone was buzzing.

'It's him,' she said, looking stricken. 'It's the ACC. Oh hell, Lola. What do I say?'

'Lie to him,' Lola said. 'Tell him you tore a strip off me and sent me home to think about my behaviour.'

Elaine gave her a dark look then nodded.

'Will it be easier if I get out of the car?'

'No!' Elaine said. 'Please stay. Just don't sneeze.'

She pressed answer and put the phone to her ear. 'Hello, sir.'

Lola heard Thompson's voice, but not the words he spoke.

'Yes, I did, sir. Yes. I went there and escorted DCI Harris from the premises and drove her from there to Helen Street . . . Yes, that's right. No, she didn't have anything to say for herself.' She said this while giving Lola a dose of ironic side-eye. 'I instructed her to go home and to return at ten a.m. tomorrow morning to meet with me to discuss her behaviour . . . Yes, sir. I shall look into that. I agree there could be grounds for suspension.' She gave Lola a reassuring shake of her head. 'I agree, sir. I shall visit Prue Carstairs myself tomorrow to apologise for DCI Harris's conduct . . . Yes, sir, I will keep you informed at all times. And I'm sorry it's come to this.'

She came off the phone and let out a long, pained sigh.

Something had occurred to Lola while Elaine was talking to ACC Thompson. Now she peered along the row of cars parked across the road from them.

'What is it?' Elaine asked her.

'One minute,' she said to Elaine, then climbed out and looked along the line of cars parked in front of and behind Elaine's, and at those parked on the other side of Queen Margaret Drive.

'Coast's clear,' she said to Elaine when she got back into the passenger seat.

'Meaning what?' Elaine asked.

'There was a car parked across the road from the university as we came out,' Lola said. 'I got the impression the driver was watching us. I looked over and the driver pulled down the visor and drove off.'

'What kind of car?' Elaine asked darkly.

'A black Mercedes.'

'I see. Did you catch the registration number?'

'It was FS3-something. I think there was an X in it.'

'I know someone who drives a black Mercedes,' Elaine said grimly, eyes on her phone.

'Oh?'

'ACC Thompson.' Elaine had the phone to her ear. 'Hello, Sandra,' she said. 'It's Elaine Walsh here. ACC Thompson sometimes parks at Helen Street. Could you look on the parking log and remind me of the make and model of his car and his registration number? It's okay, he knows I'm asking.' She turned to Lola, stony-faced while she listened. 'Thank you,' she said, a few moments later, then hung up. 'Black Mercedes, registration number FS13 TXN.' She fell silent for several seconds. 'Lola, you were right. I should never have let him pressure me like that earlier.'

'What do we do, boss?'

'We make a plan and we act,' Elaine said. 'And we don't waste any more time.'

CHAPTER NINETEEN

7.35 p.m.

'You trust Anna, don't you?' Elaine asked Lola.

'Absolutely.'

'Do you think she'd help us, even if it means defying the ACC's orders?'

'Without a doubt,' Lola said.

'Then ring her. Tell her to be ready to undertake a number of tasks at short notice.'

Lola called, but from outside Elaine's car, standing on the bridge looking down at the Kelvin. Anna had been about to leave the office for the day but sounded delighted at the prospect of helping.

'I think I know who Anthony is, by the way,' she told Lola now. 'I just got an email back from Tiina's friend in Australia. She found his name *and* address on a return label on a parcel he'd sent Tiina. He's called Anthony Watson-Black and he lives in Cumbernauld. I've already found a couple of results online, including a possible address.'

'Excellent,' Lola said. 'Confirm that address and fast.'

'Will do, boss.'

'Also, try to find Jen Crossley. Possibly lives in Glasgow but could be elsewhere. I'd hoped to get her details from the university but ACC Thompson has effectively stopped all access. I've got a phone number for her but it now seems to be switched off. I'll text you the number in case it helps with a search.'

Back in the car, Elaine was ready with handwritten notes.

'We need to build a picture of evidence so compelling I can take it direct to the chief constable,' Elaine said, 'and get his permission to override the ACC's instructions. First and foremost, we need to talk to the South Korean student. We need her to confirm what she did and who organised everything. I think we should get a statement from Min Tan as well about Chan Wen and the bought essay and the fact she was blackmailed by this Jen person.'

'How can we prove the ACC is mixed up in this?' Lola asked.

'Through Lawrie Dixon, I think,' Elaine said. 'The ACC has been talking to a man I now consider to be a suspect in a network of organised crime. We believe Dixon knows where his son is and that he's hiding him to stop us establishing a DNA link between him and Tiina Valk. You know these people, Lola. Where's Dixon's weak spot?'

'His wife, Marta,' Lola said. 'He tried to keep her a prisoner in her own home, and since Adam's gone missing he's been keeping her drugged. Him and Marta's friend.'

'What friend?'

'A woman he used to work with. Sarah Finnie. Lawrie asked her to befriend Marta when Marta first moved here. She's a prickly character. She told me herself she'd given Marta a sedative. She was round at the flat earlier today.'

'What do we know about Sarah Finnie?'

'Nothing yet,' Lola said.

They watched one another.

'Another name for Anna to look into?' Lola asked.

'I think so,' Elaine said. 'I'll drive us to Yunhee Kim's apartment. You call Anna on the way.'

* * *

7.52 p.m.

But Anna wasn't answering her phone. It would have to wait. Elaine parked in a road round the corner from Yunhee's apartment block, then Lola led the way to the main door. Yunhee's blue Mini was in one of the residents' spaces, so she was probably at home.

'She's on the fifth floor,' Lola said, and pressed the service buzzer. Someone in the building unlocked the door and Lola pushed the way inside.

The lift was already waiting for them and they ascended in grim silence.

The fifth-floor landing was quiet, apart from the sounds of a TV coming from one of the flats.

'Block her access to the fire escape,' Lola whispered to Elaine, then knocked at the door.

They heard nothing for several seconds, then there was the sound of a door opening inside the flat. Lola heard shuffling steps very faintly. The steps came closer to the door.

'Who is it?' an anxious voice called.

'Friends, Yunhee,' Lola said. 'We just want to talk to you.'

Silence.

'You're not in any trouble, but there's a chance you'll be targeted by some pretty nasty criminals and we want to keep you safe. One of those people being Jen Crossley.'

More silence, but Lola sensed she was listening.

'Yunhee, are you there?' she tried, in the kindest voice she could muster.

Lola heard a sniff, then a muffled sob.

'It's okay, Yunhee,' Lola said. 'It's going to be okay.'

A second later, Lola heard a bolt turning, then the door came open.

'My God,' Lola said, unable to help herself when she saw the bruises on Yunhee's face, the swelling round one eye and the blood matted in her hair over one ear. 'My God, Yunhee, what happened to you?'

* * *

8.05 p.m.

Lola made Yunhee go with her into the bathroom, where the lighting was bright. There she inspected the cuts and bruises, though Yunhee seemed embarrassed and unwilling to be fussed.

'I don't want to go to hospital.'

'Then we'll organise for a doctor to see you,' Lola said. 'And we can arrange for you to stay somewhere else for a few nights.'

'No, I'm not leaving here.'

After some gentle argument, Lola relented. She led the way back into the hallway and exchanged worried glances with Elaine. 'I think Marcus or Jonno should stay here,' she said.

'I agree,' Elaine said. 'You phone one of them while I make us tea.'

'There's green tea in the kitchen,' Yunhee said.

Lola called DC Jonno Gillies, who said he would be there in fifteen minutes, then she went into the living room to find Yunhee curled up in a corner of a sofa, a blanket over her.

'One of our constables is on his way,' Lola said. 'He'll stay with you when we leave.'

Yunhee nodded, looking half-resigned, half-grateful.

Lola sat on a footstool and looked about the room. It was long, with floor-to-ceiling windows on one wall. Blinds were pulled halfway down, but Lola glimpsed a section of the Forth and Clyde Canal and people moving on its towpath. Yunhee's

197

furniture was beautiful and expensive-looking and the rugs were thick and luxurious.

'Do you live here alone?' Lola asked, and Yunhee nodded. 'Do you rent it or do you own it?'

'It's mine,' she said. 'Well, I have a mortgage.'

She winced again and put a hand to her bruised temple.

Elaine appeared balancing three cups. She put them on a side table then took one to Yunhee and passed another to Lola. Then she sat in a small armchair and nodded to Lola to ask the questions.

'Who did this to you, Yunhee?' Lola asked gently.

'A man,' she said quietly.

'When did it happen?'

'Not long after you came here.'

'Where did it happen?'

'Outside. In an alley. He followed me and pushed me into the alley and started to beat me. But then two other men were coming up the alley. One of them shouted and he ran off. I ran too. I ran as fast as I could to get back here.' She put a hand to her mouth but failed to contain a volley of sobs.

'Who was the man, Yunhee?'

Her face crumpled in pain and fear. She shook her head — because she didn't know his name, or couldn't bring herself to say? Lola changed tack, but determined to ask again in due course.

'These are cruel people,' Lola said, moving on for now. 'Evil people who treat young women — and children — like utilities. I'm sorry you're in this position. We'll help you, but we need you to help us first. Okay?'

She pulled a face, as if she was wrestling with a difficult choice.

Lola asked steadily, 'How much did they pay you to carry a baby?'

The woman huddled under the blanket closed her eyes.

'I imagine it was a lot,' Lola went on, 'if you were able to put a deposit on this place and that lovely car parked downstairs. It would have to be a lot for you to carry a baby, to break surrogacy laws — and to risk your study visa.'

'Will you take it off me?' Yunhee asked.

'I don't know what will happen,' Lola said.

'They made me promise never to say,' she whispered miserably. 'They made me sign a — a—'

'A non-disclosure agreement?'

'Yes. They said . . . my life "wouldn't be worth living" if I ever told anyone.'

'Why did you do it?'

'For the money! Why do you think?'

'Was it Jen who organised it?'

A tiny but definite nod.

'I know all about it,' Lola said. 'I know all about Jen and Dear Green Place and how it works.'

Yunhee seemed to accept her at her word.

'I've been so frightened,' she said now. 'I knew there was a problem when I saw the news online. I saw that woman from the university had been killed. I thought, *Oh God, she must have found out.* I knew they'd killed her. They said they would, if ever anyone got in their way.'

'Did they? Did they threaten you?'

A nod.

'How did it begin?' Lola asked.

'At an event,' Yunhee said quietly, her eyes reading Lola for a reaction. 'Jen organised it. It was at a church in the West End. A church that's now a bar.' She said the name and Lola nodded to say she recognised it. 'It was for second-year students. A chance to meet potential employers. Jen called it speed-dating but it was less formal than that. You just chatted to people and had nice food. She introduced me to . . . a man.'

'Go on,' Lola encouraged.

'He was a businessman. He had his own company and he employed a lot of people, he said. He had an office in Seoul and his wife was Korean. He was Scottish but he spoke some Korean and we chatted. Jen seemed really pleased we'd made friends. She sat us at a table with another man, an older man, who was very charming and seemed to know all about me. He said he'd heard I was a good student and said I was going to do well in my studies. He suggested the businessman might give me a job and even introduce me to his wife. We went out for dinner the next night.'

'Who did?'

'This man, his wife, Jen, the older man — and me.'

'I see.'

She relayed it all in such a matter-of-fact way, but Lola shuddered at this first-hand account of grooming.

'His wife was so nice,' she said in an incredulous voice. 'We chatted in Korean, then in English so the others could join in. The man, her husband, said he wanted to employ me in some way and asked what I thought of that. I said, yes, I'd love to earn some money. He said he'd be in touch. The next day Jen asked to meet. She told me how much the couple liked me. I said I liked them too. Then she told me the wife couldn't have children and how sad it made them. Jen said it made her upset too. Then she came out with it. She said the couple wanted to pay me to have a baby for them.'

She took a sip of her tea.

'I was like, "Wow, okay, but what exactly are you talking about?" and Jen said they'd pay me — a hundred thousand pounds. She said it wasn't technically legal, but nobody would find out.'

'What was your reaction?' Lola asked.

'I was shocked. I guess I was flattered too. Jen told me how special everyone thought I was.' Her lips curled in a small smile. 'And then I said I wanted a hundred and fifty thousand. They agreed. Can you believe it? Enough to put a good deposit on this place and buy a car — and send twenty thousand pounds to my mum.'

'Why did they pick you?'

'Jen said it was because I was so like the wife. I was from the same place — the same city, even — and we spoke the same and even looked very similar. And it was true. She was older than me but not by much. She said it was very important to the couple that their child was the same mix as them: half Scottish, half Korean. It was important to both of them, and especially to her family, that everyone thought the child was theirs.'

'I see,' Lola said softly, and in her mind she saw Marta Dixon and Ingrid Valk, so similar in appearance . . .

'We had to meet several more times. The couple and Jen and me. Then the couple and me. And then . . .' She lowered her voice to a whisper. 'Him and me. I was given a hormone injection beforehand to help things along.'

'You and he — slept together?'

'Several times in the course of a week. Even when . . .' She cleared her throat and gazed at Lola. There was challenge in her eyes, misery too. 'Even when I didn't want to. Even then.'

'And you became pregnant?'

'Yes.'

'When was this?'

'The baby was conceived in December of my second year. He arrived late August, too early. It was a difficult birth. I was very unwell. That's why I was late registering for my third year.'

'Who knew about this?' Lola asked.

'Jen, her colleague, the man and his wife. A private doctor and a private nurse. That was all.'

'The doctor and the nurse — where did you see them?'

'There's a clinic next door to Dear Green Place. It's very exclusive.'

Lola recalled seeing it in Queen's Crescent.

'You moved out of your shared accommodation in April?'

'Yes. I'm only small but I was beginning to show. Jen told me to inform people I was moving in with a boyfriend, called Ewan. I changed my next-of-kin contact details to his on the system. But Ewan never existed. It was a phone Jen kept. I moved to a house Jen owns.'

'Oh? Where was that?'

'Cardonald,' she said.

Cardonald, where they'd traced the van to . . .

'Do you remember the address?'

'No. I was tracking our journey on my phone, but Jen saw and asked me to put it away.'

'What was it like, Jen's house?'

She shrugged. 'Ordinary. Big, though. Not connected to any other houses. A big garden.' Her expression changed. 'I remember the number of the house,' she said. 'It was number twenty-eight.'

'And how long were you there?'

'Till the birth. They came for the boy the next day. The doctor made up a birth certificate to say the wife had given birth herself. They were so grateful. So very grateful.' She stopped and wiped a tear on a sleeve of her black top.

'And you got your money?'

'Yes.'

'Do you know the names of the couple who took your baby?'

'She was Sun Hee. His name is Carl — with a C, I think, but it may be a K. I don't know their surname.'

'Where did they live?'

'I don't know that either. I think—' she frowned — 'I think he's an engineer. She might be a lawyer.'

Her gaze dropped and she looked suddenly very young. Tears were welling in her eyes when she looked wretchedly up at Lola again and asked, 'Do you think there's a way I'd ever get him back?'

Lola glanced at Elaine, who gave her a dismal look in return.

'I don't know the answer,' Lola said. 'I'm sorry.'

She nodded sadly, seeming to accept the fact.

'You're still in touch with Jen, aren't you?'

'Not really. But when I saw the news, I sent her a message. She told me not to contact her again. But then you came here earlier and I panicked, so I went to the university. I spoke to someone and then left, but he followed me and two streets away he jumped on me and did *this*.' She touched her temple again and winced in pain.

'The man who attacked you works at the university?' Lola asked. She glanced briefly at Elaine, who was listening, hawklike.

She nodded.

'He's the one who finds all the information about foreign students for Jen,' she said. 'He makes sure everything's right on the university system.'

'What's his name, Yunhee?' Lola asked, ready for it.

'Danny,' Yunhee said. 'Danny McDougall. His boss is the lady who was killed.'

CHAPTER TWENTY

9.07 p.m.

Jonno arrived a few minutes after Yunhee's disclosure. Lola told him what he needed to know then introduced the two of them. As soon as they were out of Yunhee's apartment building, Elaine called an Edinburgh number and asked to speak to the chief constable as a matter of urgency.

Lola saw a message from Anna on her own phone, asking her to call.

'One minute,' Anna said. Lola heard a door open and close. Anna said, in a quieter voice this time, 'I'm with Tiina's friend Anthony Watson-Black at his home in Cumbernauld. He's in bits, boss, and ready to talk.'

'Did you go there alone?' Lola asked.

'Kirstie's with me.' She cleared her throat. 'I'm sorry, but I told her what was going on and she insisted on helping. Boss, I think you should hear what Anthony's got to tell us. Can you come?'

Lola turned to see Elaine had come off her call.

'Text me the address,' she said. 'I'll be there as soon as I can.'

She hung up.

Elaine said, 'The chief constable's at a dinner. Someone's going to get hold of him for me.'

She was breathing hard and Lola realised she'd never known her this tense, this nervous. Lola told her Anna was with Tiina Valk's friend.

'I'll come with you,' Elaine said. 'I'll stay in the car, though. That way I can speak to the chief constable when he calls.'

'Want me to drive?' Lola asked.

'Please,' Elaine said, and handed over her key.

It was as they were joining the M80 towards Stirling, possibly because her racing mind was calmed by driving, that Lola remembered something Yunhee had said about the couple who'd bought her baby: the fact she hadn't known how the man had spelled his name, whether it was Carl with a C or a K — and a split-second later she had a memory of Marta Dixon at the safe house, stumbling over her words and seeming inordinately embarrassed for doing so, flushing red.

'Sarah Finnie,' she said aloud, her heart racing. 'Her again!'

'What do you mean?' Elaine asked.

'Look up Sarah Finnie, would you, boss? Try to find a photograph. She told me she has a property sales company.'

Elaine began tapping at her phone.

'Sarah Finnie, Crescent Properties,' Elaine read off her phone. 'Registered address of the company is . . . in Cardonald.'

Lola's hands tightened on the steering wheel.

'I'll just look on the Companies House website,' Elaine said, and tapped away some more. A minute later, she said, 'Yes, the company director is Sarah Genevieve Finnie—'

'Gen!'

'And here's a photo,' Elaine said. 'Do you want to stop and look at it?'

Heart battering in her chest and mouth dry, Lola indicated and pulled into the hard shoulder. She put on the car's hazard lights and took Elaine's phone from her.

'That's her,' Lola said. 'Can you send that photo to Yunhee? Ask her if that's Jen Crossley.'

Lola drove on, the world around her seeming clearer but darker too.

A minute after Elaine sent her text, Yunhee replied.

Elaine read: '*Yes, that's Jen.*'

'Bingo,' Lola said. 'I should have known. I should have suspected when I first met her at Jeanie Quigley's. She was so different from Marta and yet claimed to be her friend. She spun a good tale, though, about having known Dixon and how he'd asked her to take Marta shopping as she had so few friends here. But then at the safe house today, Marta made a mistake. She called her Jen. She corrected herself quickly, as though she'd meant to say "genuinely". I thought her phrasing was odd at the time. She was mortified by her mistake and went bright red. Sarah — or Jen — was annoyed too, I could tell.'

She looked at the GPS map and saw she had to turn off in three-quarters of a mile.

'Someone's calling me,' Elaine said, eyes on her phone. 'It could be the chief constable.'

She answered. 'It's Superintendent Elaine Walsh, speaking . . . Yes, hello, sir. Thank you for calling me . . . Yes, it is extremely urgent.'

***

9.35 p.m.

By the time they were parked outside Anthony Watson-Black's small house in a quiet cul-de-sac in Cumbernauld, Elaine had received permission — of a kind — to continue investigating.

'Say nothing to ACC Thompson,' the chief constable had instructed her. 'Collect evidence. Call me again when you have it and I will decide what to do.'

Anna opened the door for them and directed them into a small living room. Anthony Watson-Black, his face drawn and sickly pale, stood to meet them.

'Anthony,' Anna said after Lola had introduced herself and Elaine, 'can you tell my colleagues what you told me?'

The young man retook his place on his black leather settee. He hugged himself and recounted his story:

'I knew Tiina Valk from when I worked in Australia,' he said. 'We worked for the same company and became friends. Then I moved back here and started a web design business and we didn't keep in touch. One day about six weeks ago, Tiina contacted me, saying she was very worried about her sister Ingrid, who seemed to have gone missing here in Glasgow. She was particularly worried because just before she vanished, Ingrid told Tiina she was having a baby as a surrogate — and that she was being paid a lot of money to do it, even though that was illegal. She asked me to try to find Ingrid, but I failed. Tiina told me she was going to come to Scotland herself, via Tallinn. She arrived and stayed here at first, then she rented a place for a few weeks in Dennistoun.

'I owed Tiina a lot,' he went on. 'She helped me when I lost my job in Sydney. So I was pleased to help her when she came here.' He looked miserably at Anna, as if appealing for her to tell the story rather than him.

'Tiina was very good at computers,' Anna said. 'She managed to trace Jen Crossley and realised that she was running some kind of scheme, with help from the university. She found out Lawrie Dixon and his wife had paid Jen for Ingrid's baby — and she got evidence of a text conversation between Jen and Lawrie Dixon, in which Jen warned Lawrie that Ingrid had decided to keep her baby. Jen said she was going to deal with Ingrid.'

'Which she did,' Lola said darkly, remembering the post-mortem report on that unidentified woman found at Lancaster and the details of how she'd died.

'Tiina was heartbroken and very angry,' Anna went on. 'She vowed revenge on Jen, but first she wanted to get Ingrid's baby back.'

'What was she planning to do with him?' Lola asked the young man.

'Take him to Estonia,' Anthony said, dismal-eyed. 'She said she'd bring him up herself.'

'And so Tiina and Anthony made a plan,' Anna said. 'Tiina spent days scoping out the house in Giffnock. Except Marta saw her and panicked and told her husband. He improved security at the house. So Tiina decided to take another tack.' She looked at Anthony, inviting him to tell what had happened next.

'Tiina spoke to Marta herself,' Anthony said. 'She told her who she was and what she believed Jen had done to Ingrid.'

'When?' Lola asked.

'The day before she took Adam,' he said.

Lola stared.

'She rang the intercom on the gate and said she was the sister of the woman whose baby Marta and her husband had taken — and Marta came out to talk to her. She was horrified when Tiina told her she believed Ingrid was dead. She told Marta she could go to prison and Marta broke down. She told Tiina she loved Adam but didn't love her husband, who was cruel. She knew he only wanted Adam for the inheritance that would one day be his. So Tiina pretended to make her a promise: that if Tiina could take Adam back, then Marta could see him whenever she wanted. That they could even bring him up together, in Tallinn. So Marta agreed to help Tiina. She gave Tiina the code to unlock one of the doors and she turned off the burglar alarm. She also warned her that Adam wore a tag.'

'What sort of tag?'

'So they could find him if he ever went missing — or was taken. It was locked onto one of his ankles, like they do to people who are under bail conditions, I expect. Marta said they'd need to get it off him somehow.'

'I see,' Lola said. 'And you helped Tiina?'

'I had the car, you see? But I went to Dixon's office the evening before, to warn him we were going to take the kid back and find out what had happened to Ingrid. I'm not really sure why I did it. I think I wanted to give him a chance to own up to what he'd done. But he wasn't having it, so I left. I realise now I shouldn't have done it — I'd warned them, you see. It meant they were on their guard. I — I didn't tell Tiina I'd done that.' He closed his eyes, wincing with regret. 'Later that night, I drove Tiina to Giffnock. I went with her into the woods at the back of the house, then sat with the car in the next street, ready to drive. She'd got a fake gun — a replica Beretta, I think. She'd tried to get a real one but couldn't. Apparently it's pretty hard to get a gun.' He made a sheepish face. 'Then, when I was waiting, a woman opened the passenger door and got in beside me. I'd seen a van pass by and park behind me, but I never thought it was someone coming for me. She had a gun and this one was real. She opened the cartridge and showed me the bullets. She told me to drive away from there, and I panicked and did what she wanted. She kept the gun against my ribs, here—' he pointed to his left side — 'and she made me drive at least a mile. Then she made me get out of the car and took my keys and my phone. She drove away and I was left standing there.

'I panicked. I started to run back to Giffnock, except I didn't know where I was. And then—' another sheepish look — 'I stole a bike. A man was riding it and I flagged him down. He was older and I threatened him and he just let me take it. I'm not proud of myself, but I was desperate.

'I found my way back to the house and I could see people were awake. Lights were on. More than an hour had passed. I rode around, trying to see if I could see Tiina. In the end I gave up. I've got a friend who lives in Shawlands. I woke him up. I asked to use his iPad so I could look at the news — and then I saw something on social media — news that a woman had been found dead at Darnley Glen. I looked at a map and saw how close it was to Giffnock. I rode there on the bike to try and find out what had happened. Oh God . . .'

He gasped and covered his face with both hands.

'The photo,' Lola said quietly to Elaine.

Elaine went into her phone, tapped a couple of times, then passed it to Lola.

'Anthony,' she said, holding the phone out. 'Is this the woman who got in the car with you?'

He took the phone and his eyes widened.

'Yes,' he said grimly. 'That's her.'

Anna said, 'Anthony has already agreed to make a statement in relation to all of this. DC Campbell will take it down now.'

'Thank you, Anthony,' Lola said.

She got up and turned to Elaine. 'Ready?' she asked her.

* * *

10.22 p.m.

'What do you want?' Lawrence Dixon barked when he saw who was on his doorstep.

'To talk to your wife,' Lola said, pushing past him.

He stood aside and DC Marcus McVittie came into the flat too. Elaine had called him while Lola drove. She was currently in the car, filling in the chief constable. Anna had gone with Kirstie to Sarah Finnie's address in Cardonald, while DS Aidan Pierce had gone with a uniformed officer to arrest Danny McDougall.

'You can't,' he said, with the touch of a sneer. 'She's asleep.'

'Drugged again?' Lola asked.

'No!'

'Sarah Finnie not here tonight?' she asked.

He shook his head, but looked wary.

'Or should I call her Jen?' Lola added mildly.

'What?' His eyes went like saucers and his jaw trembled. 'What are you—?'

'We know, Mr Dixon,' Lola said. 'We know about Jen, about Danny McDougall. About your friendship with Alec Thompson. And we know what happened to Ingrid and Tiina Valk. In time we'll find out what happened to Wendy Baker as well. The game's over, sir — and you're under arrest.'

Marcus came forward and Lawrie Dixon's shoulders slumped.

Marcus read him his rights and took him out of the flat. Lola hunted for Marta, expecting to find her comatose in one of the bedrooms or even the living room.

But Marta Dixon was nowhere to be found.

Back downstairs, Lola rejoined Elaine in the car.

'The chief constable will suspend ACC Thompson tonight,' Elaine said. 'He's calling him now. I saw DC McVittie emerging with Lawrie Dixon just now. What about the wife?'

'No sign, boss.'

'Any word from Anna or DS Pierce?'

Lola looked at her phone. 'Not yet.'

'I'll drive us to Helen Street, shall I?' Elaine asked now.

'I think so, boss. It's going to be a long night.'

CHAPTER TWENTY-ONE

Saturday 1 November
1.09 a.m.

Lawrie Dixon was in a cell at Helen Street. Danny McDougall was in another, awaiting the arrival of a duty solicitor.

'McDougall was loading up his car when we arrived,' Kirstie had reported. 'He burst into tears when he saw us.'

Anna and Marcus had found no one at home at Sarah Finnie's address in Cardonald.

'It's a big old place with a huge garden,' Anna said now. She and Lola were in the canteen with coffee and KitKats. 'Trees everywhere and very private. We had a look in the windows but couldn't see anyone. There was a gap in the door to the garage, though. Marcus shone his torch through and there's a van in there. Marcus reckons it's the one he tracked on CCTV. Obviously we'll need a warrant to search it.'

Jonno appeared through the canteen doorway.

'Dixon's solicitor says his client is refusing to speak — including to him. Going by the look on the bloke's face, I reckon he's had quite enough of him.'

'What do you want to do?' Anna asked Lola. 'We haven't got enough to charge him yet, have we?'

'Hold him,' Lola said. 'By mid-morning we'll have warrants to search the Dixons' place and to access his devices. Shouldn't take long to find something.'

Kirstie came into the canteen now, carrying her laptop. Even she, who seemed to have boundless energy, looked weary. She spotted Lola and Anna and came over.

'What is it?' Lola asked.

'A photo of Sarah Finnie,' Kirstie said. 'I found it online.'

'We know what she looks like,' Lola said drily. 'That's not the problem.'

'All the same, boss, I think you'll want to see it. It's who she's with.'

She set down her laptop, opened the screen and put in her password, then brightened it.

Lola and Anna flanked her, looking at the image of a fancily dressed pair at a high-society event. Sarah Finnie looked glamorous and self-possessed in a wine-red dress. The photo must have been from a few years ago, though, because she looked younger and her hair was long. Next to her was a small, older man in a dinner jacket and with voluminous white hair, smiling a dead-eyed, thin-lipped smile. Lola stared for several amazed seconds before lowering her gaze to read the caption:

Gerald Linklater, MBE, with his daughter Genevieve

* * *

2.21 a.m.

There was little point in bringing in Linklater during the night. They'd get him in the morning and, somehow, manage simultaneous interviews with him, his daughter, Danny McDougall and Lawrie Dixon. It might work in their favour if they choreographed the extraction of information well, and let it be known to the other interviewees that their conspiracy was coming apart at the seams.

Lola got home, ate a couple of Ryvita, then took a shower before finally crawling into bed and checking her phone one last time.

She and Sandy had exchanged texts during the evening, and she'd broken the news that she may not be leaving Police Scotland *quite* as quickly as she'd thought. He might need to wait a while longer before they worked together.

He was still awake now and had texted to check she was home safe.

I am. How are feeling about tomorrow?

Nervous as hell, if I'm honest, he replied. *What if we don't get on?*

Only one way to find out, Lola texted back.

I wish you were coming, he wrote, *but I understand why you aren't.*

She sighed to herself. *Where did you decide to meet?*

The café at the Rural Life museum in East Kilbride at 5 p.m., he replied.

You'll be fine, she typed. *You'll handle it. Come round here for your dinner after if you like. Now — I have to sleep.* x

She was sound asleep when her phone buzzed again. She reached for it, and saw someone was ringing — from a mobile number she didn't recognise. She stared at the number, then at the time — it was past 3 a.m. — then answered.

'Hello?' she answered.

'Hello?' a quiet voice said. 'Is that . . . DCI Harris?'

'Speaking,' Lola said, sitting up now and turning on her bedside lamp. 'Marta, is that you?'

'Help me,' she whispered now, making Lola's skin come out in goosebumps.

'Marta, where are you?'

'Help me, *please.*'

'Tell me where you are.'

'I came to get Adam,' she said. 'I had an idea I'd collect him and take him to Estonia in the morning . . . but then—'

'Where's Adam?' Lola tried, now standing and considering her sleep-heavy face in the wardrobe's mirrored door.

'At Gerald's house,' she said, still whispering.

'Gerald Linklater? And are you there too?'

Shit. They should have gone to get him tonight.

'I'm at the top of the house. It's the only place I can get a signal. I think they know I'm here. Oh God . . .' Her voice shook. 'They'll kill me.'

'What's the address?' she asked.

'It's in Milngavie,' Marta said. 'The Old Manor on West Lane, near the reservoir, but it isn't easy to find. You have to go round a bend and find the entrance to the driveway in the bushes.'

'Where exactly are you in the house, Marta?' she asked.

'In the attic,' she whispered. 'Adam's in one of the bedrooms, though they keep moving him. I can see the tag on my phone, but the doors are all locked.'

'Stay where you are,' Lola said. 'We'll come and get you — you and Adam. Don't move from where you are, do you understand me?'

She cut the call, found the address on the map on her phone and then called Control.

'It's DCI Lola Harris,' she said. 'There's a mother and child in danger at The Old Manor on West Lane in Milngavie. I'm heading there now, but from the Southside. I'll need back-up — including firearms. Can you seek authorisation from whoever's on call just now?'

Next she rang Anna, praying her phone wasn't on silent. But it was. She checked to see if she had a landline number for her but didn't.

Shit.

She threw on clothes and was out of the house and in her car in three minutes. Anna and her husband had a villa in Dumbreck, only a mile from Lola's house in Pollokshields. Lola found it no problem, having been there a few times before, and rang the doorbell.

Anna's husband Nick came to the door a minute later, wide-eyed with alarm, then he recognised Lola.

'I'm sorry, Nick,' she said. 'I need Anna to come with me.'

He gave her a look that suggested he doubted her sanity, then disappeared back into the house. Lola heard voices, then a minute later Anna was flying down the stairs, still pulling on a top.

'Marta's at Linklater's place in Milngavie,' Lola told her. 'Adam's being held there. She'd hiding in the attic, terrified. I've called for back-up to meet us.'

Anna nodded and was in the passenger seat of Lola's Audi in a flash.

* * *

3.42 a.m.

Milngavie was at the very extent of Glasgow's north-western suburbs. It wasn't the easiest place to reach quickly from the Southside, and every set of traffic lights seemed to be against them. By the time they were passing Anniesland, Anna was talking to Control again. She came off a moment later.

'We've got authorisation for a covert armed response,' Anna said.

Lola didn't reply, just drove.

Anna looked at her phone. 'My message hasn't reached Marta,' she said. 'It says "undelivered".'

'She said the signal was bad unless she was at the top of the house.'

Anna followed the GPS on her phone, cursing when it tried to make them drive through a barricaded building site. They lost minutes but eventually found the place: a pillared gateway half-hidden by dense foliage.

Lola found a place to park a little further along the lane.

Anna's phone rang. It was Control again, confirming a sergeant and two constables were on their way. The ARV would be with them shortly.

216

'Thanks,' Anna said, adding, 'I'll send you Google map coordinates to pass on to them. This place isn't the easiest to get to.'

She sent a message then turned to Lola. 'Do we wait till they arrive?'

'That would be the sensible thing,' Lola murmured in the darkness of the car. She went into her phone and dialled the number Marta had called from, but it went to voicemail. 'I might take a peek at the house,' she said and got out.

Anna got out too.

Lola led the way back to the pillared gateposts, glad of light from the half-moon, but also glad it was shaded somewhat by a layer of high clouds. There were no gates between the gateposts, just a gaping blackness. She used her phone's torch to see a few metres along the driveway and made out a sinister tunnel made by overarching trees.

'You stay here,' she said to Anna. 'Keep an eye out for back-up.'

'Boss, don't you think—'

'I just want to get a look at the house, try to get some bearings. You stay here.'

The driveway seemed endless, curving between monstrous rhododendrons. The moonlight didn't break through the vegetation, so she used her phone torch to light her way. At last the rhododendrons parted and the house stood before her across a lawn the size of a field, a Victorian Gothic pile, all towers and windows that reflected the thin moonlight like dying eyes.

The house had at least three floors, including the attic from which Marta had called her, and possibly a basement too. There was a main doorway and a door to the side. How many bedrooms? Several, possibly. The kind of house that had once accommodated an extended family and servants. She wondered whereabouts Marta was now. Marta and her baby.

Except Adam wasn't her baby. He was Ingrid's.

She was about to turn and go back along the drive to join Anna and wait for their back-up, when a light went on at the side of the house. A door opened and a figure stood there, looking out. A woman, Lola thought. Marta? It could be.

The figure came out of the house and started towards an outbuilding to the left. The moonlight showed it was indeed Marta. Lola ran, then called, 'Marta, stop!' in a sharp whisper.

The figure halted and the head turned.

'It's DCI Harris.'

Marta froze and Lola saw her mouth working silently.

'Help me,' Marta managed.

'I will,' Lola said. 'But you need to come with me. I've a colleague waiting and a car.'

'Not without Adam,' Marta said. And then she lifted her hands. Lola saw what she carried in one of them and went ice cold.

'Give me the knife, Marta,' she said.

'I can't.' Marta stepped back and thrust the knife behind her back. 'I have to protect myself. I have to protect Adam. They'll try to hurt me. They'll hurt him too.'

'Marta, listen to me,' Lola said, stepping forward. 'You're safe if you come with me. But drop the knife.'

'No!'

Lola looked at the screen of her phone to call Anna, but there was no signal. *Damn it.*

'Marta, give me your hand. Give it to me. We'll walk down the drive to my car. You'll be safe then.'

'But I can't find him and he's somewhere!'

'More officers are coming,' Lola said, stepping forward and reaching for Marta's frail wrist. 'They'll find Adam for you.'

'You don't understand,' Marta said in a wretched whine. 'I killed her, and I stabbed him too. Now I've got to get Adam and get away before the others find out.'

Lola asked, as calmly as she could, 'Who did you kill, Marta?'

'The nurse. The woman they had looking after him. And then,' she added in a quiet, happy voice, 'I killed the old man too.'

'Gerald Linklater?'

Lola made out her nod in the gloom.

'It's his house, you see. I hid until I thought it was safe and I went to the nursery. They hadn't even locked the door. I went in. Adam wasn't there but the nurse was. She was going to give me away. She started to scream, so I had to kill her. Then I went to find Adam. I knew he was somewhere because I could hear him crying when I was in the attic. I went into different rooms and then Gerald was there, coming along the landing. I ran at him.' She let out a little giggle, then her tone darkened. 'He didn't stand a chance. But she's in there still. And there's another man too. One I don't know.'

'Who do you mean by "she"?'

'Sarah,' she said. 'My so-called friend.'

'Give me the knife, Marta.'

'No!'

'Where were you going just now?'

'There,' she said, and used the blade to point at the out-buildings. 'It's a cottage. He must be there.'

'Then we'll look there first,' Lola said soothingly.

Marta smiled, pleased.

Lola took her chance and lunged, grabbing for the wrist above the hand that held the blade and twisting it.

But Marta was stronger than she looked and wrenched away, yelping — then she froze as the sound of a crying child came from the main house. Marta turned, eyes reflecting moonlight as she gazed up.

She pulled free of Lola's grip and took off towards the house. Lola caught her left shoulder but Marta spun round, blade out, and lunged hard.

Lola felt an electric jolt in her shoulder and recoiled. She staggered back, but her attacker was already gone, arms flailing as she returned to the house and the light of the open door.

Lola scrambled for her phone but there was still no signal. From the house, the child's cries sounded louder now. Another light had gone on, this on the first floor.

She panted, hand clamped to her shoulder which burned now. She became dizzy, trying to think. How long would it take to return to Anna? Three, four minutes?

Wetness oozed between her fingers over the wound. From the house the cries intensified.

Marta had claimed she'd killed two people. She'd said there were others in there. Now she was in there with a knife, hunting for a child she believed was hers. She could hurt the child, herself too.

Back-up was due any moment. When Lola didn't return to the road, Anna would know to come in, wouldn't she?

There was nothing for it. She had to follow Marta into the dark house.

* * *

4.03 a.m.

The door led into a pantry that adjoined a large, old-fashioned kitchen. Another door led from the kitchen into a passage. Lola turned the light on, knowing the time had passed for creeping about, and went along the passage to where it emerged in a hallway beside a grand staircase.

She peered up and saw the balconied landings of two floors above. The child's cries seemed muted now, but they came from somewhere upstairs. Lola steeled her nerve and climbed the stairs, taking a left turn where the staircase split. She stopped again and listened. The cries were a little louder and coming from somewhere on this floor. And now there was a new sound, a keening singing. Marta singing a lullaby? Had she found the child?

While she listened, the crying and singing stopped and silence took over the house. The pain in her shoulder intensified, making her wince and want to cry out. Biting her lip, she craned her neck to see her shoulder. Her jacket was ripped and soaked in red. She eased it off her shoulder, then lifted the edge of her top, gasping at the sight of the wound, which was red and raw and bleeding. She looked away, squeezed her eyes shut and took deep shuddering breaths.

A new sound came from higher up in the house. Slow footsteps that made floorboards squeak.

Lola remembered Marta had called her from the attic, where she'd had a signal. If Lola could get up there, she could text Anna and tell her she was inside the house — and to call for paramedics, not just for anyone who'd been at the wrong end of Marta's blade, but for her too.

But how could she get up there? And how much time might that cost? Sarah Finnie, aka Jen, was somewhere here, though possibly sleeping. There was a man too, Marta had said. One she didn't know. Who?

The crying began again, a high wail of protest.

It came from a room down a passage to Lola's left. Above her, the floorboards creaked again. Someone was moving along the top landing. If she peered up she might see that person, but something stopped her: a deep dread.

Hand still clamped to her burning wet shoulder, she ducked into the passage and followed it to the right — then stopped dead when she saw the prone form of Gerald Linklater blocking the way. He was in gold pyjamas, his feet bare and his white hair matted with blood. Blood had spread on the wood floor behind his head and his eyes stared lifelessly at the ceiling. The crying came from up ahead, possibly from behind a door at the far end of the passage. Lola stepped over the body, groaning as fresh pain flared in her shoulder.

She arrived at the door, then paused, uncertain of her next move.

Marta's soft singing started up: a tune Lola didn't recognise, and words that weren't English.

221

She lifted her hand from her burning shoulder and tried the handle. But the door was locked. She rapped on a panel and the singing stopped. Lola listened.

'Marta,' she said quietly, mouth close to the door, 'it's DCI Harris. Let me in so I can help you.'

Silence for what seemed like an age. Then she heard something from behind her, back along the passage, beyond Linklater's corpse. A door softly closing?

'Marta, we have to get out of here,' she hissed. 'Come on, open up. Let me in and I'll help you. I'll help you get away.'

The singing began again, plaintively now. The baby's crying had ceased.

She shouldn't have entered the house, she knew now. She should have returned to the car and to Anna, and to help. Now she was trapped at the end of this passage with a woman who was deeply unwell, singing to a stolen infant behind a locked door, while a dead man lay sprawled behind her.

And there was someone else in the house. More than one person probably.

She reached for her phone — and saw there was a signal. Her heart leaped at the sight of that single bar. Notifications for missed calls appeared, three of them, each from Anna. And two text messages:

Boss, where are you?

Back-up is here. We're coming in.

She began to type a reply, to say she was in the house, when she heard a key turn in the lock. She froze and waited as the door was drawn slowly open. Marta's pale, thin face poked through the gap. She peered at Lola with oddly unfocused eyes.

'Marta, let me in,' Lola said, and Marta moved back so Lola could push the door wider.

Marta stood aside, head drooping as Lola took in the room. It was a nursery, old-fashioned and gloomy. In the middle of the room was a wooden cot. A baby lay wriggling in it, under an old tin mobile that turned and glinted. Against a wall lay a woman's body, sprawled and surely dead. The nurse Marta had mentioned.

'Help me . . .' a voice groaned from a corner half-hidden by the door.

Lola turned, her shoulder sparking pain again, and saw Sarah Finnie slumped in a corner of the room, her face bone-white in its frame of red curls. She clutched her abdomen with both hands, hands that were as white as her face but stained dark red with the blood that ran from her.

'Marta, did you do this?' Lola asked.

Marta peered up at her, head still bowed. She nodded.

'Where's the knife?' she asked.

Marta turned her head to the left and nodded. Lola moved and saw the blade glinting on the floor.

Pain bloomed bigger, making Lola gasp aloud. She fought dizziness and reached for her phone with her bloody hand. The single bar was still there. She pressed on Anna's name and held the phone to her ear. Her own blood smelled so ripe, her head swam.

'Anna, I'm in the house,' she said, though her own voice sounded odd, and far away. 'Call ambulances. There are deaths and — and a woman who's been stabbed. I'm injured too.'

'We're coming in, boss.'

'I'm with Marta and the baby. There's someone else in the house. Take great care.'

She pulled the phone from her ear.

A grimly familiar voice came through the doorway behind her: 'Who were you talking to, DCI Harris?'

Lola turned, unsteady on her feet now. 'ACC Thompson,' she said, wincing with pain. She heard Marta whimper behind her.

There he stood, one of the most senior officers in the police force, in jeans and a shirt, the same dead-eyed expression on his face he'd worn in Elaine's office.

223

He came into the room, closed the door behind him and turned the key in the lock.

'Alec,' Finnie pleaded. Thompson looked at her then away, unmoved.

His beady eyes seemed to spot the dead nurse.

'Dear, oh dear,' he murmured. 'Was this your doing, young lady?' he asked Marta.

But Marta had retreated across the room and was crouching with her back turned.

The knife. She's going for the knife.

But when Lola tried to speak, the words wouldn't come out.

'What are you doing?' Thompson demanded of the young woman, then Marta rose and he saw the blade in her hand. 'Oh dear.'

Lola's thoughts swam in a sea of pain. Her mouth was dry and she knew she couldn't stand for much longer.

'I really don't think so,' Thompson said smoothly.

He reached into a back pocket and drew out a pistol. Lola recognised it as a Beretta. He lifted it and pointed — at which Marta let out a yelp and dropped the knife so that it clattered.

'You,' Thompson said to Lola. 'Move back. That's right. Over there.'

Lola moved near to a wall and put out a hand to steady herself.

From the floor, Sarah Finnie let out another groan of pain. Lola's legs seemed to soften. They buckled and she sank to a crouch then put out her legs so she lay resting against the wall.

Thompson bent for the blade. He went to a window then lay the knife on the sill while he tugged up the sash, then he picked up the knife and dropped it from the window. He let the sash drop back into place.

'That's better,' he said in sing-song voice. Then his tone changed. 'But what to do with you two?' he asked, looking from Lola to Marta. 'And what to do with that brat?' He nodded to the cot, where the baby was grizzling.

'He's my baby,' Marta whined.

Thompson eyed her, mock pity in his gaze. 'Then take him and be gone,' he said. 'But remember, Mrs Dixon, you've killed people tonight. You can't get far.'

Marta went to the cot and reached into it for the baby. She lifted him and held him against her. Some of the blood from her hands stained his little outfit. She went to the door and turned the key, then stepped out and was gone.

Thompson went to the door and kicked it shut after her.

'And now it's just us,' he said to Lola. 'Oh, but don't worry about her.' He waved the gun towards Sarah Finnie. 'I doubt she'll last long.'

The pain in Lola's shoulder was different now. No longer burning, but cold and throbbing. Her shoulder and arm were heavy. There was blood all down her left side. Unconsciousness couldn't be far away. There was something appealing about giving in to oblivion. But then . . . But then Thompson would have won.

So, willing her strength to last, she focused on her thighs and made them tense — enough to slide her up the wall, to a half-standing position.

'Really, DCI Harris,' Thompson sneered. 'I don't think I've ever seen such a pitiable sight in all my years in policing.'

'Is that right?' Lola managed.

'You came here without back-up. You entered a house. You got yourself injured — and for what?'

'To stop you,' she said.

'But you won't,' he said. 'You can't. While you're a failed detective, complicit in your own sorry demise, I'm a senior policeman, celebrated for my career achievements, and leading the Force to new heights in the modern age — sorry, what did you say?'

'*Fantasist*,' Lola gasped, her breathing hurting as much as her shoulder now. 'I said you're — a fantasist.' She paused to fill her lungs, squeezed her eyes shut at another deep throb of pain. 'You're corrupt. You — you exploit women. You

225

sell babies. You kill the women who fight back.' She stopped to breathe more painful air, trying not to cry out, aware of nausea rising.

He didn't speak, just stared at her, sneering as if she was something to be reviled.

'But now,' Lola managed, 'your career will be over.'

'Will it?' He sounded amused as well as sceptical.

'People know,' she said. 'The chief constable knows. He's going to suspend you.'

'So that's why he called . . .' Thompson mused. 'Good job I didn't pick up.'

'There are other officers on their way,' she said, pushing herself further upright, so she was almost standing again. 'They know too.'

'Is that so?' he sneered, but she could see from the way his eyes darted that her words had bothered him.

'How will you explain this?' she asked. 'Two dead bodies, a dying woman.' She gestured to Sarah Finnie, who had begun to wilt to one side, her head hanging.

'Marta Dixon did it,' he said. 'She lost her mind. She stabbed people, including you and then . . .' He lifted the gun. 'And then she found Linklater's gun—' he smiled and lifted the weapon so it pointed Lola's way — 'and shot you with it. I was nowhere to be found when officers got here.'

He smirked, enjoying the power the weapon gave him.

'Why?' Lola asked, wincing again, fearing she might faint at any moment. 'Why did you involve yourself in . . . in *this*?'

He tilted his head, seeming to give it some thought. 'Power,' he said at last. 'The idea I was trusted and respected, and at the same time . . . running an enterprise.' He smiled. 'I've always admired gangsters, you know. Not your Glasgow ones. The Italians. The Americans. The ones who are businessmen at heart. The ones whole cities *fear*. It was Sarah who convinced me, and her father. They showed me how it could be done, how you could hide behind a smokescreen of "good work", of trusted institutions. They helped Janet and me find our son and to buy a stake in something bigger. A web that connected *everything*.'

'And the women who had the babies? Ingrid, who . . . who wanted hers back?'

'Easily dealt with,' he said. 'Sarah collected her in her car and said they were going to meet the Dixons to discuss taking Adam back. Then she and her young friend Daniel *fixed* the problem.'

'It was you who was advising Dixon throughout the night, wasn't it?' Lola managed. 'His "police friend".'

He didn't reply and she knew she was right.

She spoke again but struggled to get the words out. The pain was immense now.

'What did you say?' he asked.

'I said . . .' Lola said with strain. 'I said, *you're evil.*'

From somewhere below them, there was a low sound, like a door closing.

'Possibly,' Thompson said, and his lips curled into a cat's satisfied smile.

Another sound: a woman's voice raised in panic, then the cry of a child.

Thompson was immediately alert.

The woman's voice — Marta's, it must be — came again. Then she shrieked as if she was fighting someone off.

Anna and the officers. Lola felt the strength leave her legs. She allowed herself to slide back down the wall, until she was slumped like Sarah Finnie. She concentrated on breathing, and willed herself to stay conscious though the pain was now intense, a black hole that grew and threatened to consume her.

'Shit,' she heard Thompson mutter, then he was across the room and struggling with the sash. He put his gun on the sill while he pulled it up, but then it wouldn't stay up.

More voices from below: Marta again, and a man's voice. Marta screamed out. The baby was crying again.

Thompson was sitting on the sill, keeping the pane up with one shoulder.

Suddenly there were running feet outside the nursery. Then the door crashed open. Thompson was halfway through the window with the gun in his hand again.

Anna was there, a uniformed male officer behind her. Anna's eyes widened in horror when she saw Lola slumped and bleeding.

'Stay where you are,' Anna yelled at Thompson who lifted the gun.

Adrenaline surged in Lola. Her body tensed and her strength came back. She pushed herself up from the floor. Then in a flash she was along the wall to the window. Thompson realised and pointed the gun, but Lola was on him, hands grabbing at his shirt in a fury she'd never felt before.

'Boss, no!' she heard Anna cry.

'I won't let him!' Lola yelled, scrabbling and managing to wrench Thompson away from the sill.

'But he's got a—'

She didn't hear the last word. She didn't hear anything more.

A single flash and darkness fell.

TWO WEEKS LATER

Sunday 16 November
2.02 p.m.

Anna Vaughan collected Elaine Walsh from the pick-up point at the rear of Queen Street Station. Elaine had brought the flowers and lay them on the back seat of Anna's Volvo.

'They're beautiful,' Anna said, looking round. 'I remember Lola saying yellow roses were her favourite when she was younger. They look so nice with the white and purple.'

'I'm glad you like them,' Elaine said, pulling on her seatbelt. 'Did you speak to Frankie?'

'I did,' Anna said. 'Everything's in hand.'

'Good. Frankie will want to make sure everything goes smoothly.'

When they were on the A77 heading south, Elaine asked how Anna's time off had been. She'd been to England for a wedding. Anna told her about her mother-in-law, who was difficult at the best of times and who was now threatening to move to Scotland to colonise their Dumbreck villa.

'You'll have to be assertive,' Elaine said. 'Seriously.'

'Not that straightforward, unfortunately. So, any progress on the case?' Anna asked, making it sound light when in truth she was itching to know.

'The Procurator Fiscal is happy the evidence is strong,' Elaine said. 'Especially now we've got Marta Dixon's statement to add to the mix. And of course, Danny McDougall has been singing like a canary. The ringleaders were Gerald Linklater and his daughter. Of course, he's dead, and she's barely said a word since being in the hospital, though she's recovering fast. We'll charge her and she'll be moved from there to prison. She'll be charged with murder, along with extortion and other charges relating to the surrogacy racket, the same as McDougall. McDougall killed Wendy Baker — he's admitted that. He's told us Wendy Baker contacted Sarah Finnie to talk about her concerns about Ingrid Valk. Finnie told her she'd pick her up in her car at the top of Garscube Road in an hour's time. It seems Finnie turned up and told her to get in, but Wendy took fright and set off walking back to the campus. Finnie called Danny. Danny came out to head her off at the pass. He dragged her into the alleyway and beat her head in with a hammer.'

'And what about the Dixons?' Anna asked.

'Dixon's still refusing to speak, even to his solicitor, it seems — so he's stewing on remand. I'm not sure the charge of murder will stick, but we'll get him on attempting to pervert the course of justice, for sure. As for Marta, she's been detained under the Mental Health Act. I went to see her myself. She's proud she killed Linklater and the nurse — Nita Adams was her name, by the way. Recruited through that private clinic next door to Dear Green Place. She looked after the baby when Sarah Finnie and Danny McDougall brought him to the Cardonald house, and a few days later they moved him to Milngavie. That house was far more private.

'Oh, and Dear Green Place is no more, by the way,' Elaine went on. 'Mary Shulman arrived from New York, met lawyers and closed the place down. A real shame. Paolo

DaSalvo appears to have known nothing about the shenanigans. I think, on balance, I believe him.

'As for the ACC, he's suspended, as you know. There'll be a disciplinary process but it'll only be a formality to rubber stamp his sacking. Not that he'll ever work again. The charges he's facing, he won't be out of prison till he's a very old man.'

They drove for a mile or two more in silence.

'What will happen to the children?' Anna asked when they reached the roundabout to come off the M77. 'Is there even a precedent for this kind of case?'

'Social services are all over it,' Elaine said, 'but the women's families are getting involved, too, so there's an international dimension. In Adam Dixon's case, at least, there's a possibility that a cousin of the Valk sisters might take him and bring him up in Estonia — but there's a complication in that Lawrie Dixon is Adam's biological father. It's a mess, no doubt about it.

'Oh, and Prue Carstairs resigned this week. She was interviewed in the *Chronicle*, distancing herself from all of the scandal and pouring her heart out about her dismay at the university's reputation being left in tatters. She's moving to France to live with her sister, apparently.'

At last they arrived into Eaglesham, high on a hillside to the south of Glasgow, and within sight of dozens of whirling windmills that took advantage of stiff south-westerlies from the Irish Sea.

'Sandy said to park anywhere on the green,' Anna said. 'Oh — is that him there?'

'Looks like it,' Elaine said, sitting up to peer through the windscreen at the man walking down the middle of the grassy green triangle in the company of a young girl. 'And I imagine that might be Maisie,' she added.

They'd both seen Sandy several times in the past two weeks and heard about his 'new' daughter, though neither had met her.

'Good that's it's stayed dry,' Elaine said. 'The forecast wasn't very promising. Right. Ready?'

They got out of the car, then saw Kirstie a little further up the hill, hurrying down to meet them. She too had brought flowers, more yellow and purple.

The women embraced, then Elaine led the walk across the green.

Sandy spotted them and lifted a hand to wave.

'Thanks for coming,' he said, eyes on Kirstie's flowers.

'For Lola,' Kirstie said.

'They're beautiful,' he said, and managed a smiled. 'Oh, and this is Maisie.'

'Hello, Maisie,' Anna said.

'Nice to meet you,' Elaine added.

'Hello,' the girl said shyly.

She was pale like Sandy, but with his dark hair and blue eyes. She hunched her shoulders shyly and half hid behind him.

'Is everything ready?' Elaine asked him.

He nodded. 'Frankie's at mine just now. She's managed to rustle up some school friends. They'll come along a bit later.'

'Good,' Elaine said. 'Well, we're ready when you are.'

'I'm parked on the hill,' Sandy said and pointed. 'That's my car there, if you want to follow me? It's not far. Just along the road.'

***

3.05 p.m.

Frankie was waiting to greet them in the open doorway of Sandy's modern house. Cars belonging to friends and colleagues lined the street. Anna spotted Shuna Frain with a colleague.

Maisie got out of Sandy's car and went to a woman Elaine didn't recognise, who bent to speak to her. The mother, Elaine assumed, and wondered what Lola would make of that.

'Go on in,' Sandy said to her and Anna.

'It's your house,' Elaine said. 'We'll follow you.'

Sandy went in. Elaine followed, carrying the flowers, then Anna, then Kirstie with her bouquet, none of them speaking.

They stood in the hallway until Frankie was ready. Then she opened the door to the living room — and cried, 'Visitors, Lola!'

'Visitors?' Lola's voice came grumpily out from the living room. 'What visitors? Haven't you seen the state of me?'

'Och, you're fine,' Frankie said.

They filed in, one by one — colleagues, Shuna and her hanger-on, then schoolfriends filling Sandy's minimalist living room. Lola was on a settee at the back, propped up on cushions, her bandaged shoulder and splinted arm carefully resting.

'Are those for me?' Lola asked, eyes on the bouquets. 'Oh, Elaine, I love yellow roses. What's this in aid of, anyway?' She turned on Frankie. 'Your doing, I take it?'

'Actually, no,' Frankie said, and people laughed.

'It's my doing,' Elaine said and came forward. 'The chief constable's too.'

'Are you joking?' Lola tried to sit up but winced and gave up.

'I'm not,' Elaine said, and smiled. 'Only, he can't come today. We're his emissaries.'

'Meaning what?'

'Meaning, DCI Harris, that you're the latest recipient of the chief constable's Bravery and Excellence Award.'

Lola looked genuinely stunned. 'Really?'

'Really. And I'm here to communicate the joyous news. There'll be a ceremony in time, but for now, we just wanted to let you know. Shuna Frain is here to do an interview and her photographer is going to take some pictures.'

Lola's mouth fell open. She glared about the crowd, but a smile played on her lips. 'If you think I'm posing for photos looking like this, my jogging bottoms on and zero make-up, then you've another think coming.'

'Sandy's going to do your make-up for you,' Anna said.

'Aye, right,' Lola said.

* * *

4.10 p.m.

Lola was struggling to stay awake. Everyone wanted to talk to her — not least Shuna, who seemed determined to try to extract insider information about the case.

'I don't know anything,' Lola told her. 'Remember, I was out for the count for a good twenty-four hours while everything was getting wrapped up.'

People stayed for a drink and Frankie's famous vol-au-vents, then began to leave.

Kirstie left, and finally it was just Sandy, Frankie, Anna and Elaine — and Maisie and her mum, who were being discreet and watching TV in Sandy's den.

'I want a word,' Elaine said, perching on the edge of the settee. 'I'm not sure when I'll get another chance.'

'Oh?' Lola said warily.

'"Oh", indeed.' She nodded to Anna and Anna took herself off into the kitchen to help Sandy tidy up.

'Go on, then,' Lola said to Elaine.

'I got your email,' Elaine said, now wearing her serious face. 'I've read it but I haven't replied. I'm not going to . . . yet.'

'Oh? Why not?'

'Because I'm not happy about it,' Elaine said.

Lola gave her a sheepish look. 'Didn't think you would be.'

'I don't want you to go, Lola,' Elaine said.

Lola nodded.

'For a start,' the super went on, 'I'd miss bollocking you every few weeks when you break the rules, go off the rails, offend yet another of our eminent leaders . . . shall I go on?'

234

'Best not.'

'I'm being serious,' Elaine said quietly now. 'I don't want you to leave. You're a dedicated detective, Lola. You're driven and focused and principled, not to mention compassionate and deeply invested. You'd be a huge, and frankly irreplaceable, loss to the Force — and to me.'

Lola nodded, then took a moment before speaking.

'Thank you, boss,' she said, choked.

'What more can I say to get you to change your mind?'

Lola looked at her and smiled. Emotions welled but she managed to keep them in check.

'The thing is,' she said at last, 'these past two weeks, Sandy and I — we've realised a few things. A lot of things, actually. We've realised what matters, and what doesn't. To us. We want to give it a go, boss. And — aye, working together, we might end up killing each other — but it's worth trying, don't you think?'

Elaine looked about, as if searching for arguments, then she seemed to relent.

'Everything's worth trying, Lola,' she said, and smiled.

'Thought so,' Lola said.

Elaine demurred. 'Look, you've been shot and badly wounded,' she said. 'That was only two weeks ago. At least don't decide until you're back on your feet — please? In a couple of weeks you'll be making your phased return to work. Decide then. What's another few weeks, eh?'

Lola breathed.

'I don't want you making a decision you might regret further down the line,' Elaine went on. 'Because once you're gone, you're gone. It's very hard to come back, unless you wanted a desk job. And I can't see Lola Harris pushing a pen, can you?'

'Not exactly,' Lola admitted, and smiled in spite of herself.

'So, what do you say?'

'I say, "I'll think about it." But no promises. And if I do decide to go, you'll need to let me . . .'

'I will,' Elaine said. 'And we'll send you off in style.'

'Thanks, boss,' Lola said.

* * *

5.42 p.m.

Maisie's mum, Julia, left shortly after Elaine. Maisie would stay for her tea, then Sandy would drive her home later. For now it was the three of them.

Sandy brought Lola a coffee and a plate of biscuits. He'd looked after her like royalty, as he'd sworn he would when she woke up in the hospital to find him at her bedside. When she'd been discharged after five days, he'd driven her straight to his — with her consent, of course.

He'd cancelled his meeting with Maisie at the museum, and instead spent hours that Saturday at Lola's bedside. When he told her, she'd urged him to remake the meeting.

'Not until I know you're better,' he said.

'In that case, we'll go and meet her together,' she told him.

He'd looked completely floored. 'Are you serious?'

'If you still want me to go with you, then aye, I am.'

'Let's get married,' he'd said then.

'Oh, Sandy, no.'

'Why not?'

'Because . . . It's not for me, okay?' She saw his face. 'Well, not right now, it isn't.'

He'd been happy with that.

Lola had got out of hospital on the Wednesday morning, still in pain, but able to move and feed herself — and armed with painkillers. Sandy had arranged to meet Maisie at the same place the following Saturday, and they'd gone together, Lola tense but also pleased to be out of the house. She let Sandy meet Maisie for a few minutes first, idling at another table, then joined them. Sandy was giddy and emotional and

Lola found herself doing more of the talking. Julia was perfectly pleasant and self-effacing, and she found Maisie sweet and shy but lively on topics where she was most interested. To Lola's surprise she was an avid true crime fan, and harboured an ambition to move to America and join the FBI.

'Hiya,' Maisie said now from the doorway.

'It's okay, come in,' Lola called.

She crept into the room and Sandy rose from his crouch.

'How you doing?' he asked her.

'Okay,' Maisie said, a smile tilting the side of her mouth. 'I wanted to ask Lola something,' she said.

'Fine by me,' Lola said.

'But it's police stuff,' she said, looking at her father meaningfully.

'In that case, I'll leave you to it,' Sandy said, and dropped Lola a knowing wink.

'Sit next to me,' Lola said, and Maisie sat, barely making an indent on the sofa cushion. 'Now, what do you want to know?'

Maisie narrowed her eyes then turned to Lola.

'You know the Zodiac Killer?' she said.

'Erm . . . not personally, I'm pleased to say.' She spotted Sandy, lingering by the door, listening.

'Why do you think he sent those cryptic messages?' Maisie's forehead creased in concentration. 'I mean, why not just send them in English? Why hide the messages at all?'

Lola pondered but knew she had no answer.

'That's a very interesting question,' she said. 'Why don't we research it a bit?'

Maisie's eyes lit up. 'Can we?'

'If you like. You run and get your iPad and we'll have a look together.'

'Yay!' The girl jumped off the sofa and ran for the door, almost colliding with Sandy.

Sandy smiled in at Lola and Lola sent him one back.

'I love you,' he mouthed.

'You too,' she replied.

EPILOGUE

TO: VALK, Tiina
FROM: VALK, Ingrid
SUBJECT: Re: Re: Re: News
DATE: 20 August
TIME: 9.21

[Translated from Estonian]

Hello, Tiina.

I'm sorry for what I said when we spoke. I'm sorry I didn't listen to you. But you see, now I know you were right. I've made a terrible mistake and everything is ruined.

I gave birth to a baby boy at midnight last night. They let me hold him, and as soon as he was in my arms I knew I wanted to keep him. Suddenly the money meant nothing at all. He was my tiny baby and I was his mother and I couldn't stand the thought of giving him up.

But then they took him away from me. I cried for him and I could hear him crying for me. I could hear it even though we were in different rooms.

Then the people came for him. They came into my room to thank me.

I broke down and begged them to let me keep my baby. The nurse came in and said she would sedate me if I didn't control myself.

The husband touched my hand but I pulled it away. I never want him near me again. The wife didn't look at me, as if she couldn't bear to. I think she's ashamed.

I couldn't sleep and by morning I'd decided. I'm going to take him back, Tiina. I'm going to take him back from their thieving arms and go away with him. I might even take him home.

But these people are evil and I'm very afraid. Not just for me, but for my baby. So I'm telling you this now as my insurance. The couple are Lawrence and Marta Dixon. She is Estonian and her birth name was Rand. They plan to call my son Adam.

If anything happens to me, please, dear Tiina, rescue my son. And give him the name I have chosen for him. Call him after our grandfather.

Call him Taavi — because he is so deeply loved.

THE END

ACKNOWLEDGEMENTS

A massive thank you to Chief Inspector Kirsty Lawie of Police
Scotland for her tireless assistance with this (rather complex)
story. Kirsty has helped me since the beginning of my writing
career and has been an ardent cheerleader for Lola — which
is why I'm dedicating this, the final Lola Harris story, to her.

Suzanne Daly told me about her work as a university
registrar and explained the law and processes around visas for
international students, for which I am grateful.

Bernice Chan talked to me about naming conventions in
China and Hong Kong. YG Lee talked to me about Korea and
naming conventions there. Thanks to both of them.

Thank you to my mum Julie, and to Janice Fraser,
Katharine Bradbury, Jill Crawford, Suzanne Daly and Yvonne
Boyd, for reading and commenting on drafts of the book.
Fiona Macdonald read parts while we were on holiday in Italy
and reassured me when I was panicking.

Thank you to Katharine Bradbury and Simon Young for
medical advice, to Simon and Chris for letting me work at
their place in the wilds of Kintyre and for feeding me, and to
Niall Kinsella for looking after my website.

Local support means a lot. I'm grateful to Tom and
Kay Dingwall, to Elaine Sinclair at the gorgeous Daydreams

Bookshop in Milngavie, to Diane and the team at the Perch in Garelochhead and to Robert and the team at Skoosh in Drymen. Also to the *Helensburgh Advertiser* for their ongoing support and interest in my work. And to Kev Sage of Double Polaroid Video Production, for the tremendous book trailers.

I lost a supportive friend during the writing of this book. Lynn Sheridan was a lovely person with a huge heart. I've slipped her into the story and hope she'd have been pleased.

Thank you to Siân Heap for her excellent structural edits and to Kate Lyall Grant and Kate Ballard at Joffe Books for their support and guidance. A special shout-out to Matthew Grundy Haigh who has copy-edited the Lola books with an eagle eye since the beginning (and helped me fix the odd plot hole!).

My writer friends are truly supportive and I really value their camaraderie. Special shout-outs to Margaret (MK) Murphy, Marion Todd, Linda Mather, Sally-Anne Martyn, Michael Wood and Sophia Spiers.

My brilliant agent Francesca Riccardi is always there. I value her, her work and her wisdom immensely.

I want to acknowledge Karen Bartke's brilliant reading of the audio books. Thank you so much, Karen, for breathing life into Lola!

Thank you as ever to Gordon, on the other side of the globe, and to Rasmus, at my side unless he's sulking in another room for one reason or another.

THE JOFFE BOOKS STORY

We began in 2014 when Jasper agreed to publish his mum's much-rejected romance novel and it became a bestseller.

Since then we've grown into the largest independent publisher in the UK. We're extremely proud to publish some of the very best writers in the world, including Joy Ellis, Faith Martin, Caro Ramsay, Helen Forrester, Simon Brett and Robert Goddard. Everyone at Joffe Books loves reading and we never forget that it all begins with the magic of an author telling a story.

We are proud to publish talented first-time authors, as well as established writers whose books we love introducing to a new generation of readers.

We won Trade Publisher of the Year at the Independent Publishing Awards in 2023 and Best Publisher Award in 2024 at the People's Book Prize. We have been shortlisted for Independent Publisher of the Year at the British Book Awards for the last five years, and were shortlisted for the Diversity and Inclusivity Award at the 2022 Independent Publishing Awards. In 2023 we were shortlisted for Publisher of the Year at the RNA Industry Awards, and in 2024 we were shortlisted at the CWA Daggers for the Best Crime and Mystery Publisher.

We built this company with your help, and we love to hear from you, so please email us about absolutely anything bookish at feedback@joffebooks.com.

If you want to receive free books every Friday and hear about all our new releases, join our mailing list here: www.joffebooks.com/freebooks.

And when you tell your friends about us, just remember: it's pronounced Joffe as in coffee or toffee!

www.ingramcontent.com/pod-product-compliance
Lightning Source LLC
Chambersburg PA
CBHW011432170626
46808CB00010B/3129

* 9 7 8 1 8 0 5 7 3 3 7 5 1 *